CW00673766

05002420

About the Author

Jennifer was born in 1943 in the seaside resort of Cleethorpes.
After leaving school Jenny went to study nursing. She has been married twice and has two sons and two step sons, plus four grandchildren.
She has since retired from nursing and has completed a writing course and has written several short stories for pleasure. This is her first novel.

Dedication

To my patient and much loved husband for his support.
Keith Todd.

Jenny Todd

KEYS TO PAST EVILS

AUSTIN MACAULEY
PUBLISHERS LTD.

A CIP catalogue record for this title is available from the British Library.

ISBN 978 1 78455 466 8 (Paperback)
ISBN 978 1 78455 468 2 (Hardback)

www.austinmacauley.com

First Published (2015)
Austin Macauley Publishers Ltd.
25 Canada Square
Canary Wharf
London
E14 5LB

Printed and bound in Great Britain

Acknowledgments

My thanks to:-

Sue and Carrie Hodgett.

Linda Sproston.

CHAPTER 1

From 1921

East-Thorpe-on-Sea like many seaside resorts had its share of rich and poor people. The promises made by the men in Westminster three years previously, had failed to reach the gunnels and slums of the less affluent, they were the forgotten, the ignored.

The slums were destroyed and reduced to rubble. The ones who remained in this small court yard were still standing, if only just. The one lavatory, which served six houses, had not been destroyed; so as long as you sung loudly, or managed to wedge your foot under the door you were safe from disturbance. The one thing that you must not forget was the newspaper, which you had to beg borrow or steal, not for the joy of reading in this filthy place even if in fact you could read the time was spent tearing it up into squares to use as toilet paper.

Giving birth to Josiah Kingston in this one-roomed hovel was to be his mother's final act before leaving this world probably in search of a better one. The house no longer had a stair case it had gone leaving the partially destroyed upstairs empty except for some rubble, rats' nests and a hole in the roof.

The landlords didn't care they didn't always get their rent any way and they considered these people not worth bothering with, the quicker the buildings fell down the better as far as they were concerned. The land would be worth more to them for redevelopment. Josiah's father was also named Josiah as was his father before him, not for any other reason than that they were too drunk to think of an alternative. He was, as usual, adding to the coffers of his local hostelry. When he eventually arrived home, he found his dead wife on the stone floor, covered in blood together with his screaming lusty son. He ran into the cobbled gunnell and yelled for help.

Edna Jacks, a near neighbour and friend of the deceased made the dead woman look presentable as she had done many times before in this area, and reluctantly took charge of the child. She sent one of her many offspring to fetch the undertaker, who pushed up his sash bedroom window and told him that he would sort it out the next day. Edna had only the previous day given birth to Percy. The two babies slept head to toe in the tiny drawer which had served her offspring previously.

Josiah senior slept off the effects of the copious amount of beer which he had consumed. As it was raining both man and his late wife lay in puddles caused by the leaking roof, which at any moment may fall upon them.

The following day, a very tired Edna had little choice but to take the baby to his paternal grandmother's house not unlike the one she had just left. Josiah Jnr. was not a welcome addition. Mrs Kingston had forgotten how old she really was, but looked about eighty. After forty years of age all women looked eighty in this part of East-Thorpe-on-Sea. Her thin grey hair was tied in a bun, most of it managing to escape and hang limply around her face unnoticed. Edna was sorry to burden the old lady. The next day Josiah's father turned up, he promised his mother that he would get a job or join the army before returning. Her husband had been killed during the First World War, but not as you would expect, he was stabbed in a drunken brawl. She didn't believe her son and was right not to as she never saw him again. Neither did the recruiting officer or his new born son. The only person to miss him was the landlord of the Red Bull as Josiah had left still owing him ten shillings and sixpence halfpenny.

Times were hard and money was in short supply in these sorts of places. Josiah and Percy naturally formed a bond, it was usual for the two boys and others like them to go to bed hungry and to wake up feeling the same.

They rarely went to school but no one really cared. They were very streetwise and had many ways of surviving. They would go scrumping for apples, one being the look out and the other doing the stealing. This method worked very well in all kinds of situations. Corner shops and market stalls were a good source of supply. This was usually ignored by the owners as they were well aware of the boy's situations. The friends begged for 'pop' bottles and received one penny for them at the local shop. On the railway sidings they would sift through the coal dust to find some lumps of coal and sell them to people who had any money to spare, anything to get a few pence. This was the life that they expected. Occasionally after the local market had closed for the day, they would find the odd dropped and forgotten item of food which they would take to Percy's mother. On a very lucky day they would be successful in begging an old meat bone. It was amazing what Percy's mother could make out of what seemed very little. She had managed to produce another couple of offspring. How, the boys couldn't imagine, as Mr Jacks was usually at the Red Bull, which the boys supposed was better as it saved Mrs Jacks sporting yet another black eye and the children, who couldn't run very fast, a smacked arse, as he delicately put it. Thus the boys grew up. They didn't know any better for several years. It never entered into Josiah's head to enquire about the existence of any of his siblings. He had become one of the Jacks brood. He would go back to his grandmother's house at night time. She usually lay on the floor with an empty 'meths' bottle at her side, Josiah would creep into the corner and snuggle under his

13

blanket hoping it didn't rain as it often found its way into the downstairs room and onto him. The corner where he chose to sleep was the least likely to suffer. His grandmother would fail to notice anyway. Josiah was now 14 years old, or thereabouts: of that he wasn't sure. He must remember to ask Mrs Jacks. She would know she knew everything.

One day Edna Jacks was waiting to see Josiah. He and Percy had as usual been out savaging for food. His grandmother had died and was soon to join her daughter-in-law in the local cemetery. Ironically that very morning someone had given her an old scraggy chicken, a rare treat, and she had been boiling it over a small fire. She would have enjoyed eating it. With a few vegetables added Josiah and the Jacks kids did.

Edna, as usual sorted out the burial.

Josiah stayed in the house alone for as long as he could, avoiding the rent man. One day, inevitably his luck ran out. He tore up the bill which the Land Lord had given to him and with the two shillings he had been saving in his pocket and only the clothes he stood up in, he left. Work was scarce and Josiah was getting increasingly angry. He made a promise to himself that he would, by any means possible, rise out of poverty and up the social ladder. Lately he had realised that how he lived was not the only way. He went to the nearby docks and after lying about his age, he had his first lucky break. He was given a job as a barrow boy.

Josiah had grown into a large impressive youth. His nose-hugging wire spectacles, which he had long outgrown, resembled beer bottle bottoms which made his eyes appear to be enormous. His pastry thick lips hid his chalky, broken gravestone teeth. It had been so long since his mousey coloured, wiry hair had been washed or combed that he could not have remembered, even if he had thought about it, but he didn't.

The work was hard. Barrow boys had to push barrows full of cold wet fish from the pontoon to the fish market and then race back again. Josiah worked harder than any of his contemporaries, which didn't go un-noticed. After a year, he secured a job as a Lumper. This was hard night work but was very well paid. They were known as the midnight millionaires. Josiah, still homeless, had been sleeping on the beach. After all who was likely to give a room to this dirty smelly youth? Now that winter was on its way, he was pleased he had been supplied with a set of Ollies, which comprised of a sou'wester, oil frock and leggings, so he continued for some time when he finished work in the morning, to buy some fish and chips or if he has been lucky, supply the fish which had been surplus to requirements on the docks, and have it fried for a halfpenny then find a park bench. Fighting to keep his eyes open he would enjoy his vinegar-laden fish and chips. Checking that his money bag was safely tucked down his Ollie leg, he would curl up and sleep as long as he wasn't disturbed. He was out of the cold north winds and totally impervious to the smell of fish and body odours, passers-by usually gave him a wide berth.

Josiah was unaware of what was going on in the outside world. Birthdays had come and gone. King George V1 had been crowned in 1936. All he knew was sleep and work. There were rumours of an impending war, but Josiah knew that because of his eyesight, he would not be called up. It would be a different story for his friend Percy.

That night Percy sneaked into the docks while Josiah was unloading the trawlers. They hadn't seen each other for a while so he took a break to talk to him. Percy was now a small thin man full of nervous energy. He was continually moving about, gesticulating with his hands and sniffing a great deal. His voice was like sand paper probably due to the copious amount of black market cigarettes he consumed. His brown beady eyes were never still, they darted back and forth in a most unnerving manner. Percy had altered.

"Sorry I ain't seen yer, but I've bin busy, Jo. Me and my Ruby ave got 'itched. Just a quicky yer understand and then back to work. I ain't bein called up 'cos I'm in a reserved occupation," he smiled proudly and sniffed.

"Wot the 'ell job are yer in?" Josiah asked.

"I got me sen a lottie. Grows food and stuff yer see and I still do a bit of er ducking and diving, if you know what I mean."

He tapped the side of his nose winked and continued.

"I got two back gardens, belong to the Gibson-Ffiskes they do. I keep 'em 'appy with stuff and I'm near to my Ruby as works in their ouse cleanin and stuff." He sniffed.

"When yer want a chicken or a few eggs just let me know."

"Wait on, wait on a mo, Perce."

Josiah counted on his grubby sausage like fingers.

"Do yer mean that chubby lass as lived not far from us but was clean like, and ow do yer know ote about growin veg and stuff let alone knowing the likes of the G.Fs. and much as I'd like to take up your offer of chicken and eggs, I ain't got anywhere to live except a park bench and it don't include a cooking pot and fire. Lastly ave you got any room at your gaff?"

"Not a chance 'fraid, me 'an Rube live in one room, but I reckon I can 'elp. One of the reasons I came to see yer like."

"What's the catch, Perce?" Josiah asked warily.

"Know me better than that, Jo, yer do. I wouldn't give my old mate any duff info. There's a lovely old gal as lives in the Corner 'ouse next to the Gibson Ffiskes. The Gf don't own it. Miss Maisie Elder does, and she is looking for a lodger, just the one mind. My Rube does er cleanin like. She needs a strong bloke to elp her around the 'ouse sometimes. I 'elps er out whenever I can. She's worth a bob or two, but it's 'ard for 'er, rattling around that gret big 'ouse on 'er own. She needs some company and 'elp. I told 'er that I might know someone, so pop round, I've told 'er good things about yer. She needs yer to be kind 'an she deserves it, go 'an see 'er, Jo. Just one little thing, you look a proper smelly scruff bag. Lord knows what's living in your 'air and Ollies, yer go to the public baths

16

when yer finish work then round the back of the GFs and my Rube will trim your air and you can borrow my cut throat. I don't know what yer can do about clothes. Miss Elder would faint with the smell on yer but yer will av ter think of what to do about yer togs."

Josiah couldn't bring himself to believe it, a bed to sleep in if it was true.

"I'll be round first thing in the morning Perce, thanks a lot."

"Just one small thing, Jo, I needs a bit more room for me pigs see and Maisie Elder's back garden would be just the job."

"I din't know you ad any pigs, Perce."

"I ain't but I will 'ave once you get 'er to let me use 'er land."

Maisie Elder was a lovely old lady she and Josiah hit it off from the word go. A most unlikely friendship. She seemed to be so tiny to Josiah which in itself made him feel protective of her she had the hunched shoulders of an old person. There wasn't an ounce of spare flesh on her. With snow white hair and her cheeks like rosy red apples Josiah thought that she looked like the archetypal grandmother everyone wanted and he took good care of her. It was his pleasure as she was such a kind old soul.

When the air aids began in 1940 they would spend time together in the air raid shelter while bombs were falling. On Sunday evenings Josiah and Maisie would listen to the wireless when a programme called I.T.M.A (It's That Man Again) was broadcast before he went to work. Maisie would clap her skinny old hands with purple raised veins like knotted rope and fling her head back and giggle. They enjoyed walks along the promenade when he wasn't working. Maisie just reached Josiah's arm. She told him that both of her brothers had been killed in WW1 and that she had been left to care for her parents until their deaths. Then it was too late for her to find a husband, so there she stayed feeling increasingly lonely and wishing wishes, which were too late to come true.

After they had enjoyed a walk, Maisie would be tired and want to go home and have a cup of tea, on one such day she looked at Josiah in the old fashioned way she had and said.

"Josiah, get some new glasses, you look like a flipping owl in those." They both laughed.

He got himself a new suit shirt and razor as well. Maisie made him open a bank account. He knew he was making progress and for the first time in his life he was happy. He was still working on the night shift, but had the luxury of sleeping in a bed and the facilities of a bathroom were never taken for granted. His days on the cold benches, sometimes waking with a coating of snow covering his ollies were never far away. One thing concerned him. Winston Churchill was using some of the trawlers for war work which would mean less work for him and all dock workers. They would be put on short time. It wasn't to be very long before this did happen. WW2 was by this time well and truly under way. He did however manage to make some money on the black market. He had plans for the future when this war was over. He grabbed some work on the docks whenever he could, and thanked his luck in having Maisie as the best friend any one could hope for. He was on his way, to where he wasn't, sure but it was in an upward direction.

CHAPTER 2

Hector Gibson Ffiske walked over to the bay window of the drawing room with his usual air of importance, a trait which he had acquired long ago, and after a great deal of practice. It was now as much a part of him as his terribly posh accent. His childhood long forgotten and unknown to anyone, even his wife of whom he had tolerated for many years. There was a price to pay for everything. He, without any interest stared at the grey pulsating sea, which was opposite the four storey Victorian terraced house. He shared this monument to affluence with his wife Arabella, who had no need to practice her accent as she was born with it. Hector pulled down the blackout blinds. He had grown used to the crisscross of tape over the windows. Arabella hadn't. He drew the heavy velvet curtains.

As he strolled back to his red leather chair, tip toeing as he hoped that he would be allowed to read his newspaper, he turned on the light. He viewed his spoilt, selfish wife and not for the first time thought she had a dignity which required no embellishments. Despite her heavy make-up and blood red nails it was always the iridescent green eyes which dominated her face. At the moment they were closed. He was well aware that she was purely decorative. Marrying her was a small sacrifice to make for the life he now enjoyed. He, as quietly as possible, with one eye on his sleeping beauty, opened his copy of *The Times*. He read with great interest that, In the Battle of

Britain the RAF had rebuffed the Luftwaffe. He read on. She woke. He was certain that by the look on her face she was building up to one of what she described as her 'discussions'. For all of Hector's arrogant pomposity in his estate agent's office, it would be a braver man than he who would confront Arabella when she was in one of her moods. He desperately wanted to read his newspaper, but reluctantly realised that it would be best to get the discussion over with, and then, hopefully, he may have some peace.

"You appear to be a little agitated, my love," he ventured.

She favoured him with a humourless smile.

"Agitated, Hector, agitated? I'm furious," she ceased her tut-tutting and shook her magazine, which was her usual way of showing that she required his attention.

He realised that this was going to take longer than he had envisaged, so was forced to use his usual coping method. This involved putting his head to one side into what he considered to be an understanding pose, whilst fixing his eyes on her pearl necklace. He found it easier that way as he imagined Arabella would assume that he was listening to her every word.

Arabella continued.

"You really do not comprehend all the problems that I have to contend with. My life is becoming one long nightmare."

Hector watched the pearls as they glinted in the fire light.

"Those stupid girls, Sally and Maud have left to join the WAAF Would you believe it, with never a thought for me? They are well aware how difficult it is to get staff now during this wretched war. I told them, they muttered something about the war effort. I couldn't be bothered to listen. I don't normally speak to the staff unless entirely necessary as you well know."

Hector nodded, and thought to himself, he had better not mention the fact that food rationing was to be introduced. Not that it would make an iota of difference to her. (At least he had not had to buy the pearls, her mother had left Arabella; they must be worth a fortune.)

"Are you listening Hector, you have that glazed look in your eyes which tells me the contrary? And ..." Arabella carried on. "Ruby has had to do all the extra work and doesn't even have time to bring my tea on time."

As if by magic, Ruby walked in with the tea tray.

"Me and Percy are off 'ome now Mrs GF. I ain't ad time to make your dinner, I'm so sorry it is not easy with all the extra work I ave to do. Will it be possible for you to go to the chippy or summat, er just this once er please? "

Hearing no response Ruby gently closed the drawing room door.

"You see what I have to put up with?" Arabella said. "And she didn't even stoke up the fire. Chippy indeed, I wouldn't be seen dead in one. One has to maintain some sort of standards, I'd rather starve."

Hector shook his head, hoping it showed her that he fully understood even though he didn't. He would have liked to remind his wife that Percy Jacks, Ruby's husband, used their rear garden and the one next door which the Gibson Ffiskes also owned, as an allotment and supplied them with fresh vegetables, fruit, chickens and eggs, not to mention all the black market things which they both turned a blind eye to. It was because of Percy that they could enjoy their pre-dinner drink of gin and tonic and his occasional whisky. He cast a furtive eye on the newspaper just managing to notice that Winston Churchill was to succeed Neville Chamberlain as Prime Minister.

"Hector, are you listening to me?"

"Yes dear." His anger curled in his stomach, unsaid.

"I have to pay four pence an inch to have my stockings repaired, before long I will have to begin using Skin Toner and clothes will be rationed next year, I will be forced to manage on sixty six coupons annually I can't comprehend how little that will mean. Thank goodness for Madam Daphne, (Clothes for the Discerning) she is sure to help me when I give her some of Mr Jack's best eggs."

She leant forward.

Hector thought for one brief moment that she was going to get up and stand over him. Although she stood at only five foot and two inches to his six foot, he would rather she didn't. He would like to continue to keep his temper under control, and hoped that his moustache wasn't quivering as it was prone to do at times of stress. He caressed it like a favourite pet. It entirely covered his top lip and lay peacefully on his bottom one. It had, when he was younger been as jet black as his thick hair. Now one or two hairs began to show a little ginger hue. He had tried to dye them with shoe polish, but then lived in fear that the residue would appear on his tea cup during a meeting at work. His hand moved to his brilliantine laden hair to make sure it covered his bald patch which, to his horror he had discovered only two day's previously.

"Desperate times, means desperate measures, Hector."

She moved backwards on her sofa, Hector poured the tea.

"So?"

She took a sip of it, little finger extended,

"You know our daughter, Suzannah? I have been thinking about her of late."

Hector with a mouth full of his tea swallowed it in an effort to reply, but not quickly enough for his wife.

"Keep up, Hector, do, this is very important, Hector, you know, our daughter, away at boarding school, which I might add, costs us a fortune."

Hector nodded, while thinking about the servicemen evacuated to Dunkirk.

"She is eighteen now I think, and it is about time she came home and faced life at the sharp-end."

"Eighteen, Golly I didn't realise, we haven't seen her in an age."

"No Hector that was because we had things going on in our lives and couldn't fit her in. Anyway I telephoned her headmistress earlier today. We had a long conversation I must say her diction leaves something to be desired. In any event, I have told her that Suzannah is to return home."

"Jolly good," Hector replied preparing to read his newspaper, surely that must be the end to the discussion. He was wrong.

When the doctor told Arabella in the spring of 1922, that she was pregnant it was a black day. Neither parents wanted any children. Each blamed the other. Arabella screamed throughout the birth. Hector was very close to the delivery suite as she insisted that he stayed in the adjacent room without a newspaper. He wasn't sure if the noise was out of necessity or for effect. Either way it mattered not as Hector removed the very creased newspaper out of his trouser pocket. They both thought little of their daughter, Suzannah Arabella Elizabeth, but felt compelled to hold an elaborate christening which involved inviting everyone who mattered plus the Bishop of Longden Dyke to do the honours. Immediately afterwards they put the copious amount of gifts in the pre-decorated nursery situated as far as possible from their own bedroom and employed a series of nurses and nannies, until they found one who would tolerate the baby's parents.

At the first opportunity Suzannah was dispatched to the most suitable boarding school. She had great difficulty fitting in and finally just spent as much time as possible on her own reading. She became more shy and withdrawn as the years went by. When the holidays arrived her parents had always made other plans so Suzannah was left behind knowing that she was a liability to the mistresses who had to look after her, the only pupil left at school. She saw little of the carers, mostly just at meal time, when a tray of food was brought to her, which she ate alone. After some years of this, she became very interested in food preparation and began to read the books which were available to her, on cooking and baking. The years dragged on. Academically, Suzannah was quite bright because she spent so much time with her head in a book and studied hard in class. Each school year she usually had some different girls in her class and hoped that she would be able to make friends with someone but she lacked the confidence to approach any of them. As she got older she would view with envy the girls who were chums and went out of the school to the shops. She went into the local town to buy mostly books on cookery and the latest novels, Aldous Huxley's *Brave New World* and *Waves* by Virginia Woolf two of her favourites. She just kept her head down and pretended to be reading as the laughing school girls went out. She watched them from the window as they disappeared out of the school gates. One day when all the other girls seemed to be giggling in a circle Suzannah, feeling left out and miserable, decided to go for a walk around the grounds. Taking her book with her she stared at it as she walked. She wasn't reading she was crying. In the evening in the dorm she did the same, feeling that by pretending that she was engrossed in her book she would appear to be invisible. A new girl had just transferred to her school and walked over to speak to her. She was a "Jolly Hockey Sticks" sort of girl. Her long greasy hair was plaited and her large red face seemed to have more than its fair share of spots. The prepubescent type; her gym slip strained under the stress of her well-developed chest department.

Suzannah's heart felt that it would jump out of its chest.

"Hello there," she said. "I'm Miranda Birkinshaw Scott, I'm new.

It's awfully quiet around here."

She sat down clumsily on Suzannah's bed. The bed not used to this amount of weight groaned. Before Suzannah had time to say anything Miranda continued.

"I mean not so much quiet as unfriendly. There you are sitting here reading and that terribly chummy crowd over there pretending to be so very, very super-duper when they would scratch each other's eyes out if given the chance. So you are not part of the IN crowd I imagine. Had some sort of tiff have you? Show them what's what, even if you are scared to your guts. What's your name by the way?"

"Suzannah Gibson-Ffiske. And no I have never been part of the crowd, I wouldn't fit in, they don't care for me and I have never been asked to join them."

"Never been asked? Asked, asked, one doesn't get asked to that sort of crowd one just joins in make them think you are an "in charge sort of person" without being bossy."

"If only," Suzannah thought, but kept it in her mind.

"I guess you are a quiet sort of girl, shy. Is making friends difficult for you?"

Suzannah nodded, she was near to tears.

Over the next few weeks Miranda showed her lots of things and Suzannah was very grateful. She was beginning to feel more confident day by day. All seemed to be going well. Her life was starting to have some purpose. She walked with her head held high much as she had been nagged to do by her teachers. She was even acknowledged by the "In crowd", she had so many things to thank Miranda for, the glow of happiness being one of them.

All this changed with one telephone call from her mother. Miranda and Suzannah said their tearful goodbyes promising to keep in touch Unfortunately they never did.

.

As far as I could discover." Arabella continued to tell a disinterested Hector.

"The only lessons which Suzannah has learnt are how to alight from a car without exposing her bloomers, the recipe for Wooton Pie, whatever that is, and a hundred ways with parsnips."

"I do hope that we are not to be disturbed by those dreadful sirens and awful noises tonight. It is such a bind having to squeeze oneself under that table encased in wire like a caged animal. I know that I have a slim figure but it is so undignified and it plays havoc with one's hair. And now we have to accommodate Suzannah I dread to think what one will have to endure."

Hector thought maybe that if she had a walk on the beach during the bombing she may be happier. He chuckled to himself.

Suzannah viewed her parents as strangers whom she didn't particularly want to get to know. She had been allocated the tiny loft room and placed her few belongings into the drawers. The first meeting with Ruby was difficult for them both. She was determined to act on the advice from Miranda. Suzannah hadn't been told what was expected from Ruby, who was ill at ease at the thought of having to work with the daughter of the house who was to be treated like a cook and a maid. Although they were of a similar age, that was all they seemed to have in common. For a few moments which on reflection seemed like a lifetime they both took stock of each other. Ruby appeared to Suzannah to be a large open faced woman; her mousy hair was tied back in a plaited bun which to Suzannah's mind robbed the rest of her rosy red face of the kindness beneath. She wore not a hint of rouge or powder. It was a kindly homely face, not the type Suzannah had ever come across before.

"Pleased to meet you Miss Gibson Ffiske,"

"Do call me Suzannah. You must be Ruby. Mother told me about you this morning when I arrived," she extended her hand.

Ruby wiped her red rough hand on her apron before offering it in return .She was indeed a large raw boned woman whose formidable chest seemed to naturally descend to a point at which her legs should begin. Her slipper clad feet seemed to be at odds with each other, pointing as they did, in opposite directions. Her lovely sparkly eyes and happy smile would cheer any one up and Suzannah who was tall willowy and stick thin, responded.

"I'm not too sure what I am supposed to do Ruby? Mother said you would tell me."

"I reckon you are supposed to do the cookin and a few other cleanin' jobs. But don't try to get into your father's office it is locked, and only 'e 'as the key, and if you go anywhere near it he gets angry," she felt extremely embarrassed.

Suzannah shrugged her shoulders and said.

"Do you have a clean tea towel to cover my hair please Ruby? then I will get my bearings and find something to cook for tonight's meal. Do you stay for the evening meal? "

"Me, oh my goodness no, me an' Percy go 'ome for us teas, 'e is outside on his allotment now."

Suzannah encased her shiny swishy hair in the tea towel, turban like and went into the pantry in search of food.

The back door opened and Percy, not seeing Suzannah, despite Ruby's gesticulations came in.

"Got a brew on yet Rube I'm fair clamped? It's bloody mellow out yonder."

Suzannah came back into the kitchen, Ruby was red with embarrassment.

"Perce, this is Miss, er, Suzannah."

He spat on his muddy hands and rubbed them down his trousers before clasping Suzannah's hand.

"What an excellent idea Percy, I'll go and find the tea and milk, I expect there won't be any biscuits, I'll see if I can make some later."

Percy and Ruby exchanged glances, Suzannah returned with a tea caddy and some milk. She felt so very odd she didn't have to sit on her bed and pretend to read, thanks to

Miranda she was free to do and say what she pleased and this was her domain.

"Er" Ruby said "We usually take Mrs GFs tea tray first then when she's finished we add a bit more boilin' water for us to 'ave."

"That is dreadful, I don't intend to drink stewed up tea. We will have a nice fresh cup."

"There is a shortage of tea, so that is the reason Mrs GF wants it that way."

"I will take mother's tea myself. Then we will enjoy a fresh cup. When we run out of tea we will all either do without or try to get some more." From that moment on the pair bonded.

That night Suzannah cooked liver and onions with vegetables from Percy's allotment. Her mother wasn't pleased at the lack of a sweet and made her feelings obvious. Suzannah made no comment. She didn't care much for these people whom she hardly knew.

After the first day Suzannah, Ruby and Percy had developed a friendship with one another, Suzannah hadn't ever had a friend apart from very briefly with Miranda her mentor, and Ruby and Percy hadn't ever imagined that they would be treated as equals by anyone who they considered to be above their class. That was more than could be said for the relationship Suzannah had with her mother. She rarely saw her, and even less her father as he was mostly at work or his club. On the odd occasion they came into contact, he would continue to read his newspaper, or talk to her as a remote person whom he hadn't any option but to be pleasant to. Suzannah didn't care in the slightest and spent as little time as possible in their company.

"Aren't they an odd couple, don't you think Ruby?"

Ruby was flabbergasted and at a loss as what to say.

"You know them better than I do so you must have formed an opinion, Ruby, surely, unless it's just me."

She hadn't seen the people who lived in the next door house which the Gibson Ffiskes also owned so she offered to go and collect the rent one day to introduce herself. It was one of Ruby's tasks. She felt a little of her past nervousness, but it seemed to go well, the people seemed nice and Suzannah congratulated herself. She also got to know Miss Elder next door the other side at the Corner house. As she usually made vegetable soup for lunch she would include her. Suzannah was very fond of the old lady who was so grateful for any small thing anyone did for her, unlike her parents. Winter seemed to be hanging on, and outside Percy's sprouts and leeks curved under the weight of its frosted jewels.

The low sun danced and glistened on the dark sea opposite the houses, the wind howled and seemed to find any small cracks and crannies in the houses and entered uninvited.

Maisie was sitting by the fire in the in the parlour as she had a bit of a cold. She seemed quiet and looked pale, but she had refused to see the doctor. Suddenly the door opened and the back of a blond head appeared.

"It's only me Miss Elder I've brought your usual soup and a warm roll fresh straight from the oven."

Suzannah turned and jumped when she realised that Josiah was there. "Oh dear me," she said. "I'm most terribly sorry, but I didn't see you there." They had never met before as Josiah was usually at work.

Josiah was speechless he had never seen a more perfectly beautiful girl in his life before.

"I'm Suzannah Gibson Ffiske, from next door. I didn't mean to be rude. You must be Josiah. Miss Elder has told me how kind you are to her," she looked at him with her large green eyes and flashed him a smile. "Would you like me to get you some soup?"

As time went by Josiah joined Ruby and Percy as treasured friends of Suzannah's. She continued to take food to Maisie and Josiah when he was at home. The old lady had developed a cold and nasty cough, it worsened and despite

Josiah and Suzannah's pleading she refused to have the doctor to come and see her. Suzannah had to increase her visits as she was so concerned about her, despite knowing that if her parents found out that she had been visiting Maisie they would forbid her to do so. Josiah and Suzannah were growing more and more concerned about Miss Elder's health, she seemed to get worse each day. Her clothes hung on to her body unwillingly, her vanity long forgotten.

Josiah had the chance of some work on the Docks one day. Work was little and far between. He asked Suzannah what he should do. If he turned the offer down he maybe wouldn't have any in the future, but he didn't like the thought of leaving Maisie. Suzannah told him he must take the work and she would come to see the old lady as much as she could. He stoked up the fire and put the kettle on the fire pullout then, reluctantly left her, knowing it wouldn't be long before Suzannah came.

She arrived less than an hour later with some hot soup, a bread roll straight from the oven and a scone, only to be greeted by the old lady's rasping cough. The kettle was boiling so Suzannah made some tea and sitting on the fender, she noticed that Miss Elder's feet were cold to the touch and blue as well as being very swollen. She quickly went into the kitchen and got the cream stone water bottle which she filled and placed by Maisie's feet. She fed her the soup and gave her some tea. Maisie in a shaky voice told Suzannah what a good girl she was and that since she had known her and her beloved Josiah she had never been so happy. Suzannah smiled but couldn't stop worrying. She returned home knowing that Josiah shouldn't be long before he returned. She was also well aware that if her mother discovered what she had been doing, she would be very angry. Not that it particularly bothered her but she didn't want to create any friction if she could help it.

A little later Josiah returned; he couldn't settle at work and had made some excuse and left. As soon as he opened the front door he had a feeling of dread. Maisie Elder had taken leave of the mere portion of the world which she had occupied. Josiah wept like a child as he held her frozen hand.

She was buried on a cold funereal type of day attended by only Josiah, Percy, Ruby and Suzannah.

When Arabella found out that her daughter had been to the funeral, she wasn't pleased,

"I didn't know the old lady, never ever spoke to her myself so her death obviously means nothing to me, so I am surprised it does to you."

Suzannah didn't think the statement warranted an answer so she gave none. In her will, to Josiah's surprise Maisie had left all that she owned to him, and there were two other bequests.

He had to make sure that Percy Jacks used the rear garden as long as he wished, and that he took care of any needs that Suzannah and Ruby had.

His beloved benefactor had changed his life for ever, but he would have willingly given it all away in exchange for Maisie's company her lovely smile, the way she clapped her hands and laugh out loud. Everything about the memories moved the big man to tears.

With Suzannah and Ruby's help he sorted out the small amount of her belongings they also found clothes which had belonged to her long dead brothers which all went to the Red Cross. Josiah refused to part with Maisie's tea set, pictures and kept the rooms exactly how they had been when she was alive. That way he thought it made him still have a part of his old and much loved friend with him.

It took a long time for Josiah to cope with what had happened, he had never cared so much for any one before and he spent a great deal of time moping around the house recalling her sweet face, and thinking of all the times they had enjoyed together.

Gradually the weather improved and with it Josiah's mood.

Suzannah continued to take Percy and Josiah, when he was at the house, the usual soup. Allotment soup Percy called it. They were all admiring Percy's pigs one lunch time Josiah seemed preoccupied and suddenly he told them he was thinking of getting a lodger.

"It'll 'ave to be a bloke of course and no riff raff neither a nice refined sort of chap"

"Good idea," Suzannah said.

Percy didn't take a great deal of notice as he scratched one of the sows.

"I'm joining a pig club," Percy announced. There are going to be twelve of us. I'm looking forward to that," he sniffed and wiped his nose on his shiny sleeve.

CHAPTER 3

There came a loud knock on Josiah's door, he knew it would be his prospective lodger. William Season held out his hand in greeting. He was a smartly dressed man, about twenty five-ish with dark curly hair and a nice friendly manner. Josiah thought fleetingly that his smile was somehow not genuine, but quickly dismissed it. He had his false set of nashers so he could flash them if he so wanted.

"I'm Josiah, cum in and sit yer sen down," he led him into the parlour, feeling pleased that Ruby had done such a good job cleaning the house.

"You will need to know a little about me, and a little is all I am able to divulge to you," William began.

Josiah wasn't taking a great deal of notice as he had seen William's shiny shoes and wanted some the same.

"I am involved in military intelligence. As you will no doubt be aware, living in close proximity to the sea and within a short distance of the Docks. Trawlers move in and out of the port."

Josiah, had already decided to have him as a lodger, and didn't care what this man did for a living.

"Since 1940" William continued. "We have known that enemy aircraft have been present in the Humber. Gun fire has been heard and puffs of smoke regularly seen. These and certain other activities have been monitored closely and appropriate action taken to ensure maximum security and safety, one must keep one step in front of the enemy."

Josiah kept quiet; he was wondering if William was partial to a fish and chip supper which Mr Churchill had kindly exempted from rationing, providing of course there was any fish to be had.

William flashed a smile showing his white even teeth and pulled up the crease in his trousers. He then leant forward and lowered his voice.

"Can I be sure that you will keep this information to yourself, Josiah. It is vital to our war work that I can depend on you. I tell you this in case any-one asks any awkward questions."

"Me lips is sealed, William."

As Josiah hadn't understood or indeed listened, the secret was safe with him.

"Now would you like a cup of tea the tray is already set so it won't take a jiffy?"

William raised a hand.

"In a moment if you please Josiah, I have another couple of things I would like to tell you."

"Good lord luv us," Josiah thought. "I'm fair parched." But he just nodded.

"Some trawlers have been issued with Lewis guns for protection, but magnetic bombs are always a problem and are hazardous to shipping. The enemy are devious in the extreme." William sat back on the sofa once more.

"Are yer ready for a cuppa now?"

In a matter of seconds the tea was made as the kettle had been boiling for a long time.

Accepting his cup of tea William said,

"Do the Gibson-Ffiskes live next door to here?"

"Yer, do you know 'em?"

"Oh no, of course I don't actually know them. Does their daughter live there too? I would appreciate an introduction."

"Consider it done, William."

"Now can I ask you a couple of questions? Do you want to see your room and do you like fish and chips?"

"The room will be fine Josiah Can I assume that you are willing to take me on as your lodger? Now I must be going thank you."

He left his tea to go cold. Josiah saw him out and thought to himself, he still didn't know if 'e liked fish and chips.

A week later, William was in situ. Josiah was walking along the promenade on his way to the bank. He was feeling very happy with himself, he had a new pair of shiny shoes to go with his attire and he also had a lodger. He could now walk with his head held high. He thought for a moment about what had happened the previous day. William had been so anxious to meet the Gibson Ffiskes, for whatever reason. Apart from Suzannah they were nasty people who were best avoided. Josiah had taken William over to their house to introduce them. Hector's behaviour was very strange. He refused to shake hands with William and walked straight out of the door leaving Arabella to apologise. William didn't appear to be at all surprised at Hector's attitude.

Josiah reached the bank and headed for the cashier. Whilst idly waiting he glanced around, his eyes lit up when he caught sight of a thing of outstanding beauty. April Grantly, a very well dressed but unattractive lady wasn't the object of his desire. It was the huge diamond ring which she was wearing on the middle finger of her right chubby hand. His transaction completed, he made sure that the came into contact with the lady in question

"Oh I ham terribly sorry, madam," he said. Allow me to open the door for you." They chatted outside for a moment. She was older than he had first thought, but so obviously rich and Josiah liked that in a woman. They made arrangements to meet again the following evening.

Three of Percy's chickens had not produced any eggs for over a week. So he bought a clutch of yellow chicks and wrung the necks of the three errant birds.

Suzannah whilst cleaning and plucking them contemplated repeating the process with her parents and William Season. After William's humiliation on his first visit at the hands of her father, she was amazed that the experience hadn't deterred William at all.

Her mother typically, encouraged him to visit when Hector was at work. She fluttered her eye lashes at him in a ridiculous manner like an ageing vamp. Suzannah would take the tea in to them at her mother's request, but declined the offer of sharing a cup with them. There was something about the man which she couldn't explain. She only knew that she didn't like or trust him. He seemed to be forever just appearing in front of Suzannah and for no reason he would stand closer to her than she felt comfortable with, and ask her out. She always said an emphatic no, not caring how rude she appeared to be. He would just smile that irritating smile of his, and tell her that in the end she would say yes, which only served to make her more determined to never give in.

Before the front door closed, heralding her father's return from the office, Suzannah had been reading Eliza Acton's *Modern Cookery Book for Private Families*. She really did enjoy cooking even if her parents didn't appreciate her efforts. Ruby had finished for the day so she had a moment or two to read before setting the table in the dining room. She overheard her father and mother arguing so she stopped to listen.

"The blasted man had the impertinence to come to my office today, and he told me that he often pays you a visit and that you have made him very comfortable."

Her father's mood persisted throughout the meal. Suzannah's chicken pie was not mentioned, just eaten. She ignored her father and thought of all the trouble she had taken to follow the recipe, it tasted delicious and there was still a lot remaining for another meal and the bones she would use for stock.

Suddenly Hector turned to her it was the first time that she had been acknowledged as actually been present. "I forbid you to have anything to do with that man, Suzannah."

"Yes, father. Does anyone want tinned fruit for dessert Percy managed to get us some?"

"Is that the extent to your culinary skills, Suzannah? No I don't want any," her mother said, and turned to her husband, red in the face.

"Hector, I have my reasons as well you know."

"I have my reasons, too."

"Then kindly keep them to yourself, the world and his wife doesn't need to know, and I am doing what I consider to be for the best."

That night Suzannah went to her room in a very good mood she hadn't understood any of the conversation but took with her the contents of a tin of peaches, a spoon, her cookery books and a huge smile.

Josiah and April had been walking out together for some time. This was never going to be a love match as far as Josiah was concerned it was purely a means to an end. April was eleven years his senior and looked every day of it. Her fat dough like cheeks made her small eyes and blood red mouth sink into almost oblivion. She had a mole on her chin which proudly supported a single whisker. She did however have very good dress sense and was always corseted in like a ram rod. April was self-opinionated. She had strong thoughts on everything and was never shy at sharing them with anyone. Josiah had very few which was probably fortunate. He also had the ability to turn his mind to more important things while occasionally telling her that he agreed with whatever she had said even though he had no idea what it had been.

They were, this particular day on their way to her parent's imposing detached house for Josiah's first meeting with Major Cecil and Lady Bonny Grantley. He had as would have been expected, been given his instructions, accordingly he had scrubbed his hands with bleach and cleaned his nails with an available screw driver.

Cecil and Bonny had long since given up the notion that they would ever off-load their irritating unattractive daughter, Long ago they had envisaged a handsome suitable sort of chap, but as the years had disappeared they had been forced to lower their expectations. Not, they imagined to the depths of Josiah Kingston. Cecil had done his research on this man and was not very happy with what he had found out. Apart from the fact that he owned the well situated handsome house opposite to the sea front, there was very little else to recommend him.

April introduced Josiah, he appeared to be well dressed, admittedly he wasn't very appealing to the eye, but that was of little significance. Josiah had been, many, many times told how to act on this their first encounter. He was trying to recall all the instructions which he had been given.

"I am very pleased to meet you. Thank you for giving me the opportunity," he'd forgotten the rest, so proffered his very white rough hand.

"Indeed, yes indeed." The china-faced and more attractive version of April replied. Her smile didn't reach her eyes. "Do sit."

The tension in the air was palpable. Bonny rang for some tea. They were all relieved when Dora appeared with the trolley.

"Shall I pour, madam?" Bonny raised a condescending hand and Dora returned from whence she came.

"Josiah is involved with the fishing industry, and after the war he intends to be the front runner of a building project for East-Thorpe-on-Sea," April told them.

Sweat broke out on Josiah's neck and forehead.

"Splendid, splendid," Cecil remarked.

"How do you take your tea Josiah?" Bonny enquired.

"Milk no sugar"

April told her mother, before Josiah could say.

"In a cup."

The meeting seemed to be interminable to Josiah. Everything appeared to be a strain from the itsy-bitsy, crustless sandwiches with an unknown filling, to the cake which stuck to the roof of his dentures and no amount of tongue probing would shift it. The handles on the china tea cups was so small, he was terrified that he would spill the contents as it was impossible for him to get his sausage-like fingers through the handle. The moment that April suggested that the meeting should come to an end, Josiah was up out of his chair. Ignoring the cake crumbs which cascaded from his knees together with the bit of cloth which April had placed on his lap and disappeared onto the thick carpet beneath, he said his thanks. He recalled that April had told him to call her father Sir, but was sure that he hadn't been told to call her mother Madam. He shook hands once more smiled and hoped that cake wasn't stuck to his front teeth and was out of the house loosening his tie.

Cecil and Bonny reflected on the visit.

"Not the sort of chappie one would have hoped for, what did you make of the fellow?"

Cecil said when the door had been closed behind their guests.

Bonny thought for a moment.

"I do agree, but what does one do? I'm not sure, that we have a choice, unless we have a life time of April, and that thought is more than one can contemplate, but would the alternative be worse. Let's face it who in their right mind would take her on? What would one's friends say? It is such a problem. He is apparently, according to April, a friend of the

Gibson Ffiskes, lives next door in fact, and they are the biggest snobs around."

"We had better give this matter a great deal of thought. On one hand Josiah could be very useful to us. He doesn't appear to be a bright sort of fellow, and I'm sure that we can sort of persuade him to move in the right sort of direction and be of some use to us. We shall have to see."

Josiah had had his first experience in the black market partially because of his friend Percy and also through his work on the docks where things were more readily available, so he continued. People got to know him, he was always wary until he was certain that he wouldn't be caught and so far he had been very lucky. He began by getting fish and bartering for all sorts of food which he would mostly share with Percy and Suzannah. He then began to get more ambitious. He had it in his mind that, post-war; the seaside town would become a thriving resort with ice cream parlours, amusements and fish and chip cafés. He also knew that because of the war damage, housing would be needed desperately, and he intended to provide some. He wasn't quite sure how he would manage it yet but he would find out. He had a large amount of things which would be very useful for the bazaars which he intended to open, this assortment of suitable things were hidden under the floor boards in one of his rooms in the Corner House.

That evening he was meeting a young man in a crowded dock lands public house, 'The Fisherman's Arms'. It was to be the lad's first attempt at selling and he looked nervous. That suited Josiah as he was a master at it. Josiah sidled up to the youth and said the pre-arranged signal.

"I believe you have some time for me."

The youth opened up a large case revealing hundreds of ladies and gentleman's watches.

Josiah's mouth went dry and his heartbeat quickened.

"All good quality stuff, mister, rescued from fire damage," the lad said nervously.

Josiah knew quality when he saw it, but the game had to be played out carefully. He gave a sigh, and rubbed his chin pensively.

"Mm ... don't know if watches are what I'm lookin for, difficult to shift watches are, ow do I know that they are in workin order?"

"Take any one you like guv, they are all kosher, my word on it."

Josiah burrowed underneath and selected one, it worked perfectly. He shook it for effect and selected another and another.

"Ow much was yer thinking of for the lot?"

"An undred quid." The spotty faced youth said, not very convincingly.

"What?" Josiah said wide eyed.

"I reckon you are wasting my time. I'll tell yer what I'll do to tek 'em off yer 'ands, you are a young shaver and I'll try to give yer a leg up, twenty five quid."

"I paid more than that for em."

"You were robbed, young man, OK; my best offer thirty smackers and first refusal on any other stuff you want to shift."

"Josiah got his wallet out." Knowing that there were several hundred pounds of watches just beyond his fingertips, but he always played the game well.

"You'd better make yer mind up sharpish before a search party arrives."

The lad thrust the case in Josiah's direction snatched the proffered white five pound notes and was gone.

Josiah wanted to get home as soon as possible. He intended to catch a tram, which dropped him off right in outside his front door. So he hurried to the main road, it dropped him off right outside his front door. Looking back to check that he wasn't being followed, he saw in the distance over the dark sea a German plane with smoke pouring out of its rear. It lost height and rapidly crashed into the water. It was then that the sirens began to sound and darkness wrapped around him. He knew that no more trams would run that night and that he would be faced with a long walk home with a very heavy case of which no-one must know the contents. Explosions sounded from all directions, for a split second the sky was alight. One by one the stars became visible against the graceful half-moon which felt unreal. The bombs with their tales aflame lit up the road, darkness once more descended on the roads and houses. He could hear voices which were raised in panic and distress. Buildings were ablaze and the smell of disaster and smoke was everywhere. He walked as quickly as he could towards the main road. Windows where blown out and the ground was covered with rubble, There was a terrific explosion behind him where only minutes before he had been, and despite the heavy case he ran, his arm felt as if it was being pulled out of its socket. It was agony but the terror which he was feeling somehow seemed to put the pain into the back of his mind. His lungs felt as though they, too, would explode. He could run no more he had to get his breath back so he sat on the ground and prayed to a God which he didn't know if he believed in, and asked Maisie Elder for some help – in case she was up there looking down – to protect him from standing on a butterfly bomb. He began walking again; he had never in his life been so frightened. The case seemed to get heavier with every step, he frequently changed hands. He realised that after walking for about half an hour that he would never be able to walk all the way home, he was exhausted. He saw the pier in the distance and he had an idea, so he forced himself onward until he reached the beach railings and walked down the steps.

He walked ten strides from the black metal pier struts, dug a hole in the soft powdery sand next to the high sea wall. He knew well enough that the tide didn't reach as far as this. The adrenalin kept him scooping out the sand whilst he was aware of the background noises of bombs and explosions. When he considered the hole to be large and deep enough he placed the case at the bottom and quickly filled it in, finding a stray oyster shell he placed it on top for good luck. He knew that as the case was heavy even for a man of his size, without it he would be able to run as fast as he could to get home and also if he had been stopped by the police, he may have found it difficult to explain away the contents of the case. Back on the promenade he began to run. The last thing that he remembered was a blinding flash and a severe pain in his leg.

CHAPTER 4

After a night of bombing, in which Suzannah had spent the time encased in the air raid shelter with her mother. She would have gladly swapped places with her father who had been on A.R.P. duty. When her mother wasn't complaining, her snoring overpowered the noise of the sirens and bombs. Her father looked tired and drawn as he told them of the terrible damage inflicted particularly in the docklands area The Fisherman's Arms pub had been totally obliterated many with people had been killed or injured. Arabella wasn't listening.

"Hurry up and make some tea, Suzannah do, there is just so long that one can manage without sustenance especially cooped up in this cage, I didn't get a moments sleep."

Suzannah went to make the tea without making any comment, it was easier that way and after all these months she now failed to be shocked at the extent of mother's selfishness. When she took the tea into the drawing room her mother was on her back on the sofa, mouth open, snoring. Suzannah left the tray on the side table. Her father after freshening himself up, quickly drank his tea and went to work.

On Mondays Ruby spent some of the day cleaning at the Corner House. She popped her head around the door to say 'Hello' to Suzannah and also told her that Percy had gone cockling.

For Percy the smell of smoke was still hanging around on the beach. There were pieces of shrapnel scattered on the sand. Further along some boys with a donkey which had panniers on either side of its back were collecting cockles. Percy shouted at them to be careful as there may be some unexploded bombs under foot, one step on them and they would be blown to kingdom come. They waved and thanked him. Percy filled his sack and also collected some dabs the small fish which were left behind in shallow pools as the tide receded. He would give these to Suzannah and once the cockles had been cleaned he would keep some and use the rest for bartering.

It was May and the beach was so peaceful any one could easily imagine that the war was just a bad dream. Percy was reluctant to leave, he looked at the stream on the beach it had created a deep wide gully through the sand. The water in the stream was as clear as crystal, untouched by the war. There was hardly a ripple on the surface.

"It's only me," Ruby shouted as she went into the Corner House.

As no one answered she assumed that Josiah had gone to the docks to see if they needed any help after last night's raids. It had been a sad night for the dockland area. William would be at work as usual. She began to clean the kitchen whilst singing a tuneless version of 'The White Cliffs of Dover'. Firstly washing up the copious amounts of dirty dishes, she gave the yellow shallow sink a good scrub with some Vim and shone the lone brass tap. She took the coconut matting outside and gave it a good thrashing, and washed and polished the cardinal red tiled floor. After the rest of the kitchen had been cleaned, she as usual stood back to admire her work, knowing that it would be just as bad next Monday. She finished the rest of the downstairs rooms and went upstairs

Most of the bedrooms didn't have to be cleaned as they had never been opened since Maisie Elder had died and probably long before then. William's room usually she left until last, as it was generally locked anyway, and she didn't have a key. As he was a very meticulous man it only ever needed a dust, sweep and polish. She continued to clean Josiah's room which was always in a mess; she didn't know how any one man could make so much mess even if he tried. She stripped the bed and remade it with clean sheets. As she passed William's door she just gave the knob a quick turn, just to check that it was in fact locked, but to her surprise, it wasn't. She knocked and then hearing no reply she entered.

Ruby was shocked to find that his bed was covered with old newspaper cuttings and some sepia photographs. She looked around to see if he had left her a message telling her what he wanted her to do with them, there wasn't any. She glanced at the papers and photographs briefly, the words, Ruddlingden, Police search, and Missing, jumped out at her but they meant nothing. On closer inspection they did seem to be in some sort of order by the dates, so she assumed that was how William wanted them to be left. She carried on with her cleaning. When she heard the front door close she assumed it would be Josiah she shouted,

"I'm up ere I'll mek yer a cuppa in a sec."

The stairs began to creak and to her surprise she saw William Season.

What the hell are you doing searching my room?" he pulled her roughly by the arm and slammed the door behind them.

"Get out of here now," he told her and pushed her towards the stairs.

Ruby was terrified by this show of pointless anger, but William's sense of reason had, for that moment, deserted him. All that was in her mind was that she had to get away from him, panic had taken hold, and she ran. Suddenly William's attitude altered.

"Ruby, Ruby, Ruby stop, I'm sorry please stop."

Ruby wasn't taking any chances and continued to run, but he caught her up and grabbed her arm with a vice like grip. His face was ashen.

"I'm sorry I acted in that way it was thoughtless of me. You see I was worried that you may think me to be an untidy fellow leaving all those papers on my bed. You did see the papers didn't you, Ruby dear?"

He gave her a small unconvincing grin.

Ruby nodded. This excuse couldn't hide the certain dishonesty in what he was saying she knew instinctively that he was telling lies

"I was just doing me usual Monday work, your door was open so I just went in to clean, I didn't touch your papers or owt."

"The open door was an oversight on my part, it had been an eventful night for us all, you included, so I completely forgot about it. Let us just sit for a moment to compose ourselves.

"Now Ruby."

He said releasing his grip on her arm.

"Did you read any of the newspapers?"

"I'm not good at readin' I didn't' ave a lot of schoolin' yer see."

"You are sure, dear, have a little think about it."

All that Ruby could think about was getting out of the Corner House. She shook her head.

"You see, Ruby, my work is secret for the War Office, these newspapers are the very latest edition just printed, they contain sensitive information about the enemy and the state of war, they weren't of any interest and I was just going to discard them, so there is no need for you to remember them at all is there? Let us pretend that you didn't see them shall we?"

William had made a culpable mistake by assuming that Ruby's lack of education had taken away her common sense and ability to know a liar when she met one.

"Can I go now, I've finished me work."

William got his wallet out.

"Of course my dear you have been most helpful and co-operative."

He handed her a £1 note and carefully folded her fingers around it.

"Treat yourself to something nice," he said in a condescending sort of voice.

Although this was nearly the same amount of money which the Gibson Ffiskes paid her for a week's work, she said.

That is very kind of you, Mr Season, but I don't want any money that I ain't worked for and Josiah and Mrs Gibson Ffiske, pays me for that."

She made a hasty retreat. Suzannah saw her coming from the kitchen window.

"Jolly good, Ruby," she said as the back door opened I was hoping that you would soon be here, mother has her tea and I'm sure that Percy is thirsty so we can have ours now."

Ruby didn't reply. The shock at what had happened was just registering, she began to shake and feel faint. Once Suzannah noticed this she pulled out a chair.

"Whatever is it, Ruby, I have never seen you like this before are you ill?"

Suzannah knelt on the red tiled floor as Ruby sat down on the proffered seat.

"I've just ad a bit of a shock, that's all I will be fine in a mo."

Suzannah gave her a glass of water, Ruby's hand shook as she accepted it. Percy opened the door asking for his usual cup of tea. He saw his wife's chalk white face. "Wot's up wi yer,

Rube. You're not in the family way are yer, that would be a treat eh."

"No, Perce. I just felt a bit out of sorts I'm OK now."

Suzannah made the tea and Percy went back into the garden taking his tea with him, he didn't like getting involved in things concerning female problems.

The colour was slowly returning to Ruby's face. She accepted her cup of tea and drank it down.

"Would you like to go home and rest, or do you want to tell me what has upset you so?"

Suzannah asked her.

"I think I do need to tell yer, Suz, you are the only person I can tell, but I made a promise yer understand. I didn't 'ave a choice though I feared for me life, so does that promise count?"

"You tell me anything which you feel comfortable with, Ruby. I will fully understand."

For a moment Ruby was silent, and Suzannah waited, she got up off the cold floor and sat on a seat beside her.

"Was it Josiah who has upset you?"

She asked.

"Josiah, Lord no, I've known 'im since e woz a raggy arsed nipper like us, either me or Perce ad soon bash im if 'e said owt, never saw sight nor sound of Josiah. It woz that William Season as upset me."

Ruby told Suzannah of all that had happened, finishing off with

"I knew 'e was a liar but I'll never be able to prove it, e said they woz new papers and they weren't they woz old; e thinks I'm stupid and just cos I ain't ad a lot of learning, but I know a lot about folk and life, more 'n e'll ever know."

Suzannah spent some time thinking about what Ruby had said she needed all of her thoughts to rearrange themselves and to make sense of them. She wondered why she had taken an instant dislike to William and why her father seemed to share her opinion of him. Her mother seemed to think him charming but her mother thrived on flattery so that need not come into the equation. It was a mystery. One thing of which she was sure, William Season was not what he appeared to be. Knowledge was never wasted, with patience it would surely be expanded on as he inadvertently revealed more information about himself. The trouble was that he was very, very artful.

"I'm so pleased you told me Ruby. We must keep vigilant where Mr Season is concerned I don't know as yet what secret he holds but we will find out, I'm sure. You go home now and have some rest. Percy has given me some Dabs so that has solved the problem of dinner. He will take you home."

Suzannah decided to take a walk on the beach to clear her mind. She walked down the bouncy wooden planked steps and onto the fine sandy beach which was dotted here and there with broken sea shells. She had noticed that men had been onto the beach to explode the bombs and were just leaving. She took off her shoes for the sheer pleasure of feeling the sand between her toes and gazed out towards the incoming tide. It seemed like a moment which was suspended in time, the near perfection of it all appeared to come together and take with it the stresses and sadness of her life which she had taken for granted. It was one calm unearthly moment to be treasured for as long as she was able to hang on to it.

The seagulls with their haunting cries circled above, some brave souls were tempted into the sea. One or two early holiday makers sat on stripy deck chairs pretending that the war and its problems didn't exist. Suzannah reluctantly left the beach her problems hadn't diminished but at least she had enjoyed an hour's respite.

She began setting the table and wondered if there would ever be a time when she would be able to do what she wanted instead of the dictates of her parents.

The front door banged heralding the return of her father from work. She was just on her way back into the kitchen. Her father didn't usually acknowledge her as he would be more interested in pouring a pre-dinner gin and tonic for himself and Arabella. Despite the war, there was still plenty of alcohol to be had if you were prepared to pay over the odds for it and ask no questions. Hector was.

"Suzannah, a word if you please."

He sounded angry Suzannah assumed that it was tiredness.

"What is it, Father, I am in the middle of preparing dinner."

"Has our maid been into the Corner House to look through William Seasons private and confidential papers?"

Suzannah put a pan of fat onto the hob, trying to control her rising temper.

"Do you mean Ruby, Father, she has a name you know. How and why would Ruby be remotely interested in anything concerning that odious man?"

In one moment her father had taken away all the pleasure of her walk on the beach.

Her mother's voice echoed through to the kitchen.

"Hector, your gin and tonic is waiting and might I add, I had to pour it myself."

When the meal had been served and every one was seated, Suzannah was aware that her father was still angry, she ignored him.

"Are you sure that Mr Season's private papers haven't been tampered with by our maid."

Before she had chance to answer, her mother said,

"Suzannah, you have forgotten the napkins."

Hector banged on the table.

"Bugger the napkins, I want an answer."

Arabella and Suzannah's eyes opened wide.

51

"Hector, I will not tolerate foul language in this house."

Suzannah opened the drawer and threw the napkins onto the table. Arabella continued.

"I really do not know what has become of this family you are both acting like a pair of gutter snipes, and what may I ask is this?"

She pointed to her meal.

"I'm sorry, Mother, but there is a war on and we are out of caviar, so this is just fish."

"Sarcasm doesn't become you, dear, I just hope that it tastes better than it looks, although I doubt it."

"As a common, and may I add unpaid servant, I think it would be more appropriate, if I ate my meals in the kitchen from now onwards."

Suzannah picked up her plate and left the room, she couldn't remember ever feeling so angry and also so very tired and stressed. When she had completed her jobs she went to bed.

Just as sleep was wrapping its comfortable blanket around her, the thought jumped into her head. How did her father know about William, Ruby and the papers? Then oblivion took over and she slept.

CHAPTER 5

The phone rang Ruby answered it, and told Suzannah that April Grantley wanted to speak to her.

"Hello April, how are you?"

"It's my Josiah, I can't find him anywhere, have you seen him lately?"

"I'm very sorry April I haven't seen him for some time I assumed he may be in Langden Dyke doing some business."

April was agitated and crying.

"I have not seen him since the night of the bombings, but thankfully the destruction didn't reach this far along the beach, he is always so kind and considerate I can't think that he would go away without telling me."

Suzannah, although fond of Josiah, couldn't see these attributes applied to him, but then they say that love blindeth all.

"Have you rung the police, or the hospital?"

"I did ring the police a few times but the line was too busy to answer, should I ring again do you think?"

"I think that would be an excellent idea April, ring the hospital, too, let me know if I can do anything to help."

That afternoon the front door bell rang. Suzannah knew who it would be, and answered it herself.

"Good afternoon, Suzannah, How nice it is to see you," he placed a hand on her shoulder. She quickly turned without any eye contact.

"I expect that you want to see my mother, William," she opened the drawing room door, knowing that her mother was expecting him by the smile on her face,

"Tea please, Suzannah," she said before greeting William.

Back in the kitchen Ruby had already set the tea tray and was putting boiling water into the pot. She said

"I'll tek it in, Suz, I don't want im ter think as I am scared on im."

Later when Ruby had left for the day and Suzannah had cooked the evening meal, she grinned to herself. The table was set and her parents were called into the dining room, the remains of their gin and tonics still in their hands. Suzannah said.

"It is so nice for you to share your afternoons with William, mother, it must give you a break from the monotony."

She closed the door quickly and listened to the raised voices.

Back in the kitchen she ate her solitary meal with a cookery book in front of her; a recipe for a banana pudding based on parsnips caught her eye she would make it for pudding tomorrow. Sure was that her mother wouldn't enjoy it, she laughed to herself.

The sound of calm voices and an unpleasant antiseptic sort of smell seemed to be somewhere in the distance, then as quickly as it came, it disappeared leaving a void only to re appear some time later, how long there was no way of knowing. A faceless voice spoke but the words were meaningless, then the void once again. A rough hand gently shook him. His legs hurt.

"Can you hear me now, can you tell me your name. You are in hospital?"

His mouth was so dry and his tongue felt far too large to fit inside. The nurse gave him a drink.

"Better now, are you Josiah Kingston?" he nodded.

"You have a visitor."

April pounced on him and covered his face with tears and kisses.

"Ger off me."

"I've been so worried about you for three days, my darling, why didn't you let me know?"

"Cos I dint know me sen until just now and me legs urt, wot yer on about any road, get me another drink I'm fair parched."

Having satisfied his thirst she told him that he had been hurt in a bombing on the promenade, and that they only discovered his name from his identity card.

"What on earth were you doing on the promenade in a bombing raid?"

Suddenly it all came flooding back to him, the case ten paces from the pier struts he must get out of here.

"I don't remember why I woz there, I've bin ere three days yer say, oh my Lord I can't stay ere no longer."

"Don't shout, my love, and do please try to refine your language a little, I have told you and that is the main reason why mother and father find it so difficult to accept you as a future son-in-law. I know that I am over 21 but I would like their blessing."

And their money, Josiah thought I'll find a way, in the meantime how am I going to get the case when I can't move.

"Nurse, nurse he yelled, get us sommat for this pain in me legs will yer?"

She came with a kidney dish to give him an injection. Pulling the screens around him she told April that it was time for her to leave.

"Wots up we me legs any road nurse why, do they urt?"

"You received an injury from a bomb, some bones are fractured or broken, you were very lucky you could have lost both your legs."

The pain was beginning to ease. He must go and find his case before some-one else did, but how? There must be a way. He couldn't ask anyone to do it for him not even Percy, he would want half and he wouldn't be able to keep his gob shut.

When the tearful April arrived home and told her parents about her ordeal. Her father asked her if Josiah was likely to die from his injuries, April burst into tears and ran upstairs.

Bonny said, "That was a thoughtless thing to say Cecil; if he died we would still be stuck with April."

It was one week later that a very worried Josiah left hospital and even then it was against medical advice. He couldn't stand the worry any longer. He had arranged for a taxi to pick him up. He still had one leg in plaster and the other thickly bandaged and an appointment card in his pocket.

"Tek me to the Pier if you please."

He informed the driver. The driver was a little bewildered as the hospital had told him to take him to the Corner House on the Promenade, which was in the opposite direction, but he did as Josiah had told him as it would be him who paid the bill at the end of the journey.

At the Pier Josiah asked him to wait and with great difficulty he climbed out of the taxi, he did feel a little dizzy but it soon passed.

Josiah struggled down the steps and onto the beach. He had to wait a moment as he seemed to be out of breath. With his crutches walked the ten paces, he was concerned that either the paces were of different lengths walking with crutches than they had been without them, and also had someone got there before him?

He was exhausted but as he saw that the oyster shell was still in the same place that he had put it, his energy returned. He laid his crutches onto the soft sand and began to scoop up with both of his hands it took all of his strength to ignore the pain in his legs. It seemed that the sand fell into the hole faster than he could scoop it out, he was sweating and tired, but he had to continue. At last he caught sight of just a tiny bit of the brown case which increased his efforts. He pulled the case out and with a huge amount of effort placed it beside his crutches. Exhausted he leant against the tall sea wall for a moment to rest. He thought of that night and how many people had been injured or killed. He was one of the lucky ones so many were not as fortunate. He stood up with the help of the wall. And hooking the case around his crutches he began his return journey. The head of the taxi driver appeared over the iron railings.

"Are you sure that you want me to wait mate, only the clocks ticking and it will cost you a lot of money?"

He saw that Josiah was struggling to carry the case and walk with crutches up the steps from the beach. He noticed that he didn't look well, so he ran to him grabbed the case and with his other hand helped Josiah up the steps.

At the top Josiah managed to thank the taxi driver and as he leant on the railings he said.

"I'm about buggered."

They finally arrived at the Corner House. And the taxi driver helped him inside.

"I'm afraid this is going to cost you", he told Josiah, "Don't worry thank-you for your kindness."

He pushed a ten pound note into the man's hand.

"Yer never saw me or tuk me to the beach, did yer?"

The man was so surprised he said.

"Are you sure? This is an awful lot of money it will set me and the wife up nicely we have a little one on the way so if it's a boy we will call him Josiah, and no I haven't seen you before."

Percy had managed to supply Suzannah with some sugar and butter. She asked Ruby if she thought it would be a good idea if they were to make some biscuits and shared them. Percy's chickens were not laying eggs very well and the small amount the chickens had been willing to part with was substantially reduced Suzannah did have some dried egg from their rations. So the biscuits were made from that. She found some rather old dried fruit and added it to the mixture. They turned out to be really delicious. The tea was made and Ruby went out to call Percy in. During the cold weather he liked to come inside to enjoy his tea.

"Guess who I've just seen?" he told them.

"Jo, e'se oblin on crutches, so e is and e'se coming ere for a brew."

The back door opened to reveal the wounded soldier.

"Oh my Lord."

Ruby said.

"Wot as appened to yer?"

She rushed to get one of the empty pig swill buckets to put Josiah's legs on as he sat down.

"I've bin in the wars so to speak,"

He accepted his cup of tea,

"April let yer know dint she."

"Is them ome made biscuits I can see?"

Suzannah handed him a plate full.

He began to tell them of his terrible ordeal, omitting the part about the case. He also repeated that couldn't recall how he was on that end of the promenade in the first place.

All the biscuits had gone save for a few crumbs which, when he stood up, cascaded to the floor.

"I have bought you ladies a little gift."

He gave them a pair of stockings each. Then with a large burp he left.

"I don't reckon that there are any biscuits left to share."

Ruby said.

"Never mind, the stockings are worth it don't you reckon, Ruby?"

April and Josiah walked up the Grantley's gravel drive and into their large impressive hall.

"Feet." April said and Josiah obediently wiped his feet on the door mat.

Cecil and Bonny appeared, and after shakings hands they proceeded into the drawing room.

"How nice to see you again," Bonny said. "Do sit."

Josiah, as he had been told, answered accordingly. Cecil was standing rubbing his hands together, and told Josiah how pleased they had been that he had survived his near death experience, Bonny had organised some tea in anticipation of their visit. The tension in the air was apparent. Josiah cleared his throat.

"We 'ave sommat to tell yer," April butted in. "I'm going to have a baby."

Bonny's jaw dropped, her eyes seemed to bulge out from their sockets. April smiled, Josiah stared at his shiny shoes and Cecil got to his feet in haste.

"You bounder Kingston how could you take advantage of our daughter."

"He didn't have to tie me down, Father." Bonny seemed to collapse, Cecil fanned her with a copy of *Ideal Homes* which revived her.

"I do not believe it, I simply cannot take it in, a daughter of mine, and before marriage one cannot contemplate it. We will have to organise a wedding quickly. Oh April how could you?"

"We can blame the war?" Cecil said.

April poured the tea and passed it around. Josiah thought of his continued success with the yanks.

"Madam Daphne (Clothes for the Discerning) will have to be called upon to make my outfit and April's wedding gown not to mention the brides maids and everything else which will be left to me to organise."

"Bad show, very bad show, I will have to explain it to the Masons, the golf club, not to mention the council"

"Oh yes, Cecil, just think of yourself, never a care for me, people do get married quickly in the war I suppose, but getting the appropriate attire is not easy."

April stood up red in the face,

"Be quiet both of you. It is me and Josiah who are getting married and all you two go on about is clothes and the war, you have wanted to get rid of me for ages and now you can, so shut up. We don't care about all that rubbish."

Josiah, who hadn't been listening, realised that April was standing and thought it was time to leave.

"Are we going to see 'Casablanca' at the Plaza?" he glanced at his watch

Things at the GibsonFfiskes were equally as heated. Hector had arrived home early in the evening in an angry frame of mind. He banged the front door and dropped his briefcase noisily on the black and white tiled floor and marched into the kitchen. Ruby was washing up in the sink, her last job before going home.

"Where is my daughter?" he shouted

Ruby didn't turn around.

"She's gone to tek Percy the pig swill out yonder"

Hector's face was one of horror.

The door opened and Suzannah returned, empty galvanized bucket in hand.

"A word if you please. Not in front of the staff."

"I'm off any road," Ruby said.

Suzannah followed him, and pulled a funny face at Ruby, who turned to the sink and silently laughed.

"Do you want us to go into your office?"

She knew this would make him angry but she no longer cared. He swung round and jabbed his finger into her shoulder.

"Do not ever, ever think of going into my office. It is my domain and only I have the key."

"Why?" she asked knowing that it was a pointless question.

"Suzannah, I ask the questions in this house not you, do you understand? Has that man been here again today?"

"I suggest you ask my mother as I couldn't possibly say."

She left him feeling as if she had scored some sort of a point. She could hear raised voices as she set the table for their meal. Minutes later the door banged and she dashed up to the landing window, she saw her father heading for the Corner House. She returned to the kitchen. Her mother rang her bell even though she knew that Suzannah was the only other person in the house.

"I'll have my meal your father will be some time as he has some pressing business at the office." Suzannah lacked the enthusiasm to argue.

Josiah, now recovered, had made arrangements to meet a man in the 'Ships Tavern' The 'Fisherman's Arms' was now just a pile of rubble. Most of the former customers had, without a great deal of trouble, transferred to this pub, after grieving for their drinking partners, now dead. This was war, and after a few pints they could numb the pain of loss and hope that the next time it wouldn't be their turn. Josiah looked around the crowded pub recalling the last time that he had been in the same situation. This time he had brought his own suitcase.

There was a tap on Josiah's back, he had been told to meet a bald stocky guy called Tiny, and he certainly was, Josiah knew that this ugly man had some equally ugly larger men in the pub. He wasn't going to be a pushover this would require nerves of steel.

"Interested in Nottingham lace?" Tiny, as he called himself, asked Josiah.

"Do I look like a bloke as is interested in bleedin' lace?" Josiah retorted maintaining eye contact.

When Tiny spoke his mouth didn't move, something like a ventriloquist. His bald head was as shiny as a mirror and Josiah noticed that Tiny shrugged his shoulders a great deal, large shoulders for such a small man, probably made of padding and not muscle.

"To sell, not to bloody wear," he said.

"Let's 'ave a butchers at wot yer got."

Josiah wasn't going to look as if he was being intimidated, he noticed a gents. just behind the man, he recalled being here before.

Tiny opened a large cardboard box which he handed to Josiah.

"No rubbish, it's all pure Nottingham lace, saved from a burning factory so it's good stuff."

Josiah went to the bottom of the box and gave each item a tug, certainly good gear,

"H'm not easy to offload this sort of gear, I'm not sure that I could take the lot, Tiny"

"If you don't tek the lot I got another bloke comin in arf an 'our as will."

Josiah stared Tiny in the eyes.

"Is that a fact he said." Tiny blinked so Josiah knew that he was lying.

"Let me see what I can do, you look a nice sort of chap and so do your minders, mine are outside in case you wondered, ow many do yer reckon that there is in this ere box?"

"An undred or more, I counted em this morning me sen, lost count when I got to an undred."

"So I reckon on fifty quid."

Josiah laughed.

"Is that your best price or are yer avin a laugh? I reckon yer ave got yer sums wrong, easy mistake, I reckon 10 quid is about right."

"Yer ad be robbin me at that."

Josiah held his nerve and continued to stare down into Tiny's eyes.

"I tell you what, Tiny, because I want to do business wi yer again 10 quid an 10 pairs of ladies stockings," he held out his hand. Which Tiny grasped. Josiah handed him his stockings and cash, grabbed the box and disappeared into the gents and out of the fire door at the other side. The tram was just leaving as he managed to jump on board.

When he arrived home, he examined the 95 assorted magnificent Nottingham lace items he was pleased especially as he had only given Tiny 7 pairs of stockings. He would be off as soon as was possible to Langden Dyke. The yanks were partial to Nottingham lace to send home to their mothers.

Bonny Grantley was stressed. She had visited Madam Daphne (Clothes for the Discerning) and after coming to a compromise concerning the lack of coupons and a great deal of cash, ordered her outfit. April had been measured up for her wedding dress after explaining to Madam that she was putting on a little weight because of her over eating, as she was so excited. Madam smiled but knew that it was not the eating which was the reason for the weight gain.

Josiah had provided some parachute silk for the two bridesmaid's dresses. One was the mayor's daughter and the other the offspring of the master of the lodge. A beautiful three tiered, cardboard wedding cake was made to hide the small one underneath. It would look impressive on the wedding photographs and in the local East-Thorpe-on-sea Gazette. All this seemed to be in order; it was Josiah's choice of best man which Bonny was concerned about, Josiah had chosen Percy Jacks, now Percy was a jolly good chap when one needed anything which was difficult to obtain but as a best man. He didn't actually fit the bill.

Luckily Percy was dreading the thought of being best man and in the end Ruby told Josiah of her husband's plight. This didn't concern Josiah and he asked William Season to step in. William was overjoyed and spent some considerable time rehearsing his speech. Josiah's problem was, having to spend a year's supply of coupons on his suit and accessories. In the end he didn't have any choice but to give in, and he thought that after the wedding he could always flog it. Cecil lent him a pair of gold cuff links. Josiah hoped that his prospective father-in-law would forget about the loan, but knew that he was day dreaming.

April smiled as she held her father's arm. The music from the great organ met them as they walked slowly down the cardinal-red carpeted central aisle. Each of them thinking for differing reasons that they didn't ever believe that this day would come. The safety pin on Aprils dress didn't show. The wedding however, was not exactly as the Grantley's would have liked, but as Cecil repeated it was because of the war. William Season made an excellent best man's speech. In fact Bonny nudged her husband to tell him that half an hour was more than enough and some people were in danger of leaving or going to sleep. Cecil repeated that the rushed wedding was because of the war, which no-one believed but clapped anyway whilst making a note on their calendar. The reception was held at their home.

Sir Cecil and Lady Grantley gave the couple a detached house which was in the town and they already owned, as a wedding gift. Josiah could never understand why they had couldn't live together in the Corner house, and was finding it all a bit tedious. It had been bad enough having to read out the speech which his father in law had written for him and that he couldn't understand, but shaking hands with people he didn't know or indeed did not want to know, was more than he could cope with. Then there was the obnoxious bridesmaids to thank. He continued to ask his blushing and rather large bride when they would be able to leave.

CHAPTER 6

For whatever reasons, William still seemed to be a regular visitor of Arabella's Hector seemed to be resigned to the fact and was far more affable with William and sometimes even quite friendly, Suzannah often thought that her father seemed wary or frightened of him. She however dismissed the thought as she was far too busy with the Christmas preparations to dwell on the subject. The butcher had done his work on three of Percy's pigs, bearing in mind that he was only legally allowed two. One Percy gave to the butcher one he kept to sell and the remaining one was for them to share with Suzannah.

Ruby and Suzannah made two small Christmas cakes and puddings which contained a lot of bread crumbs but with the help of Josiah's whisky would taste good.

Suzannah continued to eat her evening meal in the kitchen with only the cookery books for company, she enjoyed it that way. Hector's attitude to her was much improved, she recalled him actually talking to her in a civil manner and even on one occasion calling her dear. Suzannah assumed that it was because she had stood up for herself, maybe he now respected her for it or perhaps there was another reason. Nothing should be taken for granted with her parents. Anyway it didn't concern her as her feelings for him would never alter.

A week before Christmas, she was told that she was wanted in the drawing room to see her parents; Suzannah was just about to begin to clear up after the evening meal had been eaten. She imagined that it must be to discuss the Christmas dinner arrangements, and she was anxious to get it over with quickly so that she could go to bed and read a new Marguerite Pattern cookery book.

Her father stood in front of the fire with his arms behind his back, Suzannah wasn't concerned until she noticed that his moustache had begun to quiver.

"We have been thinking about Christmas dinner, my dear."

"There is no need to be concerned," Suzannah interrupted.

"It will be pork and stuffing apple sauce and fresh vegetables followed by Christmas pudding. And hopefully some sort of sauce for which I was hoping that you would sacrifice some of your brandy which you bought from Josiah and is at the back of the cupboard. I'm afraid, that is all it will be as there is a war on."

Her mother said.

"Suzannah, your hands, dear, they look like they belong to a house maid, you must take more care of them. I will get you some hand cream if there is any available, that will do for your Christmas gift."

"That meal sounds awfully good," her father told her.

"But that is not the reason for asking to see you. As William Season will be alone on Christmas day we want to ask him to come here for his dinner with us, you will of course join us too."

"What are you saying father?" she began to think that she had misheard what he had said.

"You hate the man as I do, only mother likes him because he flatters her, I refuse to cook for him or even sit with him on Christmas day."

Her father came closer to her in the threatening manner which Suzannah had long ago thought amusing, but there was something different about this time. It seemed to incorporate fear as well as desperation and anger. This time it didn't seem to be at all amusing she felt afraid.

"You will do as you are told, this is our house and so long as you are under our roof you will obey me."

She couldn't find any words to say so her thoughts of horror remained unspoken and died with a sigh before she left the room.

She only managed to hear her mother saying. "Take care of your hands, dear."

Suzannah couldn't sleep. Her mind was controlled by the underlining feeling of ominous dread, a deep foreboding pool, dark and unfathomable, she was lost in an uncontrollable whirlpool from which there was no escape and never would be.

Christmas day dawned like a day from a Dickens novel, bright white and crisp. Suzannah had decided that she had no alternative than just to go through with whatever she had been forced to do. Christmas was just one day and she just had to keep calm and it would soon be over. But would it?

With Ruby's help she had made the dining room look attractive with holly and greenery from outside, last week. The artificial Christmas tree was decorated with what was available. Her parents failed to notice all their efforts. Ruby had been so excited about the festivities at her own house that Suzannah wished that she could have joined them. She cooked the dinner with less enthusiasm then was required. The pork with crackling cooked itself more or less, the sprouts began to take on a yellow tinge, there was rather more of her father's brandy in the pudding and sauce than was required, even the gravy had a good splash. To her mother's horror the serving dishes didn't match.

At dinner she even had to sit next to William as her parents had insisted, making sure that no part of her was in any contact with him and that she didn't once make any eye contact and spoke only when addressed. The food seemed to swell in her mouth she had served herself as small a portion as she could get away with. It was nearly over she told herself then after clearing up she would be able to go to her room read and enjoy her treat, a chocolate bar which Josiah had given to her.

Without warning William pushed his chair back and knelt onto one knee, Suzannah thought that he had inadvertently dropped a knife or some other cutlery so prepared herself to fetch him another.

"Will you do me the honour of becoming my wife?"

The diamond ring which he forced onto her finger felt like a dagger in her heart.

She stood up abruptly and pushed her chair back, it fell onto the floor.

"No. No. No. No. No never," she removed the ring, and threw it in no particular direction. William and her parents watched in horror as the sparkle twisted and turned in the air before landing in the coal bucket. Suzannah didn't wait long enough to witness this, as she ran to her room and locked the door.

Another sleepless, troubled night followed, and despite William, and her parents pleas she refused to answer.

Boxing Day, came and went Suzannah did her work and then decided to have a deep bath – blow the regulations.

The following day Ruby returned.

"Oh, Suz, yer look washed out, did yer 'ave a bugger of a Christmas? I was 'opin that yers ad be as good as ours."

"Ruby, I can honestly say that it was the very worst Christmas of my life even the one's which I had at school, when every other girl had gone home or to other people's houses for the hols was better than this. William asked me to marry him it doesn't get much worse than that does it?"

"Oh my good Lord, yer did say no dint yer?" Ruby, hands over her mouth exclaimed in horror.

"Of course, but I've got this dreadful feeling that, that won't be the end of it, there is something going on, I can feel it, and I don't know what to do. Tell me about your day and it will cheer me up."

"We ad an ell of a day, Percy's dad ad just got out of prison, most of the family came except two of me brothers 'oo are fightin in the war so we said a prayer for 'em, my sisters and their kids came an all, The ouse was so full the kids ad to sit on the floor. Percy ad got some booze from God knows where, so most of em were pie-eyed we ad a good old sing song, 'We'll Meet Again' and 'White Cliffs of Dover' and the ones as was still ungry ad to mek do with bread an jam, but they dint care. It went too quick, Suz, yer know what I mean?"

Suzannah didn't, so she just smiled and told Ruby how pleased she was for her.

The day progressed. Suzannah had told Ruby that she would rather not talk about her problem for the moment, as she knew that she would be reduced to tears. Ruby did her best to cheer Suzannah up but it was hard as she felt so sorry for her.

It was nearly 4 o'clock when Hector appeared in the kitchen. He told Ruby to go home for the rest of the day. Ruby reluctantly did as she was told after giving Suzannah's hand a surreptitious squeeze.

"Suzannah, a word if you please, in the drawing room."

She had a sinking feeling as she followed her father her legs feeling like jelly. Her mother was sitting on the sofa but did not greet her. The fire was blazing in the hearth despite the shortage of coal and the room was warm, much warmer than the kitchen she hoped that the ring was burning with it. The aura of something that she didn't feel comfortable with continued to creep in from the pit of her stomach. Suzannah was sure that her mother was not in fact reading the magazine that she seemed so engrossed in.

Hector caressed his moustache the way one would stroke a favourite pet.

"I am sure that now you have had the time to consider William's proposal and that you will see the sense of it, and want to change your mind."

"Suzannah used up every bit of courage and said. "Nothing he or you said would make me change my mind I don't like him, let alone love him, you used to feel the same father, so what happened to change your mind?"

"Suzannah," her father said as he paced up and down. "Loving someone is not a prerequisite for marriage; many good unions come from companionship and respect. Sometimes we all have to do things which at the time we do not understand the reasoning of," he made a cursory glance in Arabella's direction, to no avail

"I will never feel anything but intense dislike for William Season and under no circumstances could I ever respect him. I cannot for the life of me see what happened for you to change your mind about him. Are you going to tell me?"

Her heart was beating so hard and loud in her chest that she was sure that he could hear it.

"No, I am not, it is none of your business." He paused to stroke his moustache.

"Let me put it to you this way, you have enjoyed many years of private education, and now is the time for you to repay that debt."

He wagged a finger closely to her nose. Suzannah – recalling her time at boarding school – felt her head would explode with anger.

"I am an unpaid servant; I don't think that the education of which I not only had no say in, and hated, prepared me to become a skivvy. It was because of you and my mother's dislike of me and your selfishness that, not only was I forced to stay at school when all the others went home for hols, but when you needed an unpaid servant to wait on you, I was brought home. Not for my benefit, but for you two to continue to sit on your behinds and have me wait on you free of charge."

"That's enough, Suzannah, I have never heard such rubbish."

He glanced at Arabella who refused to look up. He continued to stroke his moustache. Suzannah was shaking with useless aggression. There were so many things which she needed to say that were vying for position that none of them managed to reach her lips and died in the confusion and anger in her mind.

"You will do as you are told, Suzannah, if you fail to comply you will find out just how hard it is to manage when you are no longer required to work in this house and are compelled to look for another position. You will not be the sole beneficiary of our wills as you are at present and we will refuse to supply you with a reference. You complain about your life now, but I am sure being homeless, penniless and with little chance of any other opportunity will change your mind."

Suzannah stood speechless for a moment, her mother got up and giving her husband a very angry look, she left the room. For Suzannah it seemed impossible that her parents could hate her so much. What could she have possibly done to deserve this?

Suzannah could not remember how she got onto the beach. The scouring force of the wind which whipped up the sand and burnt her eyes, reeled before her, unnoticed. The grey pulsating sea was a swirling mass, the sky dark as steel. As she walked onward the force of the wind took her breath away. It began to snow. She stopped to look upwards at the now completely white sky, even the beach was showing signs of changing from yellow to white. She suddenly realised that she was shivering, looking down she saw she had on just a thin dress which was now not only wet but beginning to freeze as stiff as cardboard. She would have to return, she couldn't think of it as home, just the place where she had no option but to work.

She wished her mother and father were dead.

While her daughter was walking on the beach, Arabella had a stern word with Hector.

"You went too far, Hector. Even I was ashamed of you and of myself."

"I didn't have a choice did I?"

"You had a choice long ago, I trusted you, I had confidence in you, and believe it or not as far as the dreadful William is concerned I did try to avert the situation. I do not profess to have been a good caring mother as I know that I am not, but I cannot believe that anyone should be forced to marry such an evil man."

"Arabella, just think of the consequences …?"

Too late, she had left the room.

CHAPTER 7

The wedding was arranged for Saturday the 9th January 1943 which didn't give Suzannah a great deal of time to dwell on it. She refused to let the subject enter even into the periphery of her mind. She cared nothing about any arrangements which had been made, only that she had made none. Her mother constantly chided her concerning the matter, Suzannah just shrugged her shoulders.

"You neither know, nor care, what your wedding dress looks like, or who are to be your brides-maids. It has been a nightmare for me choosing flowers at this time of year and with so many flower beds being replaced with vegetable patches. May I also say Madam Daphne (Clothes for the Discerning) is waiting for me, the bridesmaids and the men, to go for the final fitting of their wedding attire. Then there is the food arrangements to be …."

Too late Suzannah had walked off, not caring about the injustice of her mother's speech. She had heard it all before so many times.

Only Ruby understood Suzannah's sorrow, and her refusal to talk about it. Josiah, who knew nothing of the circumstances, had assumed that as he instigated the meeting in the first place, he was starting to fulfil his promise to Maisie Elder. Suzannah just seemed to float in a haze and took no interest in the wedding arrangements. Her mother had chosen her wedding dress as she had refused to go to see it, also those of the bridesmaids who Suzannah had never met. The diamond ring reappeared and again was placed on her finger by a triumphant William who, the next day, had some important war work he had to attend to; so the ring resided in her bedroom window. She carried on her work as usual and felt no guilt in wishing that William would be blown up. She would present her parents with an egg floating on soggy toast for their meal, when they complained she just ignored them and returned to the kitchen. She was losing even more weight and Ruby was so sorry for her. Hector showed his displeasure by just shaking his newspaper on the odd time that he was at home. She didn't ever speak to William. He had won, she couldn't even spare any time to wonder why or even care, her brain refused to consider her future with William.

It had also been decided that they would live with her parents until the war was over, presumably she would then be on hand to continue working as a skivvy to one extra person. To that end the third floor had been allocated for their use. Decorators had, somehow been found to complete the work. Or so William had said, Suzannah, as usual let it flow over her head and to her knowledge no workmen appeared. He had taken her parent's car to be checked and filled with petrol, he told them that it was to be carried out by a friend of a friend who owed him a favour, and as this sort of thing happened during the war it didn't seem to be unusual. He had also booked at his own expense, accommodation for them at the 'Royal Hotel the most expensive of hotels in Langden Dyke, he assured them, they deserved it for all their hard work. By now no one was happy with the situation. No one, that is except William. He didn't care about any ones feelings he was on the way to complete his longed for, and to Suzannah unknown, ambition and that was all that mattered.

The day finally dawned; Ruby put on Susannah's make up and brushed her hair until it shone. She wore it loose as usual and not in the fashion of the day rolled up like a sausage, it cascaded down her back like spun gold. Even in her sadness she looked stunningly beautiful, the gown, although stupendous, was rather large for her. Suzannah gave her a big hug and thanked her for all she had done.

"You and Percy are my only friends please don't ever leave me."

Ruby cried as she assured her that she would never desert her. She saw that Suzannah was dry eyed so many useless tears had been left unshed.

At the church the organ music thundered all around them filling the great ancient building and echoing down the nave. Suzannah walked along the centre aisle, followed by six bridesmaids. She refused to smile or hold her father's arm .With the organs wonderful music, all the faces of the congregation turned to admire the sheer beauty of the sad bride to be, that is all except William. She didn't look at him and just repeated the meaningless words which she had been told to say. The hymns were sung the register was signed and photographs were taken. Then the reception was endured. Hector told Suzannah to try and look happier.

"I have done everything else that you and mother forced me to do, and that as I recall, did not include smiling, I will never forgive you both for forcing me into this life of hell, with a man I hate. I hope that you and mother get what you deserve."

As soon as the speeches and the reception were over, the Gibson Ffiskes left by car and the Seasons headed for the railway station. It had begun to snow.

The station was busy but before William had the chance to click his fingers a porter appeared and loaded their luggage onto his trolley. William thanked him with a few pence and they took their seats inside the great train. No-one joined them in their compartment and the guard waved his green flag and blew his whistle. They were off, Suzannah without a word threw her new hat, which she hated, onto the opposite seat and opened her copy of Daphne du Maurier's Hungry Hill.

Two stations later a corpulent couple joined them and sitting on the opposite side of the carriage, crushed her hat.

By the time they reached their destination it was mid-afternoon, bitterly cold and dark. They could just manage to make out the rear of the large building and a sign which read:- 'The Bridge Hotel'. The door sprung open and with it a beam of welcoming golden light.

Early the next morning, Suzannah was woken up by the loud knocking on their hotel bedroom door her husband didn't stir from his slumbers. Looking at him made her remember the dreadful humiliating activities of the previous night. She grabbed her dressing gown and answered the door. She was confronted by a maid dressed in black and white.

"Mrs Season," she said. "Will you please come downstairs as quickly as you can there is an important message for you."

"I can't imagine what it can be about I'll come when I am dressed."

She closed the door.

The manageress was wringing her hands. As soon as she saw Suzannah she clasped her in a most unwelcome embrace. A policeman was standing beside her. He was a tall thin man who somehow didn't seem to look comfortable in his uniform. He had removed his helmet and was holding it under his arm. Suzannah idly wandered why he didn't put it down on one of the many chairs, did he think that someone would steal it or even destroy it?

She was told to sit down and the maid appeared with a cup of tea.

"Are you Mrs Suzannah Season?" he asked. She nodded.

"Where is your husband?"

"Look what is all this about? He is asleep and there isn't any need to disturb him, whatever it is about I can tell him myself."

"I'm afraid that I have some very bad news to tell you and I thought that you would rather have him with you."

77

"That's not necessary ".

"I'm sorry to have to tell you but your parents have been killed in a car accident, it could have been a bomb we have been informed. They were on their way, I think I'm right in saying, to Langden Dyke yesterday afternoon."

Suzannah drank her tea, she felt nothing, no emotion what so ever. The officer looked uncomfortable.

"Do you understand what I am saying?" he bent low and looked at her, a deep penetrating look. She had noticed a print of "Bathers at Asnieres" by Seurat on the wall opposite, she rather liked it and was trying to recall where she had seen it before.

"We are most terribly sorry and you on your honeymoon too."

"Would you like some brandy, Mrs Season?" The manageress or whatever she called herself asked. She looked very concerned probably the owners of the smart hotel would not be pleased that guests had to be told of the sad demise of their parents when they were staying there. She hoped that none of the other guests would find out.

"We keep some for medicinal purposes?"

She hoped that Mrs Season would decline her offer as then she would be able to have a glass herself, she did feel in need of it.

"No thank you, what I would most enjoy is a bath."

She intended to once again ignore the five inch Plimsoll line which had been imposed on them and wallow in deep warm water. Her biggest regret was that her parents had to wait until after her wedding was over, to die.

The Seasons arrived home that same day by train, there seemed to be so many people phoning up with their condolences or coming to the house for the same reason. William who didn't seem at all surprised or upset when she had told him eventually advised her to go to bed and rest and that he would organise what had to be done and answer any phone calls, he would also tell Ruby to make her some tea and toast. Suzannah couldn't believe it, William was actually being thoughtful. There was sure to be an evil reason about it. She was pleased to go to bed as she was so fed up of repeating the same thing over and over again to well-meaning people and the newspapers. Ruby arrived with her tea and toast. They were so pleased to see each other. Ruby was the only one who could understand how Suzannah was feeling; they shared a big hug.

"I'm so, so sorry that I have been so horrid the last few weeks Ruby, you must have thought me to be a dreadful person, I just couldn't seem to function properly or have any interest in this dreadful war."

"Now don't yer fret, friend's is friend's an I understood, but I couldn't do owt, but you can always depend on me, Suz, just you remember that."

William entered the bedroom.

"I think that, that will be all Mrs Jacks, Mrs Season needs to rest now and I suggest that you get on with your jobs."

"William, I am talking to my friend."

"Suzannah, Mrs Jacks is a member of staff, now drink your tea."

She did and then lay back feeling much more relaxed as she munched her toast.

She seemed to float along into a self she hadn't realised existed. It somehow seemed to cushion her from all that had happened. Maybe she was dreaming.

The next morning Ruby bought her usual cup of tea and told her that a policeman had telephoned and was coming to speak to her and William. He must have got up early as she couldn't recall him even coming to bed. She drank her tea thinking that Ruby must have altered the kind of tea they usually had. Half an hour later she was downstairs with her husband and a police officer. She was still feeling quite odd but pleasantly so.

"You didn't have to get up, darling. I could have dealt with this."

"I am very sorry to have had to come to talk to you at this time of terrible grief, but there are one or two questions I am obliged to ask as this is being regarded as a suspicious death."

The policeman had insisted on Suzannah remaining. He had a thick grey moustache which practically covered his mouth and chin when he spoke it seemed to be like the sound was coming from another place. William stood up.

"I cannot believe that at this time of war when hundreds of people are being killed by bombs that you find this one to be suspicious."

"I'm just doing my duty, sir."

William tutted and shook his head. The police officer wanted to know where they were at the time of the death, William was well aware that the officer would know the answer but with a heavy sigh he repeated that they had been on their honeymoon.

Suzannah felt as if she were in a dream her parents' deaths still hadn't caused her any grief at all.

"Did your parents, to your knowledge, have any enemies or people who had threatened them in any way?"

He addressed Suzannah.

Suzannah's mouth felt very dry she stood up and opening the door and before answering she asked Ruby for a cup of tea.

"My parents hardly ever spoke to me so I wouldn't know anything about them."

Ruby came in with her tea which Suzannah thanked her for. William and the policeman had declined the offer.

"My wife is not well, officer, this has been a tremendous shock to her, she was an only child and we had just married, she is still not coping with the situation."

Suzannah, having drunk her tea, felt tired, all of this talk seemed to her to be a waste of time, she decided to close her eyes and pretend to be asleep.

"May I suggest that you arrange for a doctor to see her she certainly doesn't look well?"

"Her doctor has seen her and prescribed a sedative."

Suzannah recalled none of this, how strange that she had forgotten his visit, but she had felt so very odd lately maybe it could be expected.

The officer's legs must have been tired as he sat down.

"Did you have anything to do with Mr and Mrs Gibson Ffiskes car prior to their departure?

"Oh goodness me no," William said.

"Mr Gibson Ffiske was most insistent that he had it checked over and filled with petrol by a professional garage. He was adamant that he would sort it out himself. With the shortage of petrol he hadn't used it for quite some time, and even walked to work, I believe that he took it to some garage to be sorted out before his journey. He was a very particular gentleman."

"Hm, filled with petrol you say, that is very strange, we have checked all the records of every garage in the vicinity and none have filled any car with petrol, even with a supplementary coupon."

"Well maybe it wasn't a full tank. I can't remember him saying that I just er shall we say assumed it to be."

"A trip from here to Langden Dyke and back would consume between five or six gallons of petrol, do you wonder why they didn't take a train?"

William scratched his head. He was feeling decidedly uncomfortable, and was pleased when the police officer left.

A week later the funeral took place. The Church was swarming with the press and was full to capacity. To Suzannah it seemed to be a re-run of their wedding, except she wore black instead of white. She felt no emotion, dismay, resentment or compassion, nothing not even one iota of grief. This in itself seemed strange enough but even more peculiar was the fact that she didn't even feel any guilt for her attitude to what everyone around her seemed to be distraught about. After all no-one could possibly have liked them, let alone care about their demise. Even Josiah appeared to be surprised at her lack of feelings. She did think of all the people who died every day in the war and all this was for a couple of selfish, pompous people. It just didn't make sense.

The Hymns were sung the prayers said people who she had never met sobbed openly, and she watched with dispassion as her mother and father were lowered into the ground. After the unwelcome hugs and commiserations she glanced at the mountains of flowers, and thought what a waste.

Suzannah went home for a welcome cup of tea, leaving the rest of the mourners to eat sandwiches and shed tears, because that was what you were expected to do. She felt tired and just went to bed taking her tea with her and slept.

William, after telling her that she should, in view of what had happened, make a will, went away on urgent war business.

The day after he had left, Ruby told her that she needed to have a serious word with her. Ruby seemed very tearful and anxious.

" I just want to tell yer that if yer wants to get rid of me I'll understand but can yer please keep Percy on until 'e finds sommat else, Suzannah?"

"Ruby, Ruby, I have told you that I am so sorry that I have been so horrid since before my wedding. I can assure you that I would never want to get rid of you or Percy you are the only friends that I have apart from Josiah. I have not felt myself, and I can assure you it is not through any sort of grief, I have no feelings at all about them, their deaths haven't changed anything much. I'm still married to that odious man the only good thing that has come out of this is that I don't have to put up with my parents any longer. "

"William did say that after the will 'ad been read that yer may not need us any more. There is sommat else that is mitherin' me even though 'e made me promise not to tell yer, e reckons that the doctor as given im these pills for yer, to make yer cope with the upset and as I ave to give yer some in yer tea or owt else that yer eat or drink, e 'as a supply of em an all. They are called phenobarbatone."

She handed over the bottle to Suzannah.

"I don't recall the doctor coming, do you Ruby?"

Ruby shook her head.

"Please don't give me any more, but don't tell William."

A few days later she felt a lot better and not seeing William was a bonus, he hadn't returned from where ever he had gone to and not contacted her to say when he would return. Suzannah answered the knock on the door. A young quite attractive woman was standing there with a baby in her arms.

"I want to see my Billy," she told Suzannah.

Suzannah thought at first that she was from the Red Cross who she gave some money to every week.

"Come in and I'll get you some tea."

"I don't want your tea I just want the money that Billy promised me for his child, Michael, she thrust the child forward. You are married to William Season I take it? He said he was marrying some good looking rich bird. Where is he?"

"I'm sure that I am as wise as you are, I have very little money in the house but I will get some out of the bank as soon as possible and send it to you, I promise, Just give me your name and address."

"He has women all over the place but I thought that I was different. You seem to be an honest sort of person but if I haven't got my money very soon then I will be back, understand? I can't stand to be turned out on the streets."

Although Suzannah felt sorry for the girl, she was so pleased that now she would be able to divorce him because of his adultery. She danced into the kitchen to tell Ruby.

"Wot if she is tellin lies though, Suz?"

Suzannah thought for a moment.

"Well it will be her word against his wont it? There is no way of proving it either way, I can't imagine that that young girl would fib."

"The will is to be read on Thursday," William said on his return.

"Then it will be appropriate for you to make your will, get it over with eh?"

"Where have you been all this time?" she asked him.

"Secret business, my dear, you know I am unable to discuss it, so what about this will?"

"I am too tired to talk about it now, William, I have been so very tired since the funeral I can't imagine why. I'm going to lie down."

She didn't feel at all tired, a little sick maybe but that was probably the after effects of the tablets which William was supposed to think that she was still been given.

The will was no surprise, everything had been left to Suzannah.

"We must make plans now, dear, we are very rich people."

She didn't remind him that it was she who had inherited the money and not him.

Suzannah sent as promised £50 to the lady with William's baby. It was a great deal of money but the child would benefit in years to come, and she did receive an overwhelming letter if thanks in return. She said nothing to William. She was just waiting for the appropriate moment for the maximum impact.

CHAPTER 8

To avoid any sexual contact with her husband, Suzannah went to bed early and when William retired she pretended to be asleep. He didn't try to rouse her so she assumed that he was receiving sexual favours elsewhere. Fortunately he spent much of his time away, telling her that he was on war business working for the ministry of military intelligence. He said that he dealt with spy's in the country, trying to keep Britain safe for her. She really wasn't concerned, what he was doing as long at he kept away from her. It could account for the secret phone calls and fat brown envelopes which arrived, and she was not allowed to touch, on the other hand he was such a liar. His latest absence heralded the first tentative awareness of the spring which was so impatiently waiting to make its debut.

Apart from enjoying her regular chats with Ruby and Percy, plus occasionally with Josiah, Suzannah enjoyed the small amount of cooking and baking she had to do and now took advantage of her newly found freedom. She loved to walk on the beach and spent this time in contemplation. She had always been used to other people making the decisions for her, so it was very strange that she was now in charge of herself and her decisions. It was like a child learning all the things which everyone else knew. She sat on the old boat slip way, where in the summer at high tide, small boats would slide down into the water amid screams of delight, from children and their parents alike. She smiled at the thought of it. Even though her parent's house was near to this small slipway, she had never been allowed to experience the joys of anything which the sea side had to offer. Even to the long Pier her visits with her nurses were usually so brief that there wasn't time to enjoy the freedom to explore its many attractions. She looked up to the sky and felt the salty air brush her cheeks, then suddenly without warning she vomited. This had been happening all too frequently, surely the tablets which she had unknowingly taken must have worn off by now it was ages since she had been given one. She made up her mind to go to her doctor; she would walk to his surgery now to see if he was available, before she changed her mind.

"Ah, Suzannah my dear," Doctor Summers said. "As I'm sure your husband must have told you, I did call to see you but he told me that you were fine. It was just a brief visit as at your dear parent's funeral I didn't get the opportunity to talk to you."

"Did you give him some tablets for me?" Suzannah asked.

"No, no certainly not I wouldn't give any patients tablets without seeing them first why do you ask?"

"Oh no reason, Doctor Summers. The thing is I'm quite often feeling or being sick."

"Hmm," he said. "Did this begin just after your parent's death? Grief can act in odd ways sometimes?"

"Yes it did as a matter of fact but I don't think the two are connected."

She didn't want to tell him that her parent's death was a pleasant relief.

"Pop up on the couch and we will have a little look,

"When did you last have your monthly period?"

Suzannah felt a little embarrassed.

"I don't know I have had a lot to think about just lately."

"I'm sure you have. Anyway Suzannah you are going to have a baby."

He placed his hands over hers and helped her off the couch.

Suzannah said. "Me, are you sure? er I can't be, I don't like babies, they scream a lot and I don't know the first thing about them, or what to do with it."

"Do calm yourself my dear everything will become clear. I delivered you and that was just what your dear mother said. See how well she cared for you."

That was too much, Suzannah sobbed and sobbed. Doctor Summers went to ask his secretary to make her a cup of tea. Suzannah forced herself to calm down and apologised for her behaviour. She sipped her tea.

"You must come back and see me next week and then probably only once a month from then on. Would you like me to book .you a bed in the private nursing home for your confinement?"

Suzannah nodded "When will it be born?"

"I can't give you an exact date yet but we will know a little later, I expect it will be about November."

Suzannah thanked him and walked back home in a haze. He was probably wrong, she thought. It was maybe a bit of a cold or something, I'm sure I will soon stop feeling sick and then I can forget all about what he has told me. I've got too much to do. I must concentrate on that and forget about this baby thing. She had been in such deep thought that she nearly walked past her own house.

Suzannah decided that she would discuss William's behaviour with Ruby and Josiah, just in case anything happened to her.

"I can't believe that William would be such a bastard, excuse my language, your ma and pa yes, but William, and to think that I ad im for a lodger."

Josiah shook his head in disbelief.

Ruby said. "E's only after your money that's the reason e wanted you to ave them there tablets. And now Lord knows ow many bairns ese a dad to. Wot in the Lord's name are yer goin to do?"

"I'm going to divorce him," she said. She had considered this many times but was frightened as to how to go about it and put it at the back of her mind, now her thoughts had become words she would have to go through with it. The thought filled her every waking hour finally she made an appointment with her family solicitor Mr Barrington.

On the day of her appointment she walked along the promenade thinking that she hadn't felt sick for the last few days, the doctor had been wrong she wasn't pregnant at all. She looked around, the birds were singing they had realised that spring was not just a rumour.

"Do come into my office Suzannah and take a seat. I haven't seen you since I read the will."

Mr Barrington had been the family solicitor for more years than she could recall. He was a small round shiny man. Even his bald head shone, as did his office.

"What can I do for you?"

He fiddled with his leather bound blotting paper pad.

"I want to divorce my husband on the grounds of his adultery."

There was a shocked silence before he said.

"Now you are distraught, I am not at all surprised after all the upset and problems which you have had to contend with. These are hard times and men, shall we say, are easily distracted."

"You won't change my mind, Mr Barrington. I want you to do as I ask please."

The smell of leather and polish was making her feel nauseous.

"Our sort of people put these mishaps behind them they forget the occasional lapses and carry on just as before."

"I want a divorce please," she repeated "If you won't help me then I'll have to find someone else who will."

"Now let us look at this matter calmly, have you ever known anyone who has been divorced? Being divorced carries with it a great stigma, you will be ignored by people of your own class and not included in any social occasions which you would have otherwise enjoyed. You will be friendless an outcast."

Suzannah stood up.

"The reason I haven't ever met anyone who has been divorced is because I have spent most of my life incarcerated. I don't know any people, let alone divorced ones. Things are going to change, I am going to change. Thank you for your help Mr Barrington, I will find myself another solicitor to help me. It is 1943 you know, not the dark ages. Women are now doing men's work. "

"I'm sorry to tell you, Mrs Season, but I can guarantee that you will be unable to find help in this town as everyone held the Gibson Ffiskes in high regard, and if they helped you they, too, would suffer the consequences and lose important business."

Not now, they wouldn't I am the last of the Gibson Ffiskes."

She walked out.

At home after making several telephone calls, she finally managed to secure a solicitor in Langden Dyke, which was forty miles away, for the following week. She had no idea how she was going to get there or even where it was exactly. She was on the way and it felt good; Mr Barrington was wrong, there are more places than East Thorpe on Sea.

"Now for the Bank," she thought to herself.

She made an appointment to see a Mr McFinn. She didn't recognise the name as her family had always dealt with Mr

Gordon an old dour man. On the odd time that Suzannah had seen him, he had always seemed to be a bit frightening.

"Hello Mrs Season, I'm your new bank manager Richard McFinn."

He was a tall thin Scotsman who was wearing round wire spectacles his blond hair was smoothed back to his head he seemed too young to be a bank manager she took to him immediately, they shook hands. He was straight to business. Suzannah was pleased. She was tired about hearing about her perfect parents. It seemed to her that anyone who died were described as being perfect but when they were alive their perfection was not mentioned. No-one knew of the evil that her parents were capable of, only she knew that, or thought she did.

"I believe you would like us to sort out the bank accounts after the death of your parents, your recent marriage, and forthcoming divorce is that correct?"

Suzannah looked up at him in amazement this was the sort of person she could rely on.

"I am afraid that all this is new to me, I don't understand anything to do with finance so you must forgive my ignorance."

"Don't worry about a thing, madam, I will sort it all out for you to understand, you will be welcome to come and discuss any problems with me whenever you want to. Banking is a difficult thing to comprehend but I need you to trust that I am working for you and will only advise you on the best course of action. I have had a brief look at your parents', estate it is not an easy one to understand I must admit; anyway don't you worry about that, leave it to me. Right shall we begin?"

"I need to make sure that my husband is unable to withdraw any money from the account."

"Does that apply to all of your accounts; they have been transferred to your name since your parents' deaths?"

"I didn't realise that there would be more than one account." Mr McFinn laughed.

"I am afraid that having a great deal of money brings its own problems and that is the reason I have a job. Right, we will consolidate all of your assets into your name but leave each account separate. The money and assets of your parents are safe."

He picked up the phone he spoke in an attractive Scots accent which she found calming.

"Miss Norman, will you bring in Mrs Seasons current account?"

He silently and quickly scanned the papers which Miss Norman had provided him with."

"You withdrew £50 for a Miss Abbot, your husband withdrew £50 pound two days ago. And apart from the usual withdrawals for servants pay and house hold bills which we take care of, that is the extent of your withdrawals this month."

"Are you certain that it was only two days ago that my husband withdrew £50? He told me that he was away on war business."

He looked up at her. He had such clear schoolboy type of skin with a smattering of freckles and a ready smile. He checked the account,

"Yes I'm perfectly sure. I'm afraid we cannot do anything about Mr William Season's withdrawal and although it was rather a lot of money, it would probably cost more to retrieve it than to put it down to bad luck. It was a large amount for him to withdraw, and it was queried but as your situation was not at that time made clear to us there was nothing we could do, but that will be the last withdrawal he will be able to make from this or any of the other many accounts which from today are in your name only," he continued.

"As your parents didn't want to leave too much money in their current account it contains only £773 -14s - 6d they were adamant that this account did not exceed £1000 which still

91

seems to me to be excessive, as I explained to you, all of your out goings and regular expenditures, are deducted automatically at the request of your parents. Are you happy for us to continue? We have a great deal of other accounts to explain to you, but this is not necessary to do today unless of course you wish me to, we will need a few signatures from you. Do you understand so far, or am I going too fast for you?"

"I can only just comprehend what you have explained to me so far, but I think that, that will be the extent to my understanding for the time being, Mr McFinn, except I would like to make a change to one withdrawal," she explained to him.

"Oh I need to ask you one more question. Your late mother and father owned one safe each. We do need the keys and if possible the passwords. Also would you like me to have a copy sent to you about each of the separate accounts? Unfortunately that would not include the safes; I will be happy to discuss any aspect of the other accounts when you wish to. It is, I'm afraid, very complicated, your father was obviously a very clever man as far money was concerned."

"Thank you, Mr McFinn. Your help has been invaluable even if I didn't understand much about it. I have no idea so far as to where the keys to the safes can be, let alone the passwords."

"I shouldn't worry, Mrs Seasons, you are a very rich woman with or without the contents of the safes."

They shook hands and, she left feeling very pleased with herself.

By the time she arrived home Ruby was just about to leave.

"Oh I'm pleased to have caught you, Ruby. I just wanted to tell you that from next month your wages will be doubled."

CHAPTER 9

Suzannah's appointment with the solicitor at Langden Dyke was on Thursday afternoon, as she was not sure that she would be able to catch the last train home, which unfortunately was at 5pm and her appointment was at four o'clock, she told Ruby that she may find a hotel and stay the night and return in the morning.

Ruby was still overjoyed about her pay rise and was acting as though she was now a millionaire.

"You'll never guess," she said excitedly.

"Percy as found us an ouse to rent, one of the ones on East Street. We will ave all the ouse not just one room as we ave now."

"That's lovely for you, Ruby, I'm so pleased. It must have been hard managing in just one room especially as you had all your family at Christmas."

"Aye it were a bit on a squeeze. The ouse is a bit dearer than the room, it's thirteen and six a week but we can afford it now."

She gave Suzannah a big hug and a kiss. No one had ever done that to her before so she wasn't sure what to make of it and felt a little embarrassed.

Mrs Gibson Ffiske had never even spoken to Ruby unless entirely necessary. Even when she was given her wages it had seemed to be grudgingly. While Suzannah treated her and Percy as equals, she had never known the toffs to act like Suzannah and she thought the world of her.

"You deserve it," Suzannah had told her.

Suzannah was pleased to find a vacant carriage on the train. She sat on the leather seat and took out her copy of *Blood Sweat and Tears* by Winston Churchill. She wasn't quite sure if she was enjoying it up until now, it was hard going and lately she found she couldn't concentrate She was feeling too nervous at the moment and realised that none of the words were penetrating so she closed it. She put it on the rope holdall, above the seats together with her hand bag.

What if Mr Lees refused to help her, what would she do? She had told him the details on the telephone, and he had appeared to be quite happy to help her. She told herself to stop worrying about it. If he couldn't help then she would just continue to contact every solicitor in the land until she found one. She tried to enjoy the scenery and stop fiddling with her handkerchief. As the train was approaching the outskirts of Langden Dyke the damage which the war had caused was evident. She wondered when it would end and also would the high cost of human suffering be worth it.

As it was announced that this stop was Langden Dyke for some reason she began to panic she must hurry or the train would continue on its journey to where ever it went taking her with it Grabbing her belongings from the rope holdall above, she opened the heavy door, the three metal steps seemed to be very narrow and she was afraid that she, in her hurry would fall down onto the track. She had never been on a train, at school they did all there travelling by bus. She alighted amid the steam and noise and just managed to see the huge sign which reassured her that she had got off the train at the right station.

Now she must try to calm down and concentrate, she was nearly an hour early for her appointment and felt really hungry despite the fact that she had eaten her breakfast. She was sure that she was putting on weight. Walking along the unknown streets she searched for a café. There seemed to be few and far between so she asked a lady who was passing by. She told her where she could find one but explained that there weren't many apart from the Yanks bars.

Suzannah didn't understand, but thanked the lady and headed for the café. It was called the Elite, but it didn't look as if it lived up to the name. The window was dirty but she went inside, one or two of the tables were occupied mostly by greasy looking men whose corpulent stomachs spilled out over their trousers and their faces hadn't made friends with a razor. An occasional women, was visible through the haze of cigarette smoke.

She found a table and sat down, there didn't seem to be a menu so she looked around to see if any of the other tables had one, they didn't, she assumed that the waitress would bring one. The oil cloth cover looked and felt greasy a brown congealed mass prevented the lid on the sauce bottle from closing the cheap glass salt pot bore the dirty finger prints of many a former customer.

She tried to ignore that as she was so hungry. She waited for some time feeling very uneasy. The greasy men were loud one of them was wiping his plate with a large chunk of bread. Rationing didn't seem to apply in this part of the world as his plate had been full of bacon and eggs. She was just wondering whether or not to leave when a woman with her hair tied up in something like a scarf with a knot on the top and a cigarette dangling from her bright red lips approached.

We don't do waitress service if that's what you're waiting for," she said as the cigarette bounced up and down with every word she spoke.

"You have to go to the counter and order."

"Oh, I'm terribly sorry," Suzannah said. "I am not from around here and so didn't understand the procedure."

Suzannah approached the counter "Yes." The very same lady asked.

"It is alright," Suzannah explained. And left very quickly, she was feeling sick.

The fresh air hit her and she began to feel better, but no longer hungry, she thought how on earth does that sort of place stay open? Who could possibly want to eat in them?

Following her instructions she located the office of the solicitor quite easily pushing open the heavy outer door directly in front of her was Mr Lee's office. The place smelt of old dust and looked slightly unkempt. The coconut matting had seen better days.

Mr Lees had a mop of unruly, curly ginger hair and a gathering of matching freckles on his pale plump face. He seemed to be a bouncy, happy untidy sort of fellow with a ready smile and a suit the same colour as his hair.

He shook hands with Suzannah, a firm large handshake.

"Now as far as you have told me you want to divorce your husband on the grounds of his adultery?"

"I do."

She hoped that he wouldn't refuse to help her or give her a long speech about ignoring her husband's behaviour. He leant back untidily on his swing round chair and twiddled with his pencil.

"I see that you haven't been married for long, didn't you know that he was a cad when you married him?"

Suzannah was shocked but ready to argue with the man.

"I was forced to marry this man, I didn't like him and knew nothing of his past, but without going into the details I did not have a choice."

"Right, now we know what we are working with, we will soon sort this little lot out. He leant forward and found a piece of paper. The office was untidy with piles and piles of papers stacked all over; it smelt dusty.

"I expect that you have been told by your parents and others that you are making a mistake and that there will be many repercussions or you wouldn't have come all this way to consult me, unless of course you thought that it would not appear in the local press."

"My parents are dead, and no-one in my town would take my case as my parents were well known. I hadn't thought about the press's involvement."

"I will just take down all your details and then we can discuss the divorce procedure and the costs which it involves. Happy so far are we?"

Suzannah nodded her head she felt like a weight had been lifted from her shoulders. Mr Lees was actually listening to her as a person not a stupid woman.

Despite the condition of his office she had a feeling that he would help her, she trusted him.

"Firstly I will need your husband's address to send him a letter to inform him of your intention to divorce him and to advise him to obtain a solicitor of his own."

"I don't know his address, you see he comes and goes, his work is secret, he works for the Ministry of Defence or something so that when he is away I can never get hold of him and don't know when he will return home."

Mr Lees frowned,

"What a strange fellow, I think maybe you should take what he says with a pinch of salt, but I could be wrong, and I will see if I can find out myself. What is his date of birth?"

Susannah felt ashamed, "I don't know," she told him quietly"

Mr Lees lent back in his chair and laughed out loud a real belly laugh revealing a moss-green waist coat.

"I will have to send the letter to your address and you will have to give it to him yourself, he will then have to vacate the marital home.

"I don't think he will agree to that, you see he wants me to make a will in his favour and then he would maybe go."

Mr Lees quickly leant forward over the desk his mirth long forgotten.

"Do not even consider that, Mrs Season, he will have no choice but to leave, I will sort that out as and when. Any problems contact me. You will be hearing from me shortly."

He passed some papers over for her to sign.

"I would like to ask you something if I may. I am going to stay the night here in a hotel and would like you to tell me where the Royal Hotel is, as I am led to believe that it is considered to be the best hotel in Langden Dyke."

"The Royal Hotel you say. There isn't a hotel of that name in Langden Dyke. And as far as I know there never has been, I have lived here all of my life and there has never been a hotel of that name. The best hotel is supposedly the Consort. I haven't stayed there myself. There are not that many hotels in the city, the Americans live on the camp, and the rest of the accommodation consists of a few guest houses or B&Bs. It's not like your holiday resort in East-Thorpe on-Sea."

He dragged his freckled hand through his unruly hair.

"I see." So could you possibly tell me where the Consort Hotel is please?"

"I could indeed it is four doors from here on the corner on the right."

She thanked him.

The Consort looked to be quite a nice sort of place from the outside. She was booked in with a very pleasant young lady and she asked about the Royal Hotel making some excuse about her parents staying in the hotel some time ago.

"There isn't a hotel called the Royal," she said to Suzannah.

She was told where her room was on the second floor and given the keys. The room was in need of refurbishment, in fact it seemed to her that the whole of the hotel was tired looking and required some cleaning at least, if this was the best hotel what would the worst be like? Her room was, to say the least, basic. The iron bedstead and bed which dipped in the middle was covered with a blue shiny eiderdown, the floor was covered in blue flowered canvas. A wardrobe unfortunately had a door which hung drunkenly open refusing to close, which, judging by the cracks in it, had seen better days. Shrunken curtains covered the window with the compulsory blackout blind and crisscrossed tapes. The lone sink was cracked.

There was only one bathroom to each floor so if one needed to use the lavatory it meant a wait until the occupant had finished bathing.

Suzannah went down for her evening meal she was feeling hungry as she remembered that she hadn't eaten since breakfast.

It was a large dining room on the ground floor not many tables were occupied, she was directed to hers.

She looked at the menu the starter was soup, it did not specify what sort.

When the waitress appeared, Suzannah asked what sort of flavour the soup was. The waitress just shrugged and said.

"Just soup."

When she had eaten it she was none the wiser as to its flavour. For the main course there wasn't a choice it was meat pie and vegetables, she didn't bother to ask what sort of meat it was, but after eating some she thought that it was horse. The only vegetable was cabbage boiled to within an inch of its life and swimming in water. The sweet was some sort of milk pudding which was light on the milk and heavy on the water, and a cup of tea. At least she felt full.

She went to her room hoping that the bathroom would be free at this time of the evening. She quickly grabbed her toiletries, however, when she arrived at the bath room she could hear the bath tap running so she assumed that she would have a long wait. She hurried back to get her book to read while she was waiting, unfortunately someone else was by now also waiting.

"It is always like this in the evening." The lady who was waiting told her. I have just been downstairs to see if that one was available but no luck, there are three people waiting already. And if anyone takes more than their stipulated five inches the water is stone cold."

"Will you please keep my place for me?" I'm going to go down and complain to the management."

At first there was no one in sight but then she saw a waitress who was clearing the dining room tables, and asked her if she could see the manager.

"He goes home at five o'clock, madam," she was told.

"Who is in charge please?"

"No-one, madam, there is a war on, madam."

Suzannah went back upstairs the queue was now six deep. She went back to her room. She did manage to get a bath in stone cold water at twenty past midnight. If ever she had a hotel of her own this one had certainly told her how not to do it.

When she checked out in the morning, she did mention one or two details and received the expected answer, that there was a war on.

During the journey home she was trying to reason why William had told them that he had booked her parents into a hotel which didn't exist. Unless he knew that they would not in fact arrive there.

When Suzannah arrived home, Ruby was so excited about her new house. Now that she had the keys Suzannah told her to take a couple of days off to give her some time to sort things out. Percy preferred to work. He came running in to tell Suzannah that he had managed to get two large tins of corned beef, and that she could have one of them, the tins were at least twelve inches long. She thanked him. He also gave her a couple of smaller tins of Spam which she had never heard of, some potatoes some eggs from the allotment, and a substantial amount of butter. She was overwhelmed. She would try the meat and give some to the people who ran the women's rescue a house in town were people in need were helped.

Josiah appeared in the afternoon.

"How is April? It won't be long now before you are a proud father will it?"

"Yer'd think no-one else ad ever ad a little un all she does is lay on the bed and moan."

Suzannah made some tea from the large packet which Josiah had brought her, he also brought some sugar. It was her lucky day.

"Yer got any scones or owt, Suz? I'm fair clamped, and my dear wife don't know ow to make em or anything else come to that, and the ouse keeper can't cook and I thought that I could smell somatt baking in your kitchen."

"If you wait a couple of minutes you can have some straight out of the oven and with butter on."

"I knew you'd 'ave sommat, Suz, you ought to run a 'otel. Where is Ruby? She is usually buzzing about somewhere."

"Haven't you heard Josiah, they have got a new house and I gave her some time off to sort things out."

"They can ave some furniture from the Corner House, if they want as no-one lives there now since William married yer."

"I think that they will be pleased with anything. Come to that I will have to begin to sort out all my parents things when I get round to it, I can't seem to concentrate at the moment."

Percy came in sniffing as usual.

"Now then, Jo any chance of some fish?"

"Not at the moment, Perce, maybe next week, not much work on the docks so it in't easy to get fish now, no trawlers yer see, most of em are sorting out war work Mr Churchill only lets us ave the odd one or two, the rest he as pinched for war work, Mr Clever Clogs at work reckons that they are used for mine sweepers."

Percy nodded. "The cargo ships which manage to avoid the torpedoes get through if they are lucky."

"Is it time for a brew, Suz? I've bin workin me arse off what with the weaners and chicks as well as me other work."

"In one second, Percy, and you can have a hot buttered scone as well."

Suzannah buttered three and passed them round knowing one each would not satisfy the men she buttered some more.

"Yer seem to be putting on weight since your ma and pa popped their clogs, Suz." Josiah said as he took a bite from the hot scone and the melted butter ran down his chin.

"It must be all these scones, I dare say I'll manage another to save yer gettin as fat as me nobody makes a scone like you do," he winked at her.

"If you like to pop in a bit later, Jo I will have a corned beef hash for you." Josiah was made up.

William rang to tell Suzannah that he would be home the following evening.

She fingered his solicitor's letter, which was in her pocket and butterflies flew around her stomach. She spent an uneasy night going over and over in her mind what would be the best way to give him the letter as she knew how angry he would be and she was very frightened of the outcome. She hadn't told

Ruby about what the solicitor had said as the opportunity hadn't presented itself.

When William arrived home he was agitated, his usual false charm seemed to have disappeared. Suzannah after her restless night decided that she would give him the solicitor's letter as he was going off again on his war work which was usually a few days but had been longer.

"I have just been to the bank to withdraw some money," he said angrily,

She had forgotten about that with all the other things to remember from the solicitor and the letter. "I was told that I was not able to, and I want to know why."

Suzannah decided to employ a method of her own.

"Do you mean to say, that they refused to allow you to withdraw money from your own account?"

"We are a married couple Suzannah, did we not say in our wedding vows a word or two about obey and worldly goods?"

"Which of your worldly goods are you going to share with me, as so far I haven't seen any?"

She thought that she couldn't have done that better even if she had rehearsed it.

He was beginning to get even more irritated, the thin veneer of his usual pretence of amiability was continuing to slip away, revealing something unpleasant beneath. Something which Suzannah had always believed to be there lurking and waiting. She knew how he had treated Ruby.

"You know nothing, my darling, you are still a spoilt schoolgirl, and have a lot to learn about life. Our bank account belongs to us both and as you agreed to obey me, you will see to it that I have access."

"And if I refuse?"

He took hold of her arm and twisted it saying.

"You won't, I knew too much about your father and he owed a great deal to me, to keep my mouth shut and it has taken me a long time to get this far and I will not give up because of you, a silly little schoolgirl, however beautiful and full of airs and graces you are. He and your stupid mother promised me that they would leave me half of everything he owned in his will; I saw the copy and the devious couple must have destroyed it."

"I don't know what you mean William, and I don't intend to find out about your lies and threats."

She handed him the letter, he let go of her arm and she walked over to the phone and picked up the handset, while he read the letter.

"I know more than you think, especially about my parents' car accident and forcing me to have tablets to what end? I hate to imagine. I found that out, also I know about your adulterous behaviour. Now do you want me to make a telephone call?"

"You little bitch, don't think that you will get away that easily," he left and slammed the door behind him.

Suzannah was shaking as she went into the drawing room, to sit for a moment to calm herself down, then she thought, who did she intend to make a phone call to anyway?

On a sudden impulse she went up to the loft room which since her wedding had become a store room for William's boxes and suit cases. The cases were locked and fairly heavy, so it was with difficulty that she tugged one on to the top of the stairs and pushed it down. She walked down the staircase to the next floor and repeated the process. She continued to do this until the case was in the hall. She returned to the loft room and pulled another case out and continued until all his belongings were in the hall. Then after opening the door she kicked them all down the steps. Then went to lay on her bed; she was exhausted but so, so pleased with herself.

She woke up suddenly. It was pitch black. She sat for a moment trying to remember where she was, then like the flowing tide it returned, she had been sorting out William's things, and had been too tired to get undressed and she was shivering with cold. Once undressed and warm in bed, she decided that she would go to Madam Daphne's in the morning and arrange to buy something more suitable to wear. Her body was expanding and all of her clothes were uncomfortably tight. Although she pushed the thoughts at the back of her head she knew that she was pregnant She was sure that she would have enough coupons, and Madam Daphne was always understanding about those matters She would also go to see Dr. Summers and tell Ruby and Josiah when the opportunity arose. Once more feeling pleased with herself she fell asleep.

Madam Daphne was overjoyed at the news and promised that she would get all the things that the baby would need.

She then went to Doctor Summer's surgery as she was feeling guilty. He told her off but in a kindly way. She did repeat that she didn't know anything about babies and she didn't much care for them.

"You will find, my dear, that babies bring their own love with them."

Dr Summers told Suzannah of all her entitlements and gave her an appointment for a month's time.

Ruby was back, she couldn't wait to tell Suzannah about her new house and the furniture that Josiah had given them. Suzannah told Ruby that she was pregnant.

Ruby jumped up and down in excitement.

"I thought that could be the answer to your sudden weight gain."

"Let's have a cup of tea," Suzannah suggested; her panacea for all things.

She told Ruby everything that William had said and explained about the cases in the front garden.

"What do you make of it Ruby, what does he know, do you think it is the reason why I was forced to marry him?"

"I'll tell you one thing, Suz, the first thing we need to do is to get the locks changed. I wouldn't put owt past im. E's evil that's what e is, evil. Locks will be done today I'll sort it."

Suzannah decided to take a walk on the beach, as it usually made her feel better. Even though there was a war on, it was quite crowded. The deckchair man was rubbing his hands, he had definitely had a good day as had the ice cream man and the fish and chip stalls which, although it was only mid-day had closed as they has sold everything that they had. It was mid July 1943, everyone was saying that the war was just about over, and they were enjoying themselves. The men with rolled up trouser legs, which were held up with braces, and knotted handkerchiefs on their heads, read the newspaper. Then they would have a snooze for half an hour. The ladies in their new dresses bought especially for this trip sat on the stripy deckchairs with their kiss me quick hats and red faces. The seagulls made their presence felt as they circled above, hoping that a scrap of food would inadvertently fall to the ground. The children ran in and out of the water with their knitted swimming costumes which headed southwards with the weight of the water, despite how many times they were hoisted up. They were shouting happily. Sun kissed faces were everywhere. The donkeys looked forlorn as they walked up and down the beach carrying noisy children. The donkeys had donkey type names like Dolly and Kitty. Horse and carts carried youngsters with their mothers into the shallows of the waters and back again for three pence each.

Suzannah walked at the water's edge her shoes hanging around her neck. Her feet left an indent in the water-sodden sand as she continued on her way.

Ruby told Suzannah as she was just entering the house, that the locks were done and also Josiah had arrived and was looking pleased. Josiah's big familiar face looked so happy.

"I've got a son, so I ave," he looked as though he would burst with pride.

"Ese to be called Marcus Josiah Cecil Kingston, Marcus is after her brother who was killed in the war. Funny sort of name but still the other two are alright, well Josiah is."

Wonderful, Josiah, congratulations they all told him.

"Who does he look like?"

Josiah thought about this one

Like a bairn, all red and wrinkled."

"How is April?"

"She was asleep so I didn't ave chance to see er. I just came over ere to tell yers."

"I'm afraid we haven't got any champagne to wet the baby's head with, so a cup of tea will have to do," Suzannah said.

While they were sitting drinking Josiah asked,

"What are all those cases and clobber doing at the bottom the front steps, Suz?"

With all the commotion Suzannah had forgotten about them.

"Oh yes I meant to say, I did it after William had left, It's a long story, Jo. We will talk about it another time."

Josiah went to the Corner House and found some metal cases which belonged to William and brought them to add to the pile.

Suzannah had to pull his arm and tell him to go and see his new baby son and April.

Two days later the things had gone. She knew that it must have been William as there was a rather thick envelope pushed through the letter box in his hand writing. She thought at first that she would dispose of it but then she changed her mind, It may come in useful sometime especially with her divorce pending. Finding a suitable box she popped it inside, unopened.

CHAPTER 10

April was not happy. Her son was beautiful. But apart from that she had certain issues to discuss with her husband who she hadn't seen since the dreadful trauma she had suffered during her son's birth. The nurses were not at all helpful, what are we paying all this money for, she thought? They were not willing to take the baby away and feed him so that she could have some rest. Her parents were not much better telling her that childbirth carried with it certain responsibilities and feeding him was one of them. All that the nurse would do was try to get baby Marcus to breast feed.

"He doesn't like it," she repeatedly told them.

When Josiah finally arrived the first thing she said to him was.

"I'm never going to go through that again,

It was torture, a nightmare. So don't expect me to provide you with any more children. You haven't been to see your son or me."

"That's where yer wrong I came and yer were asleep and so I saw my son and even gave him a cuddle. In't e the best looking little chap yer ever did see, e recognised me as his pa I could tell by the way e looked at me."

"Go away, Josiah, and tell the nurses that I need to rest so they can look after him for a little while."

Suzannah in her new maternity dress, which felt like a tent and she hated, decided that too much time had been wasted, she must be more focused. Percy and Ruby had left for the day so she was alone. The huge house was full of her parents' things all of which she disliked She was well aware that she would be unable to buy any new furniture until the war was over but at least she should be able to reduce the amount of things that were overcrowding each room.

She decided that she would start with her parents' bedroom knowing that she would have to get someone to move all the heavy things but for now it was her intention to sort out the things which were easily transportable first. It was a big room and had a spectacular view of the sea from the large bay window, there were three other rooms and a bathroom on that landing one quite small, which she would use as a nursery, the other two larger ones which faced the rear of the property she intended for the time being, to use them for storage and make decisions at a later date. She gazed out of the bay window. The sun sparkled off the sea blue, purple and green seemed to mingle together. The beauty of it was breathtaking, but in these days of war no-one had the time to just watch and store that memory for a time when beauty was needed to be recalled. It was views like this one which had sustained her through the long months and years of boarding school. She reluctantly returned to the project in hand.

They said the war was practically over, she hoped that they were right.

Order and method her school mistress had told her, so she decided that she would begin with the dreadful pictures on the walls. She was quite sure that they would be worth a great deal of money. Paintings were only worth how much pleasure the owner got from them and in her case, it was none. Some charity or good cause would be pleased with them she was sure, they could sell them and use the money for a much better cause. The furniture and bric a brac of which her mother was fond would surely be to someone's taste.

She couldn't imagine that her parents had never done anything for the benefit of other people, so now all their belongings would make up for their life of self-indulgence.

She managed to remove most of the pictures and carried them through to one of the other bedrooms, which looked as if her father had used as a dressing room.

One of the pictures, a landscape in oils which Suzannah thought was about the nicest of all the pictures, refused to budge. It seemed as though it was screwed to the wall. How odd she thought, why would one picture be fixed in an entirely different manner to all the others? She pulled and tugged but it wouldn't move, she felt around the mahogany frame and at the top there seemed to be a little sort of lever which she pushed but it was firmly fixed. She sat on the bed for a moment and thought about it. Then she dragged her mother's dressing table stool over and stood on it. It was indeed a small silver lever which she pushed again and to her amazement it moved. Her heart began to pound she felt her mouth going dry. She told herself not to act so stupidly and to calm down. Then she pulled the picture, it moved, then opened like a cupboard door.

The telephone rang downstairs. It made her jump she ran as quickly as she could to answer it; running wasn't as easy as it had been before she was pregnant.

It was William,

"There are some things in the Corner House which are missing from my belongings which you so kindly dumped on the door step, important things which are connected with my work and I need to get them and I no longer have a key as I gave it back to Josiah."

"Why are you ringing me, William? It was Josiah who sorted out your belonging in the Corner House, call him."

"How am I supposed to know his number now that he is married?" he was yelling like a maniac and she was beginning to feel frightened.

Suzannah thought about this, she obviously didn't want to give him Josiah's number.

"If you give me your number I will get him to ring you," she told him.

"Do you think that I am so stupid as to give you my number?" he screamed.

She tried to think what to do her mind was unable to comprehend any logical thought it was full of too many other things.

"I will ring Josiah and tell him to meet you somewhere, wherever you want."

"Not for one moment am I going to fall for another of your tricks?" he said sarcastically.

"I am coming over to our house now, and if I don't get what, I want woe betide you. You cannot believe how nasty I can be when I don't get what I want. I will win whatever it takes, believe me," he rang off.

She frantically looked for Josiah's phone number. There was no answer, he was probably visiting April.

She rang Josiah again, no reply. In her panic she rang the police.

"I am alone in my house and a man has threatened to come. I am pregnant and very frightened."

The police told her that there was no-one available; she would have to find a friend to help her as there was a war on. Then they rang off. She ran upstairs and without looking inside she shut the door to the picture.

The maternity home number in the phone book was elusive, she was shaking, whatever did she do to deserve this? She couldn't cope. Someone answered the phone.

"Is Mr Kingston visiting his wife can you tell me please?"

Her voice was shaking with terror.

"It's urgent."

The nurse went away to find out. It seemed an age before she returned.

"I'm afraid he has just left," she replaced the handset and tried to calm herself and think logically.

Then there was a crack of what sounded like thunder, then the sirens, loud and clear another bang then another. Suzannah ran down into the Morrison shelter in the cellar. Shaking she sat down on the cold, tiled floor and put her head in her hands. There was a lull and then it began again, it seemed to be ever closer. Another loud thumping sound and then the ground began to shake. Suzannah was shivering from both the cold of the cellar and the ominous feeling that she was about to die or worse still the house would collapse upon her and she would suffocate. After what seemed to be a life time, the all clear was sounded.

Suzannah continued to stay where she was, she felt too shocked to move and too cold to stay. What would she find when she did leave the shelter? What if half of the house had been bombed and William was standing waiting for her. She didn't feel as though she could face anything else. So she dare not move. It was as if she was rooted to the ground still shivering with the cold from the dank shelter, she put her head in her hands and sobbed. Why hadn't she grabbed the box of things which were meant for such an event it was only next to the door of the cellar, how stupid to just dash past it in her panic. At least then she could have wrapped herself in the blanket and put on the woolly hat. It was too late to think of those things now. She had to concentrate on pulling herself together and getting back upstairs.

Eventually she managed it and tentatively walked through the house. She climbed to the top attic rooms everything seemed as normal. She went downstairs and onto the promenade. The smell of smoke was all pervading the visibility was limited. People were crying; small fires were still alight; most of the ground seemed to be rubble. A policeman appeared out of the smoke. She asked him what she could do to help.

He, seeing that she was pregnant asked her where she lived and then told her to go home.

"What has been damaged?" she asked him. Ignoring what he had just told her, she was still shaking with a mixture of fear, horror about what had happened and cold, the wind off the sea seemed to be angry. The war was supposed to be over.

"The cinema has been destroyed completely. Most of the houses a little further along have suffered irreparable damage and there is a crater on the promenade. There have been some fatalities but how many we won't know for some time. The injured have been taken to hospital."

"If there are any people who require hot drinks or shelter, I will be more than happy to provide them with what they need."

"That is very kind of you, madam; I will pass your message on. In the meantime go home and get yourself a hot drink." The policeman put his hand on her shoulder. "I will walk you home to make sure you are safe."

As they walked the short way a figure appeared out of the smoke.

"Oh no!" Suzannah exclaimed hands over her frozen face. It was William.

"Please, please officer don't leave me with this man I'm sure that he will kill me."

"Move along, sir." The policeman told him. "There is nothing for you here."

"You mind your own business, this is my wife."

He pushed the officer.

"I don't care for your attitude."

Two seconds later, William was hand cuffed.

"Go home madam, I will sort this gentleman out."

She ran as fast as she could, William continued to shout threats at her until she closed her door and obliterated them.

The policeman sounded his whistle while dragging a protesting William further along the promenade which was covered with debris, taking care not to tread on a butterfly bomb. The smoke and smell wrapped around them penetrating and intruding. Another man clad in a policeman's navy blue uniform called out to him before he came into sight.

William was to spend the night in a cold, prison cell. Surrounded, it seemed, with noisy drunken men. He was beside himself with anger, continuing to protest saying.

"Do you know who I am? You will pay for this."

The policemen had heard it all before, and were oblivious to his calls.

CHAPTER 11

The doorbell rang. Suzannah was in a quandary. She was sitting in the freezing kitchen hands wrapped around a hot cup of tea, her third. Who could it be at three am? Surely it couldn't be William, was it someone wanting some shelter and a hot drink? She seemed to be unable to make any decisions about anything at the moment, she realised when the knocking continued and the bell rang that the decision had been made for her she had no option but to answer it.

"Hello," she said tentatively to the closed door.

"Are you alright? It's me, Josiah"

Suzannah was so relieved and managed with shaking hands to open the door.

"Yes thank you, William has been arrested, I'm OK and the house, from what I've seen seems to be untouched. Unfortunately the rest of the promenade hasn't been so lucky but it's dark and obviously I can't see very much, The Cinema is just rubble so I am told. William came and frightened me but I'm fine now so long as he doesn't come back. He was arrested so he will be angry and he wants to see you."

She babbled on nervously and opened the door wider to let him in.

"I'll put the kettle on."

"I have told the policeman that anyone who has been affected by the bombing is welcome to come for a cup of tea or anything."

The doorbell rang again,

"I'll go." Josiah told her. "Oh Ruby wot are you doin comin out when it is so dangerous? Cum in you look so shocked, are yer on yer own?"

"Well as yer can imagine Perce slept through it all, but I couldn't stop worrying, I went to the phone box, it was cut off so it seemed better to just carry on and come ere."

"Oh, Ruby."

Suzannah came through to the hall and hugged her tears once more running down her face.

"I have never known people be so kind and caring. Let's have some tea."

The three of them sat at the white scrubbed kitchen table drinking the warming cup of tea.

"William has been arrested," she told Ruby

"I don't know the procedure but one thing, I am certain about is that is as soon as possible he will come back. I honestly think that he wants to murder me."

"I know everythin off by art, Suz, I've ad enough experience e will be kept in the cells overnight then e will have to go before the magistrate in the morning, e'l be told not to go anywhere near you or face the consequences, so I don't think that e will be able to come ere."

"What a relief, Ruby, I have been so frightened I was so pleased to see Josiah and you of course."

The front door bell rang yet again.

Josiah told Suzannah that he would answer it, It was a considerable number of people accompanied by the policeman who Suzannah had spoken to earlier and had arrested William. Suzannah was close behind Josiah.

She asked them all to go into the drawing room, and she Ruby and Josiah brought in some more chairs. Every one of them looked absolutely distraught, no one spoke, they were too shocked to utter a word, the small children whimpered and snuggled into their parents' arms not able to understand what had happened to them and also, why.

Josiah after being thanked was dispatched home, this was women's work.

Ruby and Suzannah managed to find enough cups to go around and they made copious pots of tea. Some of the children went to sleep out of sheer exhaustion.

Most of the adults just stared in disbelief.

Later all the people had been taken away and distributed to safe houses and relations. Suzannah and Ruby realised how tired they were, the supply tea had taken a hammering thanks to Percy and Josiah for always giving her the (ask no questions) supply. The clearing up had been done. Suzannah told Ruby that she should go home, go to bed and take the next day off. Ruby felt relieved but reluctantly agreed. Suzannah imagined that when she was alone she would be able to have a bath, and go to bed as she felt drained and it was approaching dawn.

She was in bed, warm and comfortable and in that state between dreams and wakefulness, when she remembered the picture. It would have to wait until tomorrow then she was asleep.

What seemed like moments later, the doorbell rang Suzannah thought that she had only slept for an hour or two and still felt too tired to move. Despite Ruby's reassurance it would be William surely. She would wrap the covers over her head and go back to sleep.

The doorbell rang once more it went on and on. She got out of bed and looked out of the window, with her eyes still full of sleep, she could just make out a figure as her sight improved she realised that it was Josiah.

"What do you want? I'll come down."

She grabbed her dressing gown and went to the front door, not at all pleased about the interruption when he must have known how tired she was.

She was feeling even more displeased when he said

"I couldn't get in the back door, it's locked."

Suzannah stared in disbelief at Josiah.

"Why are you here? You know how tired we were and I must have only been in bed a couple of hours."

"About twelve hours," he told her," Suzannah put her hands over her mouth.

"Oh my goodness I am most terribly sorry. What time is it?"

Josiah looked at his watch, "Twenty to eight, at night," he added. "Come in, come in do, I must just go and wash my face to wake me up a little and then I will put the kettle and the toast on."

"I want to show you sommatt, Suz. I'll show yer after we ave ad our drink and toast." Josiah told her

Half an hour later the two of them were walking down the promenade. The damage was so much worse than she had imagined. The house next door to hers which now Suzannah owned and rented to the Gibbs' family had only received damage to its loft room windows which had been blown out and a small hole in the roof as far as she could see. That would have to be repaired. The next three houses were in ruins.

Further on Josiah showed her the remains of the theatre, the roof was non-existent. What was left of the walls swayed drunkenly and dangerously in the sea breeze. The smell of smoke still remained in the air, and the dust was still rising, all the rest was just rubble, that is apart from what was left of the stage, which seemed to stand in defiance. The red covered seats were not recognisable. It seemed as though some outraged madman had thrown everything about in a terrible temper. One child's black shoe lay forlornly on what was left of the impressive red carpet.

The pride and joy of this remarkable Art Deco building of entertainment, which had stood for many years giving pleasure to thousands of people, was no more.

Only the new red 'KEEP OUT SIGN' stood proudly in the dust and debris.

"Doesn't it make you so angry, Suz?"

"Yes Josiah it certainly does, it somehow makes one feel responsible for all of this, for all this destruction, killing and hardship, is it all ever going to be worth it?"

"It don't make me feel responsible, it makes me determined to bring it back, to ow it woz and I will, fair means or foul despite Herr Hitler."

They wandered back in quiet contemplation. Just as they approached her rented house next door. The lady came out she looked very stressed and weary.

"Can I come and have a word with you, Mrs Season? It's about the house."

"I am going to get all the damage mended and anything else you want, if that is what you are concerned about I am so sorry about it all and that I haven't had the opportunity to see if you and your family were alright."

"No it's more than that, I will see you later." And near to tears she ran into the house.

"Everyone is understandably so distraught." Suzannah said sadly.

Back in the house, Josiah had given her some haddock, margarine, lard and cheese. Suzannah was so surprised and pleased and thanked him very much.

"I need to ask you for some advice but it will do another time."

Josiah left looking sad and confused.

As Josiah went out of the back door, Ruby let Mrs Gibbs into the front one, and showed her into the drawing room.

Suzannah, once more commiserated with her, she wished that she was the sort of person who could just spontaneously put her arm around anyone but she just wasn't able."

"I will see that everything in the house is returned to how it had been before the dreadful bombing."

"Well it's not that exactly, What with all these bombs and things and my husband being away in the army, my mother and father and the children don't feel happy to stay here any longer, and my aunty has told us about a house near her in the midlands which is up for rent, so er. We have been happy here but now things have changed."

"Don't you worry about it you must do what is best for you and your family. Let me know when you wish to vacate the property, take as long as you need, and don't worry about any more rent."

Josiah drove along the Top Road, a short distance from his house to the nursing home. He had mixed feelings. He was anxious to see his new son and to get him home, but as for April he wasn't sure, she could be difficult. His in laws had taken over most of the organisation one bedroom had been sympathetically changed into a nursery. Everything that a baby could possibly require, and more, had been bought. Even a nanny had been engaged, he tutted to himself, surely that was what mothers were for. He thought, not for the first time, that Cecil and Bonny had conveniently forgotten that although they had kindly given them the house, they still treated it as their own

For a moment Josiah recalled the times he had managed to drag himself up to where he was now, he sometimes wondered if it had made him any happier. The times when he and Perce had scarpered from a constable for pinching even a potato, or two. They would make a fire in a clearing in the woods and put the potatoes into it then go off exploring, it was amazing what sort of interesting things could be found in the wood, sticks to make dens, flat stones for skimming on the water, and lots of animals and birds to watch. They would then return to their fire. They knew every inch of the wood it was their playground as was the beach. The potatoes were crispy and black on the outside and soft and fluffy on the inside, just right, potatoes never tasted so good, they laughed at each other's black sooty faces and wiped them on the back of their hands.

Then there were bath nights, few and far in between taken in front of the fire, when there was coal to spare, in a tin bath filled by lots of kettles full of hot water, having a good old scrub while Josiah's poor old grandmother knitted as she sat in her rocking chair, then she would fall asleep, chin on chest, which was the signal for him to get out of the bath, after all a boy had his dignity. Happy days, he sighed.

He arrived at the nursing home and mounted the steps. April was sitting on the bed waiting for him, their baby son in her arms. He smiled what a lovely sight and bent to kiss them both.

"Where have you been Josiah?" I've been waiting for ages. Has the nanny come?" he realised that the kiss was not welcome.

"I'm sure she will be at ome when we arrive, as will your parents no doubt."

The nurse came in. "All ready are we?"

April frowned and Josiah smiled

"Well take good care of him, and maybe we will see you next year for number two, as you made such an excellent job in producing this little chap. The nurse always said that to new mums.

"I will never ever go through that again." April said and Josiah continued to smile.

The journey home was so full of complaints that Josiah found it easier to think of something else. Once they had arrived home he got out of the car to help them.

"Shall I take him while you get out?" he asked helpfully

"You may well drop him you know how clumsy you can be."

There was no point in arguing, so he left her to it and walked into the house, noticing that Cecil and Bonny's car was in the drive way, April managed to follow a few moments later.

The Nanny Miss Troy, came into the room She was as round as she was tall and had an air of importance which assured anyone who even contemplated questioning her had better think twice about it. Her sleeves were rolled up ready for work, her backside swayed like a ship in full sail.

"I'll take the little fellow."

Her large capable hands carried him away like a collected parcel from the railway lost and found.

"He will be tired and will need his sleep in a nice quiet environment for a while."

"Oh" Bonny remarked, whilst thinking that she would at least have had some time to hold her first and it seemed only grandchild.

"I will go to bed now I need my rest and those hospital ones are so uncomfortable and there is constant noise day and night, so I am looking forward to some peace and quiet."

"As I recall," said Bonny. "That is the last thing that you are able to get with a new baby in the house."

"What do you think a nanny is for mother? She comes highly recommended."

"I know I'm paying for her," her father remarked,

Bonny had hoped that her daughter may have wanted to look at the newly decorated nursery and all the clothes which she had chosen for the baby. On second thoughts she should have known that her daughter wouldn't appreciate anything, and not for the first time wondered where they had gone wrong.

"Would you like some tea or owt?" Josiah asked his Parents in Law hoping that they would say no, they did, and in less than two minutes their car disappeared down the drive.

Suzannah thought that at last she would be able to look behind the picture. The door creaked open, inside there just seemed to be piles and piles of white paper. Each bundle wrapped in string. It wasn't very light in there, she tugged at one pile and turned to throw it onto the bed, there were still lots of piles left and she didn't want to go up and down off the stool each time so she carried on just pulling and throwing until the bed was practically covered. My parents were totally crazy she thought as she got the last lot out. She was about to close the door to the picture, but in the very back where she could hardly see, something glinted, she pulled it out, it was a large bunch of keys.

These might prove to be very useful she thought as she handled them, especially if she could find out which locks they would fit. She was pleased with herself and looked forward to doing some detective work. She smiled as she got down from the stool. There was only the paper to put in the dustbin; after she had had a quick look at it then she could think about the keys.

She put the keys on the dressing table then she turned to the rubbish on the bed.

Picking up the nearest bundle she suddenly stood up and let out a loud scream .... They were five pound notes, hundreds and hundreds of them. She felt dizzy and had to sit down on top of some of the money. Surely they were forgeries.

CHAPTER 12

Suzannah couldn't sleep, she tossed and turned, she tried counting sheep and counting backwards from a hundred. In the end she went downstairs to find out if there was enough milk to make some cocoa, there wasn't nor was there any sugar, so she had to have a watery bitter one with a dash of milk to take back to bed. It wouldn't be the first time, She felt uncomfortable her stomach always seemed to be in the way. She tried to put the matter of the dubious five pound notes to the back of her mind, without much success. What if she rang the bank and she was arrested before she could prove that she had only just found them? Her eyes began to droop so she quickly drank her cocoa and slept.

She woke up suddenly, and found a cup of cold tea on her bed side table.

Grabbing her dressing gown she went to the top of the stairs.

"Ruby," she shouted, "Did you bring me some tea?" There was a short break before she answered.

"I did, but yer was sleeping so I just left it. I'll bring you another one in a sec just stay where yer are."

Suzannah lay in the comfortable bed, feeling more than a little guilty, and her thoughts inevitably returned to her immediate problems. Her brain, like a grass hopper jumped from one problem to another. Ruby arrived with her tea and some toast.

"Oh Ruby, you are so kind. How did I deserve to have you? Thank you."

"Rubbish, yer should ave a bit of pampering."

She asked Ruby if she had ever known the location of a safe which belonged to her father, obviously thinking of the one in her parents' bedroom.

Ruby looked shocked, and sat down heavily onto the bed.

"I suppose it don't matter now," she said, looking more than a little flustered.

"I ad only bin ere a week or so, I'd be fourteen at the time. Mrs G.F ad asked for a tray of tea to be taken to the drawing room. When I teks it in I saw that the master wont there so I asked Mrs G F if I should tek im a cup as I thought that e maybe be in his study. She didn't say owt as she was reading er magazine. It won't very often she spoke any road so I just poured im one and took it to im. When I knocked on his study door and went in, e woz on the floor looking under a kind of metal lid behind the desk. E went wild so e did, I was scared to death, I thought that e would sack me and I needed this job. E got up and asked me to forget about what I saw or e would dismiss me.

I told im that I would, but to be onist I dint see ote and it wern't til later in the day that I realised that it were a safe. I ad forgot about it till this day. Is that OK? I ave never talked about it to anyone even my Perce, that were the one and only time I ever saw into is study, as far as I know it is still locked and Lord knows where the key is."

Suzannah thanked Ruby, finished her breakfast and got up out of bed thinking how interesting a mistake could be. She now knew the location of two, not one safe

Her first job was to ring the bank it was no good putting off the inevitable, she asked to be put through to Mr McFinn.

"Ah, Mrs Season, lovely to hear from you, how can I be of assistance?"

"Well, I really do not know how to begin. You see I found a safe which I presume belonged to my father it contained some keys of unknown origin which isn't what concerns me, I also found a great deal of money in five pound notes, I think that they could be forgeries but I'm not sure. I can't imagine that they could be anything else as there are far too many of them, and what reason would my father have to hide them in such a place, I don't know what to do with them, I didn't put them there and I don't want to be in trouble with the police. Will you please help me?"

She felt so much better by just unloading her problem.

"Are you able to bring them to us for verification?"

"Well to be honest I would rather not unless I have to."

"Mrs Season, please do not concern yourself, you are in no way responsible, forgeries or not, we will send one of our vehicles to collect the money, the driver will have confirmation of his authenticity, you will need to sign for the items, and he will bring them to me. His name is Albert Williamson. Are you happy with that?"

"Oh yes thank you very much."

"I will of course inform you of the outcome, in the meantime try to ascertain the location of the keys some of them could belong to safes here in the bank, if you can't, don't worry, I am quite certain that we can sort this matter out. Please do not hesitate to contact me at any time."

Suzannah ran upstairs as fast as she was able and gathered the bundles of notes together. Then she looked for something large enough to put them into. She found an old box which was ideal.

Ruby had just returned from the butchers she had managed to get some sausages, liver and lamb chops, she was so excited.

"I conned the butcher out of the chops by saying that they was for you," she didn't add that it had caused a lot of name calling from the other customers. Suzannah was not popular, most people still openly disliked her. Not only were they jealous of her wealth but didn't believe in divorce however bad things were. Marriage was for life.

"Well, Ruby, we will share them; now what about some tea?"

They sat at the kitchen table and called Percy in.

"Sorry we haven't any scones or cake today Percy, just tea."

"Well as a matter of fact," he said with a supercilious look on his face.

"Guess what, I managed to get this morning? I ad to part with some of me eggs but I got some butter and a bit of sugar."

He placed the blue bag of sugar and the butter wrapped in grease proof paper on the table.

Suzannah asked Ruby if she would make the scones in the afternoon she even found some dried fruit to put in them which would no doubt improve the appearance of them. They were a bit old and shrivelled but better than nothing. She told Ruby to take half of them home with her. It was Suzannah's turn to do an afternoon at the Red Cross and she wasn't sure if she would back before it was Ruby's home time. She felt very agitated at the thought of the man collecting the money. She just casually mentioned to Ruby that a man was coming to collect something. One of them involved in forgery was enough. She would feel a little better when the box was safely handed over.

Another thick letter from William had arrived along with the post. She placed it unopened in the same place as the other letters, which was getting quite full.

The Red Cross building was on the sea front, It was an old wooden shack where the wind whistled in uninvited. No one else wanted the tumbledown building, hence the Red Cross rented it for a shilling a week. After the war was over, it would no doubt be demolished.

The volunteer ladies were always nice to her, that couldn't be said for the customers. Suzannah had donated many things since she had been a worker. When her parents were alive it had been a bone of contention, her mother, she did not approve and made her feelings felt.

The workers had to sort out the donations Suzannah usually did the clothes she found the job unpleasant to say the least. She always took with her a bottle of her mother's cologne even before her death she seldom missed it. Some of the clothes could be shaken and brushed without cologne others were in great need of it, A proportion were home to fleas, the Red Cross had a bottle which was supposed to be flea killer, it was better not ask what it contained, the smell of it was bad enough. When she was dealing with these items she would hurry home to have a bath and inspect what she had been wearing and hang it on the clothes line to give it a good blow, when she knew that it would be her turn to be on 'flee day duty' she usually wore some of her mother's old clothes so that they could be donated after she had worn them. This was impossible at the moment because she was far too large.

"You should not be working now, Suzannah dear." Trixie Hamilton Blythe, told her kindly.

"You only have a month to go you say, I think that your baby will be on the large side."

When Trixie laughed each burst of laughter was accompanied by a snort very similar to the horses she owned and loved. Her husband was a fine fellow accompanied by a monocle and a very sturdy but unnecessary walking stick. Green tweed check plus fours completed the ensemble. His laughter seemed to reverberate all around the hut. Suzannah liked him very much.

"Haven't you produced the next lord of the manor yet Suzannah?" he would ask.

Once home and when Ruby and Percy had gone. Suzannah ate a buttered scone and went to see if any of the keys would unlock her father's study. The last one, when she had almost given up hope, turned the lock.

Josiah was not very pleased with the situation at the "Chestnuts." In fact when he dwelt on it for too long, he found it difficult to control what he said to his wife and the nanny, who continued to refuse to let him hold his son.

To add fuel to the already blazing fire, April suddenly said. "What we need is a cook."

Josiah lost control.

"We already have more staff than we do people in this bloody ouse, we ave a maid a nanny and a gardener. It's about time that you got off your arse, looked after our son and made friends with the cooker."

"Daddy pays for the gardener and the nanny," she began to weep.

"Ave yer ever for one moment thought about my feelings? I don't want your bloody parents to run this ere ouse, I'm supposed to do that and I don't ave a chance, I'm married to you not your mother and father, and another thing Marcus is my son not that bloody know all nanny's and I'm sick to my arse of being a stranger in my ome."

Josiah left the room before he made things worse, and went to his favourite eatery where coupons were not required. The patrons paid for different coloured tags, green for soup blue for main course and yellow for pudding, He bought one for each of them and grabbed a tray.

The meal just filled a hole in the large man's stomach and that was all any one could say. He sat on the promenade's low wall. The autumn would soon push the summer out of the way. He watched the beach for a while to calm himself down. There were times when he absolutely disliked April and although he was polite to Cecil, he knew that he thought Josiah to be an embarrassment and was determined to make him acceptable to the most influential people, He said that he had secured a place for him on the Town Council, which would begin the next week, Josiah didn't know that Town Councils existed prior to his father in laws chat with him on what he must say and do, emphasizing, the way he spoke. He had also told him that he would soon be a member of the Free Masons. All Josiah knew of them was what he had heard, that they had a funny hand shake and walked with a stutter. Josiah now went to church at his father in law's request. He had told him that you didn't need to be a Christian to go, but it was of paramount importance that you were seen by the people that mattered. Josiah did as Cecil had advised. He kept a low profile as he could see him becoming the next Church warden and being a member of the Church Council.

What had become of this raggy arsed kid? He had wanted all this and now that he had it, he didn't want it. But he liked the money and the way people treated him so he would just ave to get on with it.

The days were beginning to get shorter. The salty wind from the sea became sharper, and people had once again to prepare for the coming months of winter. There was still a smattering of people on the beach, the tide still came in with its frothy foam twice a day that would never change. The deckchair man Syd waved to him, Josiah had known him from the hovel in which they were both born, proper friends they were not folk who wanted to alter you altogether and make you into a sort of toff. It was useless trying to fight the system, much better to do what was required of him. Syd would be battening down his deck chairs for the next season. The ice cream and cockle bars would put up their shutters. They would all be in limbo waiting to be reincarnated the next season. They would return to their run down houses, with none of the amenities which he enjoyed. Doing any jobs offered to them, until once more spring, then summer put in its very welcome appearance. The whole cycle would begin again. Was this what he wanted?

Josiah looked at his watch he was meeting a man at eight o'clock. At this time of the year sun hats buckets and spades and the like were surplus to requirements and took up storage space, Josiah wasn't short of room at the Corner House so he would employ his usual methods and no doubt do business with the seller, then store the things until the following years season and the opening of his Bazaar.

Suzannah walked into her father's study for the first time. It smelt musty and surprisingly an aroma of her father. Quite disconcerting, it was overpoweringly quiet, not the normal sort of quiet, or that which one finds in a church or library. She shivered and put the thought of it being her father's ghost out of her mind. One of the walls was covered with books, one she noticed was an ancient copy of Burke's Peerage, in the centre of the room stood a large oak desk. It had an air of importance about it somehow. A captain's chair stood at its rear, Apart from the layer of dust, it looked as though her father had just left it. The leather bound blotting paper pad had one or two undecipherable words on it, a beautiful fountain pen lay like a soldier on parade perfectly beside the pad. The walls were papered with William Morris's Larkspur in lavender blue. The desk had three drawers either side of the knee-hole. Inlaid into the oak floor was a sunken safe. Probably if one was not aware of its existence, it could have been missed. Suzannah, with difficulty knelt on the floor and began going through the keys. It was uncomfortable work. Her stomach felt so heavy. On the fifth try it opened. She stood up for some respite from the discomfort and felt very pleased with herself even though her back ached. The back door opened. Josiah shouted.

"It's only me."

She rushed out to lock the door and greet Josiah. The last thing she wanted was to be interrupted.

"Before you ask, yes, Ruby has made some scones and they even have fruit in them and the kettle is on a slow boil on the hob. I will just have to find some aspirin as my back is aching, it's caused by the hard work at the Red Cross when one is in this condition."

"Don't go an ave the bairn while I'm ere will yer?"

"That is hardly likely as it is not October until tomorrow and I won't have it until November or maybe even later. Anyway, I thought you said that you were going away for a few days soon."

"I'm off tonight. I don't know how long this bit of business will take."

"How are young Marcus and April?" she asked as she drank some hot tea and took her aspirin.

"Don't ask, Suzannah, my son is probably lovely if I could ever see im and April is shall I say April. We ad a few words earlier on, well, I did the talking and she did the cryin."

"I see. Things don't seem to be improving then?"

She buttered him several scones and passed them to him.

"Can't yer give er lessons?"

"We are all different Josiah you have to accept that I'm sure you love her as much as you ever did. And I am afraid not Josiah, I have more problems than I can cope with without taking on yours, too, and before you ask you cannot help me with any. I was under the impression by what you intimated the other day that you needed to talk to me about something else."

"Well the thing is," he took a large mouth full of his scone, crumbs cascading down his corpulent stomach and butter running down his chin, as usual.

"I know that Bonny and Cecil, don't like me much, April an all. I don't exactly fit the bill, and to tell you the truth I don't care very much most of the time. Yer know that I din't wed April for er good looks and charm, I married er for er money and because she was avin me baby. To be honest, Suz, I never loved er. I wanted to escape from the life that I would ave ad. Sometimes I wish I adent but most of the time I now know that true appiness dunt exist and we ave to ave the best we can. But apart from that I want my son to respect me for wot I've done on me own, and not wot they ave anded out ter me, just to mek them look good. For the first time since Suzannah had known him she felt a deep sorrow for him he looked so sad, his eyes were full of unshed tears. Her back ache was much improved. She buttered him another scone which he accepted.

She was just about to tell him that she had a lot of experience of not fitting in when he began to talk again.

"I ave got a bit of money saved and I've bought some stock one way or another and me plan is to open some bazaars on the prom when the war as finished. Lately though, I've got thinkin about building, nice ouses, small but we a bit of style, not like them ovvels I grew up in. There is gonna be a demand for ouses after the war, wot we bombin an so forth. I want to be in on it without Mr Grantley behind me, I'm gonna make sommat of me sen.

"Yes I can understand that, Josiah, and I don't blame you, but where do I come into all this?"

"Firstly I want you to teach me to talk proper, more like you do."

She stared at him not quite understanding why he wanted to alter, when he resented the Grantleys trying to alter him into something which he wasn't. It didn't seem to make any sense to her, but who was she to criticise

"Josiah we are what we are. People around here don't like me because I am getting divorced and they dare not do what I did. Also I talk differently.

I spent a great deal of time being concerned about this but at the end of the day if they can't accept me for what I am, that is their loss not mine. And that is the only way that I cope with it. I do my best to be a nice kind person. That will never be enough for some people. I have to accept that or I may as well be dead. If you want me to teach you to speak how you wish to, then that is what I will do."

"I ave to, Suz, that will give me the confidence I need but that is not all. I want to sell the Corner Ouse, but as I promised Maisie I would always let Percy use the rear land, I am stuck, no one wants a big ouse with pigs in the back garden and I will always keep my promise to her, I owe her my life and I still love er like a mother and always will. That will give me enough cash to start me own business and then I can tell my son that I did it not is granny and grandpa ...."

"I think all that you have said is admirable Jo but why do you need the money when you have been given a lovely house by the Grantleys?"

"I didn't want the ouse. It will always be a way of owning part of me, and April wanted it that way because she is bone idle and er parents will always cough up the readies. I want the cash to buy the old bombed theatre, but I don't want it from them."

"We will begin your speech training from now on and I will try my hardest to find a solution to your other problem, although I cannot think of one at the moment."

"I'm off to see this building bloke again tomorrow for a few days. I don't know ow long it'll tek."

"Josiah, How, not ow, and take not tek."

He left, and she felt relieved .Her back ache had returned but it was too soon to take any more aspirin. She would forget about her father's office for the moment and have a bath. She was just about to get into it when a very upset Ruby rang.

"Suz, me brother as bin killed in action and is wife is expecting er third. We just gotta go to er, but as yer know she lives miles away."

"I'm so sorry, Ruby, of course you must go, do you need any money? You stay as long as it takes and I will send you money any time you ask just ring. Love to you, Percy and your family."

"Percy's brother Jack will come and sort out the allotment, will you be ok? We don't need any money at the moment, thanks, Suz, I gotta go. "

"Of course, I'll be fine, don't worry, and I will see you both when you get back, I really am so sorry."

Suzannah thought how sad life could be, and she went and had her bath.

CHAPTER 13

Suzannah, felt weary when she had had her bath and now her
back ache had begun to go round to her stomach, maybe she
had eaten too much butter on her scone, so she went in search
of some bicarbonate of soda, and decided that she would have
to have a couple more aspirin, fill herself a hot water bottle and
go to bed. Her eyes continually drooped. She must have fallen
asleep for some time as the stomach ache had returned and
woken her up. Later, she woke again with the pain and also
found to her horror that the bed was wet through. At first she
imagined that the water bottle was leaking. But that was not so.
Where could it have come from? Surely she couldn't have just
wet herself. A wave of pain swept over her at the same time
the sirens sounded loud and clear. She was frightened. Looking
under the blackout blinds she saw that the sky was ablaze
lighting up the beach. Then as the pain struck her again the
bombs began to thud down. The pain was getting more severe,
her fear was now descending into terror. The telephone was
dead, the lines were down and she was now aware that she was
about to have a baby. She tried to calm herself. Her cold wet
clothes sticking to her were of no importance now she must get
to the nursing home which was a long way away along the
promenade and up the hill. Surely when any one saw her they
would take pity and help. She left the house and locked the
door. The pain continued to sweep over her, one moment she
was hot the next freezing cold and shivering. Another bomb

whistled, was silent, and then came the explosion. Maybe she would be better to just die now. Blood was streaking down her legs and it had begun to rain, torrents of it. The top of the hill could just be seen through the sheets of rain when the sky lit up once more. The pain was now beginning to feel different more like it was pulling her insides down, dragging at her and she began to groan. She felt that she was in a ball of pain. After stopping several times as she dragged herself up the hill, not one vehicle had past her. She couldn't help herself she just began to cry. Her face was wet with tears and rain, her clothes were sodden and covered with blood, she couldn't go on. She turned the corner at the top of the hill. The steps to the Nursing Home seemed to appear, or was it her imagination? She used every last bit of energy to carry on. An aeroplane over the sea dropped a bomb just as she pressed the bell on the door of the Nursing Home. She and let out a scream, something else had happened. Then she fainted.

Suzannah lay prone, relaxed and comfortable. She wanted to return to the place where she had, moments before, floated effortlessly, in tranquil peace. A place only a breath away, but as elusive as a sunbeam. She fingered the tight binders, where, not so many hours before, her swollen belly had been.

The door opened noisily. Suzannah remained unmoved, eyes closed, still attempting without success, to recapture the total annihilation of her present circumstances.

"We can't spend this glorious morning sleeping, now can we?"

An unfamiliar booming voice disturbed the silence. To Suzannah the question was not deserving of an answer. It appeared none was expected. She tentatively opened her eyes. The formidable figure of the nurse slowly came into vision, not a pretty sight she looked as though her whole body had been emerged in starch. A cup & saucer clattered on her bedside locker top. Large, strong arms dragged the inert patient forward. The pillows were duly thumped & pummelled into submission by rough hands.

"Knees up, push backwards" was the command.

Suzannah had little choice but to obey. With the help of the nurse's strength she swiftly moved into a sitting position. The sheets were then tucked in tightly either side of the bed, rendering any sort of movement below the waist impossible. Even her toes faced downwards like an immobile ballet dancer. The nurse gave the bed a slap accompanied by a sigh of satisfaction.

"We will have to open our eyes, if we want to drink our tea, won't we? Come along now … do."

The nurse said in a condescending voice.

"We will have to look livelier than this to greet our visitors won't we?"

Suzannah knew that she would not receive any visitors that day, or any time during her stay in the Nursing Home. Who would know that she was incarcerated in this impersonal overpriced prison of a place anyway? She however lacked the incentive or enthusiasm to reply.

A meaty hand grasped her wrist, whilst a matching one held up a fob watch which had pride of place on the nurse's well upholstered bosom. The cup of, by now, tepid tea, most of which had been spilt into the saucer, was placed, with an indignant glance, in Suzannah's hands.

The cup was thick and the tea thin. She drank it down quicker than would have been socially acceptable.

"Better?" the nurse said hands purposefully on hips.

Suzannah managed a feeble nod, & tried to regain custody of her face muscles in an attempt to smile. She neither knew nor cared if she succeeded.

The nurse marched to the far end of the room. Even the floor seemed to reverberate in her wake. With one deft movement she pulled up the bottom of the sash window. The outside noise seemed to be in a rush to enter the room uninvited. The nurse approached the cot beside Suzannah's bed. It contained a very tightly packed white bundle. The sleeping baby's pink face was just visible.

"What are we going to name this beautiful wee girly who only just managed by a few seconds to be born on this first day of October?"

Suzannah hadn't imagined that she would have given birth so soon, and in such circumstances, and was still in a state of shock, she realised that the thought of her own baby being born had been put to the back of her mind. She had never had any contact with babies, or ever had any desire to. They were something belonging to other people. With all the problems and upheavals during the last few months a name for her baby had not entered even into the periphery of her mind, a mind not yet ready for motherhood.

"Octavia," she said dismissively because of the date and added her own name for no other reason than for better or worse this baby in the cot at her bed side, was now her responsibility "Octavia Suzannah."

"Do you want to give her a cuddle?

Too late, Suzannah had once more, blissfully, joined her daughter in sleep.

Moments later, or so it seemed, an unfamiliar wail came from the cot beside her. She turned over, still it persisted.

Your baby is crying, Mrs Season," she is maybe hungry or needs her nappy changing."

The Doctor had arrived.

"You look a lot better than you did the last time I saw you," he told her.

Suzannah looked puzzled.

"You were wet through in a great deal of pain and had just given birth to this beautiful baby girl."

"I wasn't expecting her so soon you told me it would be November," she said petulantly.

"If you had kept your appointments my dear we may have been in a better position to tell you," he smiled.

She thanked him and apologised,

"Can I please go home now Dr I have so much to do and I need to get Mdm Daphne to deliver the baby's clothes and other things?"

"Oh no, you certainly cannot. In a week or so maybe longer"

Suzannah had no intention of staying in this place, she needed to get home. She would now be able to explore the safe in her father's office.

The only problem was how she could be discharged.

Josiah arrived back several days later and called to see Suzannah to tell her things he had learnt and see if the Corner house was still standing. He walked into the rear garden of Suzannah's house only to see Jack on his own.

"Where is every one suppin tea and leavin you to work eh?"

"Aint yer erd, Jo? Ruby and Percy ave gone to stay wiv me auntie, my uncle Reg as bin shot dead so e as, and I ain't seen Suz for ages, ant even ad a cup of tea or owt so I goes ome early."

"Oh my good Lord luv us. Let me know when any of em come back."

Josiah sat in his car for a while wondering where Suzannah could be, what if she had had the baby early, she ad looked like a mountain the last time he saw her.

He started the engine and drove to the Nursing Home.

Suzannah was bored, she sat up in bed just thinking of all the things she needed to do, apart from that she fed and changed Octavia when she cried, ate the tasteless food without any enthusiasm or pleasure, when she was sure no one would see her she had a stroll round the bed and looked out of the window. The days were so long and noisy and the nights even worse, So many screaming women and babies.

She looked up suddenly and to her delight she saw Josiah. She had never been so pleased to see any one in her life before.

"How did you get into this fortress?" she grinned.

"I dint see anybody so I just walked in and looked in some rooms till I saw you. Ave the bairn early did yer, wot sort is it?" She nodded,

"She's a girl. Are you sure no one saw you?"

"Positive."

Suzannah's brain was working overtime. Josiah opened his mouth to speak, Suzannah put her hand up.

"Josiah this is vitally important, don't ask me any questions just do as I say please. Go and find a nurse and tell her that you are my husband and you have employed a live-in midwife and nanny who are already at the house, so you have come to take me home, be very pushy and don't take no for an answer. Do you understand?"

"No but I'll do it," he went out of the door.

Suzannah could hardly bare the waiting, he seemed ages. Finally the matron arrived with Josiah in tow.

This is highly irregular Mrs Season but we are very short of beds at the moment, so many babies being born. You are positive that you will be alright, the midwife will call in to see you at your house and I understand your husband will be at home and staff will be living in, also he says that you have a cook and a daily help already. You do know that you can return at any time if necessary?"

Suzannah felt that she would scream with the tension. The matron looked undecided.

"I think that under the circumstances ... we can ... make an exception in your case."

Suzannah was up and out of the bed in a trice.

"Do be very careful, darling." Josiah said and took hold of her arm.

Suzannah dared not look at him in case she began to laugh.

"I will go and bring the car round, sweetheart."

Once inside the car with Octavia in her arms they set off after waving to the staff and thanking them profusely. Neither of them could stop laughing.

They arrived home and Suzannah immediately rang Madam Daphne to ask for the baby's things to be delivered to the house.

Josiah peeped into the blanket. Suzannah handed her to him this is Octavia she told him as she went to make some tea, unfortunately without any milk.

"You are a bonny little baby. It's a shame about your name though."

He also promised that when it was her appointment with the solicitor He would take them both.

Suzannah found looking after a baby wasn't as easy as she had envisaged. Feeding winding bathing and changing nappies, which they had shown her how to do at the nursing home, didn't seem to be sufficient. Suzannah followed these instructions to the letter, every four hours. It was evident from the onset that Octavia didn't seem to agree. She would cry in her crib before the four hours were up. Then take so long to bring up her wind that Suzannah would give in, and the moment she laid her down she would cry. How long will this go on? Suzannah thought, If Ruby didn't return soon she would just have to employ a nurse, knowing that she had forbidden her to do so. She had been home three days now and felt absolutely worn out. Why on earth do people have babies?

Her appointment with the solicitors was in two days' time. It took Suzannah an hour to pack her bag with all the things she thought that her daughter would need. Josiah arrived on time, Suzannah was not quite ready.

Feeling stressed and out of breath she climbed into his car complete with babe in arms who was sleeping, Suzannah hoped that she would stay that way.

Josiah said that he would have a short walk around while she was in the solicitors.

"Ah yes here we are, Mrs Season, and who is this charming little one?" Suzannah told him,

"She seems to be so small how old is she?

He tickled the sleeping Octavia under her chin. She woke, then thankfully went back to sleep with a gentle rocking of her mother.

Suzannah wanted to get on with the business in hand thought for a moment.

"She is a week old today."

"Oh my word, should you be out with her? My wife, er, er …. Oh yes back to business. Mr Season appears to be a very difficult man to deal with. We could not find an address for him, so had to send our letters to his solicitor which meant going through countless telephone numbers before finding the one representing him. He continues to refuse to divulge Mr Season's address. So I will have to send all the correspondence to him and presumably he will give them to his client. I wouldn't be surprised if doesn't cause more trouble, but if he does I will sort it out, so there is no need for you to concern yourself, or even go for that matter. It is straightforward enough. Mr Season will to be in attendance so I will explain the reason you will not be, a baby, etc. I will keep in contact with you."

"When he rang me the other week he threatened me, and I was terrified I think that he will continue to do the same thing to wear me down, I can't cope with it, as I have a lot of other things to consider. Have you told him about the baby?"

"That was one of the things I wish to discuss. Apparently, according to his solicitor, what had made him so angry was the fact that he had to spend a night in the cells and appear before the magistrate the next morning. He evidently told the magistrate that a man of his importance should never be subjected to such indignity, which I found particularly amusing. You have, I assume had all your locks changed?"

She nodded.

"Now concerning the baby; legally it would be better if he was informed, as this would give him less ammunition against you. If he wants to see her, he has every right to do so, but we will talk about if the subject arises."

He waited for her to make a decision.

"I will do as you suggest, but I don't want any money from him for her, but I would think it unlikely that he would offer any."

Mr Lees made a note of this.

"A letter will be sent to his solicitor and mention the fact that he is banned from making harassing phone calls to you, or visiting his former home."

Suzannah smiled, she was unfortunately aware of a smell permeating the room.

Mr Lees continued,

"May I suggest that if he does telephone that you put the phone down immediately, the moment you realize that it is him, without saying a word. In the unlikely event of him visiting you call the police and explain the situation, telling them that he has a restraining order on him."

"Just one more request, Mr Lees, may I use your lavatory?"

Suzannah changed her daughter's nappy and performed the necessary jobs with one hand Octavia in the other arm. She began to cry,

"Just a moment," she told her daughter. Suzannah realized that she needed feeding.

This is a smelly unhygienic place, Octavia, couldn't you have waited?"

The baby continued to wail, she evidently couldn't. Suzannah realised that her daughter would be due a feed shortly and that were an hour away from home. She explained the situation to Josiah who extended his walk while feeding time took place.

"Thank you so much for taking us, Josiah, it would have been difficult without your help."

"My pleasure, Suz, what a good baby she has been. Hardly any crying or dirty nappies or owt er anything"

Suzannah said,

"Your talking has improved, well done."

At home, once she had put Octavia in her cot she made herself a coffee and went into the drawing room and looked out of the window. Mellow sunshine of the early autumn day seemed to bring with it a certain calmness, the lengthening shadows of the high railings on the opposite side of the road seemed to be richer and more intense somehow. She could imagine the sound of the sea as the huge waves lost their impetus then gently rolled up the beach bringing with it the frothy white foam. One or two couples strolled along the promenade. A man with a dog which was anxious to go and run into the water pulled him along. She drank her coffee and felt a calmness which always came with the thing she liked most, the beach. The sound of Ruby's voice brought her back to reality. She had returned. Suzannah had missed her. She rushed through to the kitchen hugged Ruby and asked about the funeral and how everyone was. Ruby was sobbing and clung on to Suzannah.

"It woz really terrible, Suz."

Suddenly Ruby stopped and put Suz at arm's length.

"What the …?"

Suzannah laughed.

"Of course, Ruby, you weren't to know, I've had the baby."

"Oh my giddy aunt, my goodness, I can't believe it"

She sat down heavily on the kitchen chair and insisted that Suzannah told her everything. She skirted over the really awful bits, not only for Ruby's sake but she too found it difficult to recall.

"Where is she for goodness sake?"

"Where would you expect, Ruby? I fed her changed her and put her back in her cot and she stays there until the next feed, that's the way to do it isn't it? "

"I must see her." Ruby said.

"I reckon that she is missing out on something important cuddle time."

Later that evening Suzannah decided to explore the safe on the floor of her father's office, the one which Ruby had inadvertently revealed.

As she felt inside, it seemed to contain just more papers. She removed them they were very old and brown, not at all like the white ones which she had found in the bedroom safe. At the bottom was what seemed like something metal and square. It was wedged in and took quite a while to remove. When she did eventually manage to pull it out it appeared to be old sepia photograph of a boy who she did not recognise, He seemed by his dress to look a bit eastern or something different which she couldn't put her finger on. The frame was tarnished solid silver. On the back in very feint writing it said.

'My Beloved Godson, Hector Gibson Ffiske.

Lady Gertrude Elizabeth Gosling.'

Suzannah felt as if her father's past was being revealed to her by a very slow unwinding picture down the years of which she had no choice but to view. It made her feel both uneasy but curious at the same time.

The papers were very fragile. With shaking hands she unfolded them with great care.

The first one she opened was the Ruddlingden Reporter. She had never heard of the name before. The headlines read:-

'THE MYSTERY AT RUDDLINGDEN HALL.'

She couldn't imagine that it would be anything to do with her family so she turned the page. The advertisements were amusing, but that was not what she wanted. Why on earth had her father gone to so much trouble to save this paper when none of it seemed to concern him? She was just about to throw it down in disgust thinking all this time and effort and for nothing, when the words Hector Gibson Ffiske jumped out at her she read it with difficulty as the newspaper was not only brown with age the script had faded.

It read:

'The mystery of the missing Harry Gibbs continues to baffle police. As previously reported he was the general manager and factotum of the late Lady Gertrude Elizabeth Gosling of Ruddlingden Hall. Mr Hector Gibson Ffiske, Lady Gosling's godson, said. "He was devoted to my godmother she loved him like a son, It is imperative that he can be contacted so that one can reward him for all the devoted service he gave to my beloved god mother. He is approximately seventeen years old. He is tall has dark hair and speaks with a typical local accent. Anyone who has been in contact with him should report it to the police. A substantial reward will be given to anyone with any relevant information. The search continues.'

Suzannah was amazed and realised that she knew nothing of her parents' past. She had never before been interested, but now she was.

She looked at another cutting which appeared to be from a national newspaper, the article was from an interview with Harry Gibbs's parents.

The transcript had been slightly altered to enable Mr Gibbs local dialect to be sufficiently understood. She read –

'The parents of the missing Harry Gibbs have been worried about their son. His seven brothers and sisters are concerned about their brother, although they haven't seen him for about six years. He left school at the age of eleven for financial reasons and went to work at Ruddlingden Hall. He was, his father told our reporter, an exceptionally clever boy who wanted to stay on at school but owing to lack of money he had to leave. The family thought that he had gone to work at the Hall, he hasn't contacted them since. We have received a letter of condolence from Mr Hector Gibson Ffiske who has arrived home from India and was the last person to see our son.'

- And from Mr Hector Gibson Ffiske

'Harry met me at Southampton to where I had travelled on the HMS Medina from India where I was born and after the massacre of my parents and servants. I was forced to flee to the arms of my godmother Lady Gertrude Elizabeth Gosling. Unfortunately the old lady had died, by the time I arrived. I apparently inherit many acres of park land plus the Hall and with its considerable amount of valuable antiques, and pictures, as well as my godmother, Lady Gosling's own personal fortune. I am told that she was considered to be a very wealthy land owner but for many years had been a recluse. I'm afraid I have not had the opportunity to see her for many years but have corresponded regularly. Despite that, I will miss her dreadfully. Harry Gibbs adored my godmother and he sorted out all her personal effects, the feeling was no doubt reciprocated, as she wrote of him in her many letters to me. I wish that I had known him. I think that my god mother must have had a premonition that she was about to die as she told Harry to dismiss all of her staff. Mr Gibson Ffiske was clearly distraught. He pleaded for anyone who knows anything about Mr Gibbs to come forward.'

The date of the newspaper was June 1917.

CHAPTER 14

Monday morning dawned bright and clear like a spring day, although it was autumn. Suzannah heard the telephone ring, and ran down the stairs to answer it. She could hear Ruby's dulcet tones singing some war time song in the kitchen.

It was Mr McFinn the bank manager.

"Good morning, Mrs Season, Would it be possible for you to call into the office as soon as possible please, as I need to discuss with you a matter of great urgency?"

Suzannah's natural reaction was panic.

"What is the problem?" she felt the familiar grip of terror in her stomach which had never been but a breath away these last months.

"It is nothing to concern yourself with, quite the contrary," he said.

"I will be there directly."

She replaced the handset and asked Ruby if it would be alright if she left Octavia with her, as she was as usual in bed and shouldn't need a feed for about an hour. She had to go and see her bank manager

To her surprise, Ruby, without looking up from the sink said.

"No, Suzannah, I won't. That bairn never sees the light of day or as any attention from you. Put er in er pram and take e r with yer, the fresh air will do er good."

Suzannah thought as she pushed her daughter in her pram..Surely Octavia was too young to understand where she was, Ruby's judgement must be right, and it was true – apart from breast feeding and attending to her in the night she didn't realise that at her age Octavia needed anything more. She had been relying on Ruby too much for child care and that was very remiss of her. She had a lot to learn.

"Good morning, Mrs Season."

Mr McFinn said with a beaming smile which unnerved Suzannah even more.

"Congratulations, by the way, where is the little one?"

"She is in her pram outside," Suzannah replied.

"We have made exhaustive enquiries into the bank notes which you gave to us."

"Oh yes, of course the bank notes."

"Shall we go into my office to discuss this in private?"

Once inside he said. "Well we are very pleased to inform you that the bank notes which you found in your house are in fact legal tender."

His smile seemed to nearly cut his face in half. "Oh I see."

Suzannah said when in fact she hadn't understood the consequences at all. Her face didn't show any emotion at all, but inside she fought against presenting a scared image.

"Fifty thousand pounds is the amount." The bank manager told her, he still had a look of expectation on his face thinking that she would be so very pleased, when in fact she wasn't.

"That seems to be a lot of money," she said. "Is it a great deal of money or am I overestimating it? I am not very good at ...."

151

"It is a lot of money," he interrupted.

She thought for a moment as she gazed out of the window. The crispy russet leaves were beginning to reluctantly escape from their cosy home and fall to the ground only to be eventually reduced to dust. This for some reason made her feel very sad. She suddenly realised that she had not spoken.

"I don't know exactly what to say, does it mean that they are mine or what?"

"My dear Mrs Season of course they are yours, what would you like us to do with them?"

It took Suzannah a moment or two to understand eventually she said.

"I am happy to go along with whatever you consider to be the best option."

She continued.

"I am very sorry to appear to be so unwise where money is concerned, but the fact is until my parents died I had not ever had a bank account let alone any money of my own. To be quite honest I find the whole thing awfully tedious it does not interest me very much I'm afraid, I just don't know how much this amount of money represents. I do apologise for appearing to be a complete and utter fool. But the fact is that I am terribly dim where this is concerned," she splayed her hands with a look of hopelessness.

He shook his head.

"I can see that we will have a job on our hands, Mrs Season, you will need to have a great deal of support and guidance. Or else you will be an ideal target for fraudsters."

He leaned forward, his elbows on his shiny oak desk his face was rigid as he stared at her.

She was tired of all this, and felt so embarrassed at her ineptitude, it seemed to be such a burden. She had a feeling that her parents' deaths and her subsequent discoveries, were going to end in great sorrow, for some reason she didn't appear to have a choice, she was heading down a slippery slope and couldn't stop.

One of the cashers came in.

"Mrs Season your baby is crying outside should I bring her in?"

"That would be so kind if it wouldn't be too much trouble."

Mr McFinn leant back in his chair whilst trying to explain to her. He was thinking that such a beautiful rich young lady seemed to have all the worries of the world on her shoulders. If only she could understand. He had never been in this sort of situation before and tried to sound reassuring.

"A three bedroom terraced house in a row of similar houses in a nice location, would cost around about £400. This would be considered a dream come true to many people most who thought that they would never own one. Houses could be obtained more cheaply also considerably more expensive but most working class people have to rent their houses, and will never own one or any property. This is what they expect. The thing is, Mrs Season, if people's expectations are low they are usually happy if they attain them. The problem begins when we have higher expectations and they are not achieved. That is where dissatisfaction creeps in. You are able to attain everything you wish for."

But unknown to him Suzannah didn't have any high expectation, she was not worldly wise.

"May I give a considerable amount away to, I don't know, good causes, poor people or something."

"That's is a magnanimous idea, Mrs Season, but gift giving also presents its own problems and I think that you have had enough for today."

The cashier came in with a screaming bundle in her arms.

"Isn't she adorable?" she said as she handed her to her mother.

Suzannah couldn't agree with her when all you could see was an open mouth making more noise than a siren.

"Thank you, Yes, I had better go before you are all deafened."

"Go home take some rest, please do not make any decisions as far as money is concerned until you speak to me. I will put this money into a separate account and we will discuss the matter at a later date."

He stood up shook her hand and she left.

As she walked home pushing the pram Octavia seemed to calm down with just the occasional whimper. Suzannah enjoyed the walk home pushing the pram with the wind in her hair and the taste of salt on her lips.

When she reached home she waved at Percy with his brother Fred and parking the pram she went inside the house. Percy was expanding his empire so needed some help, as Fred and school weren't a harmonious combination he was the help Percy needed.

"I'm just making the tea." Ruby told her

"I'm so very sorry, Ruby, about this morning, I was wrong."

"Sit yer sen down and ave some tea, I'll call the men." Ruby told her.

Octavia began to cry Suzannah went out and brought her in.

"I'll just go and feed and change her," Suzannah said

"When you've finished bring er back in ere for me to ave a cuddle."

Later when Suzannah was alone and deep in thought about what Mr McFinn had told her, Josiah came in and placed a newspaper bundle on the table in front of her, and beamed

"I reckoned that you'd not make your sen any supper so I bought us both some fish and chips."

"How terribly kind of you, I can smell them. I'll get some plates and cutlery."

"Cum on, Suz, be common for once and eat em out of the paper."

"As you say then, Mr Kingston, she laughed "I will do just that."

When they had enjoyed their meal, Josiah told her that he wanted to talk to her about some things.

"It's a waste of breath talking to April, I feel like I've done me duty as far as she is concerned and now she couldn't care less."

"I'm sure that is not so. How is your baby son?"

"He is a right little bobby dazzler, ese gonna be big like is pa, mind you is ma ain't so small," he threw back his head and gave out a loud belly laugh

"I need to talk to someone with a brain. Cecil is alright, I'm now on the board of governors at the local school, I belong to the funny hand brigade, I am a J.P. You name it I'm on it. I'm not daft enough to think that all this is for my benefit, it is for his. Don't you think I talk a lot better? I do remember me aitches. Not always in the right place mind but I reckon I'm coming on."

"I'm sure that you are trying hard," she told him diplomatically.

"Now what else is it you want?"

She knew that he had something else on his mind she could read him like an open book.

"Well it's like this ere."

"Here, Josiah not ere," she interrupted.

"Oops, sorry, any road (she ignored that) I'm going to see that bloke again tomorrow. I've got a lot of learnin to do and he is the one to teach me, He is right good. When this war is over, I've told you before, Suz, there is going to be a right lot of house building to do and I intend to be first on the bandwagon you'll see."

He winked. It might not come to owt er anything. So I was wondering I'll only be gone for a little while, can you keep your eye on the Corner House?"

Then suddenly it was out of her mouth before she knew it, the words escaped without her knowledge as if they had a mind of their own, they even surprised her.

"I'll buy the Corner House," she said.

CHAPTER 15

It was Saturday the house was silent save for the tick tocking of the long case clock in the hall. Octavia was sleeping, Suzannah gazed out of the window. The sky looked raw, the sea the colour of pewter. Now November was nearing its end the days seemed to be like small grey spaces between the long nights when the blackout blinds were once again apparent. Suzannah decided to try and to make an effort to tackle the unwanted things in the bedroom which was once her parents until it was devoid of all memories and clutter, part of them would always occupy it. She had toyed with the idea of moving up one storey but all the work which would be involved including changing Octavia's bedroom, seemed too daunting a task to be contemplated at this moment in time. It was going to have to be done at some point so it would just be delaying the inevitable anyway. She would begin with her mother's huge dressing table, it even seemed to have retained the smell of her. Suzannah shivered. She would just have to sort out the things which it contained as it would not be possible to replace it while the war still continued. She stared at the top and could see the reflection of her own face. Ruby had continued to polish it despite Suzannah telling her that it wasn't necessary. All her mother's creams and perfumes had long ago been thrown into the dustbin. She tried to open the large jewellery box but as expected, it was locked. The key was probably on the bunch which she had left downstairs in the office, so that could wait, the top drawer was also locked.

"Damn and blast," she said out loud. "Keys, keys, keys."

A thick journal, with metal covers was as, expected, locked, it had a tiny key hole. The second drawer opened, it was full of fancy lingerie all of which was silk and wrapped in tissue paper, Suzannah scooped everything up and put it in a box which she had brought up for that purpose. It was a large box but it was already nearly full. She was uncertain as to whether to include them in the jumble sale things or if people would object to wearing second hand underwear, however beautiful. She would ask Ruby's opinion when she came back on Monday.

She moved down to the next drawer, and then the bottom one. They both contained assorted clothes all of which would go to charity. She was pleased with her progress. She would move on to the chest of drawers. All jumble sale things no need to sort them out. The howl of a hungry baby interrupted progress.

Octavia was clean, fed, winded and back in her cot in a trice, the blackout blinds were all secured. Suzannah took the bunch of keys from the office and continued with the task in hand, she selected one of the smallest keys and tried to open the jewellery box, it worked. It must be her lucky day. Inside Suzannah had not expected to be surprised as she knew, or thought she did, of her mother's vast collection of expensive jewellery,

Some of which she assumed to have been inherited, but as she had been told nothing of either set of grandparents she didn't know from whom. The amount of jewellery was beyond her expectations. She closed the box quickly. She took a deep breath and told herself that the bank would have to sort it out. She locked the box before examining the full extent of the contents. She had envisaged that she would never be surprised about anything else regarding her parents. Now she was wrong.

Suzannah yawned. She was tired but most of all she was very hungry, she hadn't eaten since her breakfast toast. What could she find to eat? Even with all this wealth she still had to search for the ingredients for a meal. How odd.

She found the tin of Spam which Percy had given her long ago and which she hadn't ever tried. What else did she have, yes potatoes and she found some eggs. What more could she ask for? She sliced and fried the potatoes cut the spam into chunks and added it to the pan then whisked the eggs and poured them into the rest of the ingredients.

Amazingly it tasted good, or perhaps it was because she was so hungry.

Monday morning arrived, Ruby, Fred and Percy with it. Suzannah was already up and sitting in the kitchen.

She had bathed and dressed her daughter and was in the process of feeding her, Ruby was impressed.

"Don't you think that as I don't have a fire in the drawing room it would be too dreadful to have one in here, it is so cold even when the hob is lit? I do understand the problems with coal shortage."

Ruby took off her coat and rubbed her hands together and began to make a pot of tea from the already boiling kettle.

"It's colder than outside in ere, Yon bairn will freeze to death we will ave a fire, I'll get our Percy or Fred to make one and look out for any coal going spare like, I reckon Josiah will know, leave it to me, Suz."

She made the tea, Suzannah had finished feeding her daughter and Ruby called in the men and snatched Octavia out of her mother's arms.

"What a beautiful baby you are, ave yer got a smile for Rube eh?"

Octavia gave her a huge toothless smile the first she had made.

"I've got a busy day ahead, Ruby. I spent the weekend sorting out my mother's dressing table I need to ask you to pop up some time and look at the things please. Also will you advise me about my mother's under clothes? There are also a great many cashmere jumpers all sorts of other items of clothing and a large casket of jewellery, which I thought I had better take to the bank out of the way, but you are welcome to take anything you want."

"Thanks, Suz, thank yer very much, I will ave to give it some thought. Talking of jewellery I keep meaning to ask you, did William give you all the jewellery and other bits and bobs that the police gave to im from the car crash, he signed a bit of paper for em cos I saw im."

"You won't be surprised, Ruby, no he didn't."

"There was your ma's pearls an all, bet they would be worth a fortune er diamond rings and er watch, If I wasn't olding this innocent baby I reckon that I would swear. Can we look at the stuff tomorrow? Today Percy's man from the pig club is comin to do for the three pigs, we are only supposed to ave two but as you know Percy did a deal."

Suzannah had to think for a moment as to what Ruby meant then it dawned on her.

"I'll make sure that I am out of the way then."

The telephone rang it was a Mr Philip Bush who announced that he was from Gibson Ffiske and Marsden Land and Estate Agent.

"Are you feeling a lot better, Mrs Season? He asked.

"I wasn't aware that I had been ill," she replied.

There was a brief silence,

"Oh er I am terribly sorry but Mr Season is constantly telling us how ill you are. Would it be possible for you to come and see us?"

She assured him that she would come that day. William was evidently continuing to cause her problems.

She rang Mr McFinn at the bank and made an appointment to see him later in the day too.

The day was cold but bright, the promenade almost deserted the gulls circled above with their mournful cries demanding attention but receiving none. Suzannah pushed Octavia in her pram.

She entered Madam Daphne's shop.

"Ahh, Mrs Season, you rang last week and ordered some warmer larger clothes for your little one. I have them ready I hope that they will meet with your approval shall I put them on your account?"

Suzannah nodded smiled, and thanked her. Then a thought occurred to her, "If I bring all the babies old clothes, as you know they are good quality and hardly warn. Could you give them to families who are unable to buy them for their own babies"?

Madam Daphne sat down on her chair at the rear of the counter, she was ashen. "Mrs Season I am sorry if I offend you but can you imagine in your wildest dreams that those sort of people would be welcomed in my shop, even on the remote chance that they would consider entering they would lower the tone and my regular customers would leave me, oh no, oh no, oh no."

Suzannah had never felt so angry even with William. She had to get out before she said something that she would regret. The large bag was placed in Octavia's pram she didn't seem to be pleased at the invasion of her space and kicked at it. Suzannah could hear the high pitched voice of Madam calling after her, which she ignored.

By the time she arrived at her late father's place of work she had calmed down slightly, she left Octavia outside and entered. Philip Bush was a tall gangly man whose legs seemed to be too long for the rest of him, as though his body had not as yet caught up his arms appeared to show far more hairy flesh than was necessary.

"We appear to have a few problems," he told her as they went into his office."

He explained that William had been going into the office frequently claiming that his wife was ill and that she had advised him to take over her responsibilities. He had made it clear that he did not want them to telephone her under any circumstances. They had become suspicious, together with the fact that Mr Season was becoming increasingly angry this forced them to make the telephone call.

She felt nothing, or exhibited any emotion or surprise.

"William and I are getting divorced very shortly, and I have a baby. He is the father of course. None of what he said is true he is a vindictive conniving liar."

Mr Bush looked extremely uncomfortable.

"I see," he said feeling most embarrassed.

Mr Marsden entered, to Mr Bush's relief.

"Ah, Suzannah I am so pleased to see you."

He shook her hand until it seemed to nearly fall off. She repeated her story to him.

His large fleshy face had a sprinkling of dark age spots his wiry, bushy hair made him seem to be somehow, top heavy. His full, dark heavy lidded eyes missed nothing and seemed to belie his innermost feelings.

"Now that we have sorted that matter out I have many things which I need to explain to you. Every November as you are probably aware we pay out our stock commissions to partners. Your father preferred to have his paid in cash, five pound notes to be precise. So we wondered if you would like that practice to continue or if you would like to make an alternative arrangement?"

So that was how the five pound notes were in the wall safe. She thought.

"I would like the money to be paid into my bank account, if that will be alright with you."

"Certainly, would you like your father's shares from this, and all the other branches to be deposited in the same bank account?"

Suzannah tried to hide her amazement not knowing what he meant, but also afraid to show her ignorance.

"That would be satisfactory, thank you."

"Now, your father's belongings are in a safe box. We will deliver it to you if you wish," she smiled and nodded. It was all a complete mystery to her.

"I intend to buy the house next door to me, the Corner house, which belongs to Mr Josiah Kingston and would like you to handle it please, I have no idea how I would go about doing so. Unless there is anything else important, will it be alright if I take the baby home now as I am sure it will only be a matter of moments before she is yelling with hunger?"

They arranged to contact her, value the house in question and deliver the safe box. They told her that they didn't have the keys to the box but the contents of her father's drawer would be placed in a container and also delivered.

She arrived home with a screaming Octavia thinking keys, keys, keys my life is dominated with them and hoped that the man from the pig club had been and gone.

Her afternoon was spent at the bank, where Mr McFinn was his usual helpful self. She gave him the rest of the keys and told him about the house purchase.

"I really don't want to think too much about the complication money is causing me. I realise how this must sound and I intend to give some to good causes but will, of course, need your help and advice. I am burdened down with all this responsibility," she said. Her bottom lip was shaking and she felt so very upset about her attitude but didn't seem able to control it.

"I can understand that," he told her. "I think that it would probably be better if we tried to sort out the keys at another time as to be quite honest I do envisage finding even more money or valuable things, and this will only add to your problems. Will that be satisfactory to you?"

"More than satisfactory; it will be such a load off my mind."

While Suzannah pushed the pram homeward her daughter stared at her mother with her huge eyes, Suzannah looked closely they seemed to be turning into green a colour like her own. She was concentrating so hard that she very nearly bumped into a couple of women chatting on the road side.

"Oops I'm most terribly sorry," she told them.

"That's all we expect from the likes of you and your sort, think you are so much better than the rest of us don't you?"

Suzannah was so shocked she had never seen these people before in her life.

"I think you must have mistaken me for someone else?"

Both the women cackled.

"No chance, Mrs high and mighty Season, or whatever you choose to call yourself, we might not have your money and your la de da talk, but we don't stoop to divorce. Everybody round about knows about it, you only aver ter cough and somebody tother end of town gets the flu."

Suzannah stood absolutely still; a feeling of pointless anger was threatening to rise to the surface, a feeling which she was trying without success to control; another time another place it would have been possible, but not now.

"You know nothing about me, my life or my problems; you have no right to judge me. So I suggest that you save your wicked tongues for the Germans. And leave innocent people who you have no comprehension of, alone, I have done nothing or indeed intend to do anything to hurt you. So kindly keep your unfounded opinions to yourselves."

She moved off shooting them a venom-laden stare.

She still felt disgruntled when she arrived home. Her knuckles where white as she had been inadvertently holding the pram handles so tightly.

Octavia still hadn't started to cry so she left her outside in her pram.

Ruby was peeling potatoes. She wiped her red sore hands on her apron and made the tea. Suzannah couldn't believe that there was a fire in the black Yorkist grate.

"Shall I call Percy and Fred in for their tea?"

"Josiah is here, too." Ruby said,

"Ese wanting one of the sides of pig and the three of em are negotiating a price, the pig man as gone. All done and dusted, Suz, it is. I ope that there ain't no air raids, as the cellar is full of hanging pork."

Suzannah called the men in for tea, Octavia looked so cold that she wheeled her pram in and put it in the hall.

Ruby watched her with interest,

"Why can't little un join us?"

"She wasn't crying so I thought that she would be ok in the hall."

"I'll fetch er."

Ruby jumped her up and down on her knee, Octavia giggled.

"She doesn't do that when I hold her."

"That's because you don't play with er, she just gets fed and put back in er cot perhaps she doesn't like it."

Suzannah thought about this and then said.

"Some horrid women were very rude to me when I was walking home."

"And it won't be the last time, Suz." Ruby told her.

Josiah joined in.

"I'm afraid that is what you will always get, Suz. You ain't short of a bob or two and divorce is not a popular word when most of the women are subject to infidelity and abuse on a regular basis and worse. They have no more sense and think that they don't have a choice, and maybe they don't."

Suzannah thought how Josiah's speech had improved. Ruby continued.

"I've been spat on and called names because I work for you. That is what life is like I'm afraid, Suz. You are so innocent and that is why we don't say anything, in't it Jo?"

"Fraid so, I'm a big chap but some of them have a go at me, insinuating that we are having an affair, if it's a bloke I punch him one, a woman I just give them a gob full; that's what William Season left you with, you will have to be very strong."

"Golly I didn't know any of this. I should have been prepared. I wouldn't have changed my mind any way so I will just have to deal with it but I do feel guilty when my best and only friends are involved, and another thing which made me very angry."

"Don't you fret about any of us, we was dragged up. This is note to wot we ave ad ter put up with." Ruby told her as she nursed a now sleeping Octavia.

So Suzannah left the tale of Madam Daphne until another time.

CHAPTER 16

Suzannah picked up and discarded the usual thick letter from William unopened, the box containing all his letters was getting fuller and fuller. She rang Mr Lees to see if any progress had been made in her divorce.

"Ah, Mrs Season I was going to ring you today to ask you if William had been behaving himself as far as you are concerned."

"Well I get the usual letters but they remain unopened in a large box I actually received another one this morning."

"Do you think that you should open them?"

"No I don't, I have enough problems and may need them in the future to prove that he has in fact written something which he then denies, then I will open them. It is my latest problem which concerns me. After my parents' deaths, which incidentally I am certain he caused, he was evidently given all my parent's jewellery from their bodies after the car had exploded. These included at least one diamond ring and a pearl necklace. He apparently signed for them. I was not aware of this until the other day, he kept these items, in fact stole them, they would be worth a great deal of money."

"I see; this matter becomes more complicated by the day. I will find out more and let you know of the outcome, any more problems, Mrs Season, do not hesitate to contact me."

She rang off.

"Can we sort out some of my parents' things this morning, Ruby?"

She agreed and they went upstairs to her bedroom.

"Now, Ruby, let us be sensible about these things. I do not want any of them. I would be so pleased if you would accept some."

Ruby sat on the bed and didn't make any comment for some time then she said.

"I can't deny that owning even one piece of the jewellery would be beyond anything that I could imagine, but, in all honesty I did not like yer mother and I don't think she would want me to ave anything."

"They don't belong to my mother now, they belong to me, if you don't have anything the jewellery will go into the bank vaults presumably never to be seen again in our lifetime and the clothes will go to charity."

"Will you give me some time to think about it, Suz?"

"You can have as long as you need, but can you bear in mind that I wish to get rid of them and move on? I still have the rest of the house to go through."

"I can tell you now, Suz, I wouldn't want any of er clothes, one they wouldn't fit me an two I couldn't stand avin er so close to me body, I should give em to the Red Cross including the underwear, I ave looked and there is so much that I reckon they will come and collect em."

That afternoon the things from Gibson Ffiske and Marsden were delivered, Suzannah decided that she would go through them when Ruby had gone home and she had time to think.

Percy staggered in with a box of winter vegetables he had also set up a stall outside to sell the ones left over. There'll be more to come he told them.

"Ere, Suz, don't put yon bairn outside it smells something awful of pig shit, I'm digging in my manure. And, Ruby, don't be too long before you show the fire the kettle. It's more en parky out ere."

Ruby put the kettle on and started preparing the pile of winter vegetables.

"There will be plenty of good veg to mek soup and stuff ere, you ought to be a lookin in your favourite cook books for recipes," she told Suzannah.

"They both worked very hard peeling and chopping the vegetables the result was a huge big pan of delicious soup. And very sore hands, Ruby and Suzannah shared it out. They also made a couple of vegetable shepherd's pies which they called Percy pies. They were topped with a mixture of grated cheese and toasted bread crumbs. (Heavy on the bread crumbs) A sprinkling of mustard powder completed the job.

Octavia was getting more difficult to settle in her cot after she had been fed and her nappy changed. Suzannah found that the only way was to ignore her crying and in the end she would give up and go to sleep. Suzannah emptied the contents of the carrier bag which contained her father's things taken from his office drawers they revealed nothing of any interest only pens ink and a diary of appointments. Glancing through she saw that WS had appeared on several occasions but of the other initials she knew nothing. She fetched her bundle of keys hoping that one would fit the small metal case which had been delivered from Gibson Ffiske and Marsden. It was then that she recalled what Mr Marsden had said about other branches, what did he mean, why was everything so very complicated?"

Eventually she found a key which fitted. She was disappointed, it contained letters from people who were unknown to her, she was uncertain as to what she had expected.

They were from offices in Brigtown, Harrindan and Ruddlingden. Where had she seen that last name before? Then she remembered it was in those papers which she had found in her father's desk.

The headed paper read:-

GIBSON FFISKE AND GOSLING
Land Agents, Estate Agents Valuers and Auctioneers
High Street,
Ruddlingden.

Dear Hector,

Please find enclosed your yearly free hold profits, as you can see they continue to be profitable year on year despite Herr Hitler. We send you our very best wishes.

Yours Mike.

It was dated, 12/4/42

The others were similarly worded.

Why would her father want to keep these letters locked up, and who was Gosling?

Then she came across another letter which seemed to have been screwed up and then unfolded it was hand written. It read.

Dear H,

I am on your trail. You don't have to look too far.

W

It was dated 28th March 1942.

Suzannah felt tired and overwhelmed, did she really need to look at things that she neither understood nor at this moment even cared about?

She simply left it all and went to bed. It was all too much for her, she didn't understand any of it and her brain felt incapable of coping with all this. She would just give it up and live her life as normal people managed to do. Why had all this appeared in her life? Then she realised, she had caused it by her inquisitiveness; so how could she let the matter drop now? At this moment she felt the need to, but in the morning ...!

She woke up suddenly and looked at her watch, Octavia was screaming. She wearily went to her room. Octavia was kicking her chubby legs, she was angry. Suzannah picked her up she immediately stopped crying and gave her mother the brightest smile.

"You think that you can wrap me around your little finger baby, but you are wrong."

Suzannah, realised that it was now only two weeks until Christmas, Octavia was ten weeks old, maybe she should be eating other things apart from her mother's milk which seemed to be drying up any way, her breasts were no longer feeling full. She took her downstairs and into the cold, cold kitchen. The embers of the fire were now grey and lifeless. She warmed up some of the left over vegetable soup and made some tea for herself, she spooned some of the vegetable liquor and fed Octavia with a tea spoon, she drank it greedily.

"So that is why you are so grumpy, you are hungry."

Octavia yelled every time the spoon was empty. She gave her more and she ate it. When she had, had her fill she grinned at her mother and immediately fell asleep.

Suzannah put her back in her cot and went to bed herself.

The next morning the first thing Suzannah was aware of was Ruby bringing her a cup of tea, it was seven o'clock.

"Thank you so much, Ruby, have you taken the baby downstairs?"

She told Ruby what had happened during the night.

"No I ain't, Suz, I looked in and she was fast asleep no wonder with a tummy full of soup."

At that moment, Octavia began to yell.

"I know the answer, Ruby, it's our soup."

Octavia yelled in temper all the way through her bath and while being dressed in her new winter outfit, despite the fact that her mother had fed her.

"She will need some National Dried." Ruby shouted above the din.

"Yer will ave to tek er to the clinic in double quick time they will give yer some orange juice and cod liver oil an all they will."

"Can't I just give her some soup in the meantime?"

Ruby was indignant.

"No get your sen off to the clinic an wrap er up warm, it's freezing out yonder, Percy and Fred ain't cum, there is note that they can do as the ground is frozen solid, I told Fred that e needn't cum ter feed the animals as I would do it. I'll do an ot water bottle for Octavia's Pram."

Overnight without any warning the snow had arrived. Suzannah pushed the pram through the clean white carpet of crunchy slippery silence. The snow continued to drift earthwards making the promenade resemble a place of dark beauty, a still adornment which almost took her breath away.

The clinic had one or two mothers with babies of all shapes and sizes waiting to be seen. She parked her pram in the covered entrance. When she entered everyone seemed to stop talking and began staring at her.

Suzannah smiled, and wished them. "Good Morning."

No one answered, but continued to stare and to mutter between themselves. She told herself to ignore them and give no reason for them to begin their abuse, which was obviously bubbling under the surface. The nurse called the first baby in, the mother glared at her and spat as she went into the surgery. It missed Suzannah and Octavia by inches, she ignored it and left the spit on the floor. Her turn came eventually, after ignoring the comments from the other mother's, she felt stressed and so very uncomfortable. As Ruby had told her she was given the necessary advice and supplements for Octavia, she was also weighed. The nurse smiled and nodded so Suzannah assumed everything was alright. She breathed a sigh of relief and quickly headed for home. She could see in the distance Ruby talking to women who she didn't know, they both looked very angry. She quickened her step. Their cold breath seemed to be like steam or was it the anger which they expelled? She saw Ruby snatching an envelope from the woman, as she got nearer she could hear the conversation.

"You know note about er, she is the kindest person that I ave ever met; if you and your sort want to persecute er for what yer ad like to ave done but didn't ave the bleedin nerve …."

"Or the bleedin money." One woman interrupted.

"All my bairns are starving cos of the likes of er."

"Ow the ell is it er fault, you stupid woman, don't ave so many bloody kids. You know by now what causes it; tell your Stan to keep is trousers on and get im sen a job, you know WORK, and may I add keep im sen out of the public ows."

"You talk out of your arse, try stopping Stan when ese ome from the pub."

Ruby put her hand up to signal to Suzannah who was approaching to go home, but Suzannah was having none of it and for the moment stood quietly listening to the conversation. The woman crossed her arms in a confrontational manner, Suzannah was so fed up, and her appearance took both women by surprise. Ruby continued.

"You stupid cow you knew what e was like before you married im, ow many broken jaws do you need before you get the message."

"What is all this about? Me I expect. I am so tired of you all judging me when you know nothing of my circumstances. I didn't choose all this, I cannot stand all this bigotry, I don't deserve it."

She opened her purse and threw two five pound notes at the women, with tears in her eyes she said.

"Take this for your starving children as it is allegedly all my fault though I cannot imagine why, and please leave me and my baby alone and free from your abuse and spitting at me. Don't come back as there is no more money and I will report you to the police for common assault."

She walked back round the corner to her rear door of her house

The woman snatched up the money.

"Oh yes, you'll tek er money you grasping cows. If I ever see yer, or ear of yer, or yur so called friends, causing er any more grief. I will see to it that people I know pay you a visit, and don't go telling anybody bout her kind donation, UNDERSTAND?"

The woman walked away.

"She can afford it, more bloody money than sense." One of the women said, and they both began to laugh as they walked in the opposite direction to Suzannah's house and they headed to the "Dog and Cat Public House."

When Ruby went into the kitchen she found Suzannah in tears.

"I got spat at in the clinic, so that I feel unable to go back, then this, it's every time that I go out someone is horrid to me, why Ruby? Don't you think that I did the right thing as far as William's treatment of me is concerned?"

Ruby stared into the kitchen fire before she spoke.

"It's very difficult for me to mek yer understand, Suz, I'm certainly not on their side, I'm on yours, but their life is so very different from yours. And they can't understand. Yer see

174

they don't expect much and when you are not the same, they all get together and talk, they are jealous, I'm not much good at explainin, but it is only what I expected, yer will just ave to try and not get upset I know ow ard it is for yer, yer comes from a different er, sort of place. Don't argue or else they will just smack you one, you will be no match for em believe me, and don't go round andin out money or yer will ave em all on yer doorstep. Your mother would never set foot outside the house she had everything delivered or she went in the car."

Suzannah listened and decided that she would try and change her attitude and be harder in future, so to this end she rang Mr McFinn and told him that she was ready to try and sort out her parents' safes, she had acted so stupidly for too long, things were about to alter. She also decided to ring the doctor and ask him to deal with all aspects of Octavia's child care, as she explained the treatment she received at the clinic. It was easier just to pay than to spend her time worrying every time she had to go to the clinic, he told her that he would arrange for a nurse to come.

The following day she gave Mr McFinn the keys after tentatively walking to the bank. She followed him into the dark, dank room which contained the safes. There was a large metal door which he undid with his own key before entering the inner sanctum the walls were lined with metal safes. The room seemed to echo in a most eerie way.

"I'm sorry that I don't have the safe codes but you did say that they could be accessed without them."

He smiled and assured her that he would use the banks own.

"Mr Gibson Ffiskes first I think."

It opened with a creak.

"Success I believe," he said.

It contained papers, lots of them.

"Why do all my parents' safes contain papers?" she asked.

Mr McFinn didn't comment as he carefully pulled them out and gave them to her, thus emptying this particular safe. She was asked to sign for them. The next one was her mother's which he opened. To Suzannah's surprise it contained a pearl necklace several diamond rings, a gold watch and earrings.

"How did they get in here?" she said in surprise.

"Are these the things which William stole?"

He handed her a certificate of authenticity which lay behind them.

"If I were you I would leave these well alone in this safe, I believe that I know the circumstances, but I think that unveiling them at this stage will only cause more problems than you already have."

"By the way on another subject; we received some moneys to be deposited into Mr Gibson Ffiske's account, which is of course now yours, looking back I noticed similar amount from the same sources appear every year, shall I give you a record of them for your own personal use or just deposit this money into the number two account."

Suzannah agreed the second idea.

She was surprised to find that Octavia, although awake, lay just looking around from her warm cosy habitat. Her eyes were definitely green.

As Suzannah pushed the pram home she felt proud of herself, and was actually looking forward to finding out what the papers from her father's safe contained. Was she turning a corner in her life? Only time would tell. She shivered, the frost was taking hold and its icy grip was once more in command. The darkness was creeping in very quickly and draining into the white cold earth. She had an unusual longing to be home. She hurried along. When she arrived Ruby was on the point of leaving for the night.

"Tea's in the pot, kettles on the ob, the fire is blazing, Josiah as bin and fetched you some coal. There is a stew in the side oven. See yer tomorrer kiss, kiss for Octavia. Oh and I fetched a rug down from one of the unused bedrooms for Octavia to lie on."

Suzannah enjoyed her stew and Octavia the sauce.

Later when all was quiet in the house and with Octavia tucked up in bed, Suzannah was alone in the kitchen she spread out the old papers on the scrubbed white kitchen table.

The first and largest was a map of some land, which was entitled Ruddlingden estate. The second was the same but with some, what looked to Suzannah like plans of houses. The third showed some sort of large building and out buildings.

''ORIGINAL.'

RUDDLINGDEN HALL AND LAND

The building is to be sold by auction subject to—

Auction of fine arts, antique figurines furniture and objet d'art is to take place in the Hall on June 29th 1917 from 2pm onwards. There will be a viewing for prospective buyers during the morning.'

The other two were similar, all large buildings with a great deal of land and many antiques.

Suzannah recalled that Ruby had not given her the letter which that dreadful woman was about to put in the letter box. The next morning a parcel of dog dirt arrived.

Christmas was only a few days away, she had declined an offer of Christmas at the Jacks, as she knew that she would not fit in and would feel uncomfortable. There didn't seem to be much point in putting any trimming up, as no one would notice, so she decided on a chicken for lunch, which Percy had given her and winter vegetables. She had bought Octavia a blue teddy bear, and placed it in her cot. She had given Ruby and Percy money which they were more than happy with. Ruby still hadn't decided about what she wanted from Suzannah's mother's jewellery so she tried to forget about it. She gave Josiah a toy for Marcus.

On Christmas Eve Mr Lees rang to say that William had admitted to the theft of her parents' jewellery and said that if she would give him £500 pounds and forget about prosecuting him for the jewellery theft he would agree to the divorce.

"What would you do?" she asked Mr Lees.

"Well, it does seem to be an awful lot of money to me considering the short time that you were married, we could try and negotiate, if that is what you wish. Mr Season insists, according to his solicitor, that you owe him a great deal more and has only agreed to this at the suggestion of his solicitor. He also intimates that he will be able to prove that he is correct. Personally I would be inclined to give in to him, just to get him off your back instead of facing the humiliation of the court."

"Hmm," she thought.

"She could afford it but didn't like the thought of giving in to him for all the things which he had subjected her to.

On the other hand would this get him off her back for good?

"If you wish to think about it over Christmas you may."

Mr Lees told her.

"Would I be able to come back to you if he caused me any more trouble in the future?"

"At any time, Mrs Season, you will find me very willing to help you. The divorce will now proceed and will most probably be in January"

"Well then I will agree."

"I will send you all the necessary papers today. In the mean time I hope that you have a very happy Christmas."

She thanked him and returned his good wishes.
She danced around the kitchen.

CHAPTER17

Summer 1944

Suzannah sat on the beach her back against the rough, grey worn wood of the groynes, the sand was soft and powdery as even at high tide the brown frothy water didn't reach this far up the beach. In the distance could be heard screaming from the children on the helter-skelter. Several people sat on the beach others had hired stripy deck chairs for sixpence a day. The backs of the chairs strained under the weight. Father would be fast asleep dreaming no doubt of the pint or two which he would enjoy later while the kids sat on the pub doorstep eating crisps and drinking pop. They would no doubt be hoping their parents wouldn't be too long before they rolled out of the pub full of jollity and beer, in need of their beds, but not before the customary bag of chips, steaming hot and covered with crunchy scraps and soaked in vinegar. Mother's lipstick had been left on the beer glass, and father, clad in braces and collarless shirt with rolled up sleeves, searched in his pockets for enough money to afford the three pence on each bag of chips. For the moment the beach and all the excitement it held was sufficient to keep them occupied. The sad looking donkeys walked up and down carrying happy children. The cockle stall man yelled.

"A plate of yer finest cockles sixpence, five oysters one shilling."

Children walked down the wooden steps carrying American whipped ice creams, white as snow, which quickly melted and ran down the cornet where they had to lick the dribbles off, others preferred the pink frothy candy floss.

They would be staying in one of the many boarding houses which displayed a 'No Vacancies' sign in the window they were not allowed back in until nine in the evening. Suzannah thought this practice to be disgusting; the whole idea of these unwelcoming places reminded her of the experience she had endured at Langden Dyke, and that was only for one night. But these people seemed to be happy enough, they could forget about the war and enjoy their week's holiday entitlement, and eat their and fish and chips, from one of the greasy cafés. Suzannah, while enjoying her afternoon, thought again about why the boarding house land ladies barred their guests all day. These thoughts had jumped into her brain many times during the last few weeks, she had day dreams about how she would run such a place if she had one. All the residents would be free to come and go as they wished, tea and cakes could be served in a large sitting room in the afternoon, then in the evening she would cook a delicious meal for them all. The thought passed. For her it was so nice to sit on the beach where no-one knew her so she could avoid the usual abuse. She had by now become used to it, or so she convinced herself.

Her divorce was over and done with, she had received the nici and the absolute was due any day. She was coping much better with the people who in East-Thorpe did their best to upset her. She now owned three large co-joined houses and after the war was over, she could decide what to do with them, providing they were still standing. She knew a little more concerning all the land and property which her father had owned, and she wanted to find out the full story. That is to say that sometimes she did, and sometimes she was so frightened of the outcome that she decided to leave well alone as it could only result in disaster.

Octavia was eating sand, one of her favourite pastimes. Her arms were getting redder and so was her face. It must be time to go home.

"No, baby no, your nappy will be full of sand and irritate your bum, stop it now, Octavia looked up. She was ten months old and not only had a mind of her own she could crawl very well and walk around providing that she had something to cling on to. She turned around and swiftly headed for the water.

"No, Tavia, no," Suzannah told her, still she travelled as fast as she could giggling all the time. Suzannah got up, she was stiff from sitting in one place and just managed to catch Octavia before she entered the water.

"You do not go near the water that is naughty. We will go home now."

Octavia wasn't pleased. Suzannah gathered up her things with a screaming Octavia under one arm she walked the short distance towards her house. Looking up it never failed to amaze her how lonely the three tall houses looked, standing as they did with a now cleared bomb site beside them, and where once, three more similar houses had stood proud and elegant; a sign of dignity in this time of austerity. The beautiful Art Deco Theatre had then occupied the opposite corner as if to finish off the facade in all its magnificence, the grand statement to East Thorpe on Sea was no more.

She tried not to think that she owned these three large houses and had no idea what she was going to do with them, so they remained, alone and isolated, similar to how she sometimes felt herself. At twenty two years old she was far too young for all this responsibility.

"I think this little madam will have to go into the big bath," she told Ruby when she returned home. Ruby took her off her mother.

"Oose bin a naughty girl then?"

She looked at her green eyes so like her mothers.

"Come on let Ruby sort you out eh?"

"Suz, Jo as bin wiv that play pen, it's folded up in the corner."

Suzannah was so hot she got herself a glass of water and sat down. Play pen she thought I don't recall one being mentioned.

When Octavia re-appeared with a red hot Ruby, she was placed in the unfolded play pen with her Blue teddy bear, she was wearing only her nappy and liberty bodice.

Suzannah took tea out to the men then her and Ruby settled down with theirs.

They both looked at Octavia as she shuffled round this strange wooden boundary dragging Blue Bear with her.

"Believe me, Suz, she is planning her escape."

Josiah burst in.

"Prefabs, we are havin no such thing as prefabs."

Ruby and Suzannah stared at each other. He pulled out a chair at the table.

"Our lads and them as have suffered deserve more than shabby pre fabs and East Thorpe are havin none of it if I have my way. They reckon that they last for 10 years. Rubbish. And even if they did that's £50 down the drain, I'm havin none of it I tell you, none of it," he repeated.

"Good morning, Josiah, how nice of you to pop in and thank you for the play pen," Suzannah said sarcastically.

"Oh, er sorry. Good morning."

"Do you think that Marcus would like to come and play with Octavia in it?"

"That's how you come to have the contraption. April wouldn't let our lad in it, said he didn't like it so she picked him up, gave him a cuddle told me to take it away. I tell you that lad won't know if he is Arthur or Martha by the time he's fifteen."

The play pen narrowly missed Ruby's ankle. They all looked in amazement as Octavia half carried half pushed the wooden play pen along the floor in an attempt to join in the conversation. Josiah bent and picked her up.

Now, my little princess, have you got a kiss for your Jo."

She plonked a wet sloppy kiss on his large lips and giggled.

He put Octavia back in her play pen and grasped the proffered tea cup. She grizzled for a few moments and then continued to move the play pen all over the kitchen.

Ruby told her off for banging the play pen into the door in an effort to get out. After three attempts Ruby picked her up and took her to the table which Octavia thought was great fun.

"You spoil her, Ruby."

"Well someone as to."

" Do you know who owns this land yonder next to yours and where the old theatre once stood, also the former Gunnell's land? I'd be very interested to know. In my circle seem to be a bit tight-lipped about it, will you try to find out for me?"

"Well I suppose so, Jo, but I'm getting a bit fed up of all these mysteries in my life. Why would you want to know such things?"

He declined to answer and drank his cup of tea, she looked at him whimsically over the top of her cup as he told them that he must go and waved good bye.

"Ese gettin a bit full of im sen ain't e?" Ruby said.

The next day Suzannah went to her father's former place of work, to see Mr Marsden.

"I have been thinking about you and have realised that because of your upbringing you aren't as I may say, fully understanding of your father's involvement in certain areas. I haven't been as helpful as I probably should have been. You seem to comprehend very little about his work and other matters. For this I can only apologise."

Suzannah thought. He is absolutely correct I don't understand anything. She remained silent.

"Stop me if I am telling you things which you already know."

He looked ill at ease while trying to look relaxed.

"You see," he cleared his throat.

"Your father was a very wise man, which I am sure you will agree, but your mother was the driving force."

"To be quite honest, Mr Marsden, I know nothing of them. Before I was sent away to school and when my mother forced me to return to be their servant, and consequently to marry a man who I hated, I can honestly say I learnt nothing more. Then they were killed, so my knowledge of my parents is negligible."

She felt so much better."

"Oh dear, oh dear, I feared as much. I wouldn't be telling you this but I have felt sorry for you and Mr William Season could be a force to be reckoned with. He had a hold on your parents over something that happened in the past in Ruddlingden that I know. Your father owned a great deal of land. I wouldn't like to speculate how much, it is scattered in many areas, he liked to play his cards close to his chest, so to speak. He inherited many acres of land in Ruddlingden, it now has several hundred houses built on it some of them leasehold, some rented. He, up to his death still owned the land so obtained the ground rent annually he refused to sell the lease to any of them. He owned Ruddlingden Estate Agents and many more which I can furnish you with if you wish, all of which he obviously earned a great deal of interest. It is now all yours. I cannot, in all honesty, say that I envy you your considerable fortune. I will see to it that this year's leasehold rent is placed in your bank account. Selfishly I am very pleased to have off loaded some of the, what I consider, to be liabilities on to you. This does not prevent me from feeling a traitor."

Suzannah needed some time to digest what she had been told, but in all honesty she wasn't too worried about it.

"Thank you for your information Mr Marsden. Please may I ask you one question? Who owns the land adjacent to mine on the promenade also the same question about the old Gunnells?"

"It is better for you that I don't tell you at the moment as the information may be passed on to people who, how can I put it, are better off not knowing."

He fidgeted and pulled his finger around the inside of his collar because he was agitated.

"All I would advise you is, not to try to find out too much of your father's past or in fact with his relationship with your ex-husband. It will not help you to know everything and most likely it will cause you a great deal of upset, it is too dangerous, my dear. Please don't tell anyone we have spoken about this."

Suzannah felt a shiver of fear run down her back. For that moment her mouth was dry.

"We won't talk of it again."

He reached across the table top and grasped her hand, his fingers were as cold as ice.

CHAPTER 18

Part 2 1911

He crawled along the under growth, he knew every blade of grass, every hollow and tree of this copse. He reached the place which he regarded as his sanctuary, a dry hard hollow of earth and crispy russet leaves. Above was a canopy of tree branches meeting as they did as a lover's embrace. The birds sang in tuneful harmony; a perfect place which he had long ago claimed as his own. When he approached the squirrels and rabbits scampered away there was no need as he bore them no harm. He lay on his back in a pensive mood thinking of what his father had told him, it was not unexpected but never the less still as devastating. He was eleven years old, far more clever than all his siblings or school chums, partly because he spent his spare time in this place reading and studying. The younger ones didn't have the chance to go to school instead. They were given tasks in the house and also had to share shoes as there wasn't enough to go round. Why did his parents have so many children, who they were incapable of caring for or afford to feed and clothe? This was not going to happen to him. He knew the moment the headmaster appeared at the door offering his father a scholarship for his eldest son to continue his studies, explaining how clever he was and how he was capable of greater things and had the ability to go far in life, be someone of importance, what the answer would be. The man tried to explain to his father about the opportunities which would be open to him in the future. The boy knew that his father wouldn't take any notice, he would want him to work he knew he wouldn't take any notice of anyone, his father was always right and anyone who dared to argue with that was in danger of being punched.

He could still recall the fire of anger and hatred which began in his stomach and rose up like a volcano until the only thing which he could do was run despite the threats which his father yelled after him.

He lay, as usual, gazing at Ruddlingden Hall and its grounds, admiring the sheer beauty of this massive building. It was sadly descending into disrepair and ruin. But Harry Gibbs adored it. He wanted it for his own however impossible that appeared to be for him, he was a scruffy homeless child without a penny to his name, but he was clever, very clever. He tried to keep up to date with word affairs by searching for discarded newspapers he came across in all sorts of places and reading street sellers newspapers at a distance. They got to know this strange, skinny, street urchin, and therefore gave him their spare papers at the end of the day which he squirreled away in his hollow and covered with leaves, until he had the opportunity to read them.

The beautiful impressive, neglected stately home with its acres of land had once been a grand Georgian redbricked building with impressive steps leading up to the huge front door. Stone lions standing on guard, it boasted stepped gables and twisted chimneys. He admired the square balustrades and turrets, the phoenix weather vane which stood proudly on the right hand side, on the top of the cupola.

The night was drawing in, and with it came the cold. The sky looked raw. A yellow moon shone casting a halo onto the ground. The shadows of the trees fell across the once green lawns now an eerie shadow of grey. Harry had made up his mind. He would not be returning to screaming children and a clout across the head, or worse with a future of unimaginable drudgery. He'd be very brave and it would certainly work out.

He piled the dry autumn leaves and old newspapers on top of him, curled into a ball and slept.

He awoke with the first grey fingers of light, the chill of daybreak touched his face, and the memory of what the day had in store for him filled his mind with fear and hope. He wondered what time it was and looked at the rising sun to make a guess. It was too early for him to pay his planned visit so he must bide his time. He walked to the stream and washed his hands and face which drove away the last vestiges of sleep, combed his hair with his finger nails, brushed his trousers down and pulled up his socks, making sure that the holes were not evident and no-one would ever know that his shoes were minus their soles. He rubbed his tongue over his teeth and scooped a drink of water from the stream. Then sitting down he went through his prepared script for the day. He imagined the answers which he may receive and practiced his persuasive replies. It was time to go.

Lady Gertrude Elizabeth Gosling's wiry grey hair, piled up on the top of her head in an unkempt manner, having never in its memory felt the tug of a brush or a comb, only dust and debris kept it in this position. Sitting erect as was her habit, born from years of discipline, her saggy, lined face, thin, unsmiling lips and her aura of importance made her the person she was, there was nothing hidden and no pretence she was a selfish, manipulating cantankerous lady, and always had been, her large pale eyes, missed nothing. When her dear husband was alive he would, to a certain extent control her temper. She loved him dearly and would never forgive the people she believed were the perpetrators of his untimely death. She continued to mourn his passing, and always would. Wearing as usual, her long black, high necked, Victorian gown. She would sit as was her habit, in an almost thread bare chair in what she assumed to be her tower facing her domain, watching and scrutinizing the few things which occurred on her vast estate. She failed to notice that both the land and the once magnificent buildings were crumbling around her. She didn't ever leave her rooms now and didn't like visitors. She had once been very interested in world affairs but now the interest had left her, no one to discuss things with. That particular day she watched the ragamuffin boy, as she did most days. He assumed that he was concealed from her but he was mistaken.

She was intrigued by him, and knew that one day he would have the courage to come to her door. Looking through her telescope, which she hid in the folds of her dress, he reminded her of her beloved godson whom she had not seen for many years as he lived with his parents in Bombay India. His father was a Civil Session judge, but her godson was cared for by his devoted Ayah and Barriers, so he saw little of his parents. Lady Gertrude had a silver framed replica of him beside her bed it was the thing which she coveted most in the world.

She watched as this urchin emerged from his woodland retreat. She knew that he would do so one day. She clapped her claw like hands and cackled.

He, walking proud and erect, approached the front door and climbed the steps.

"You won't get in that way," she thought, enjoying this. It was the most fun she'd had for goodness how long.

He knocked loudly on the door not noticing the pull bell and waited, and waited. He was just about to knock again when a girl about his age answered.

"Tradesmen go to the back door," she told him with the authority she didn't have, pointing to the correct direction.

Harry wasn't put off just more determined. He walked around the large house and down many steps until he found the rear door and knocked.

"I have an appointment with Lady Gosling."

The same maid looked astonished and cast a glance at what she presumed to be the cook. She wiped her red sore hands on her less than clean apron.

Harry stood his ground.

"You and my Aunt Sally," the cook said.

Harry very briefly thought about this then said,

"You can ask her if you don't believe me."

Although he had taken the time to observe her, high in the right wing, on his visits to the wood, little knowing that at the same time she was doing exactly the same, watching him. He was hoping that the cook didn't choose to confirm his presence with her. He stood firm. He was well aware of where to find Lady Gosling it was the highest room on the opposite side of the building which was below the cupola. This seemed simple enough. He had worked it out in his mind many times before.

"Alright, on your head be it, if you are so clever off you go and find her ladyship's room."

Harry dashed up the stone steps and opened the heavy door to reveal a huge hall which in its day must have been breath-taking, but now had lost its former glory to decay and neglect. He ran the full length of the building passing the front door and mounted a wide stair case, in past days this must have appeared luxuriant, the chandeliers hung like rain drops after a storm from the cob webbed ceiling, the red, once lush stair carpet was a shadow of its other life, it was now thread bare and the brass stair rods green and tarnished. The curtains hung in tatters the peeling walls and smell of decay was all pervading. The two other stair cases were identical. He calculated which would be the front room and knocked.

Lady Gosling cackled to herself, the day had finally arrived as she knew it would.

She said with a strong unquavering voice.

"Come."

He entered boldly.

"Good morning, my Lady," he slightly inclined his head.

He was interrupted by the old lady.

"You are that common boy who hides in my copse. Watching, always watching. Do not," she emphasized "underestimate me, I know everything."

He thought quickly.

"I am aware, of your observations of me your ladyship and I respect your great wisdom, for that reason I would like to work for you, and I know that you will consider me to be suitable I will work hard and learn from your vast knowledge."

Lady Gertrude rose up in her chair a look of amazement on her face.

"You, a dirty urchin, how can you possibly know what I, a Lady of the highest regard could possibly know?"

"Because having heard great things about you. I realise that you will make the right choice."

She was not only flattered as a lonely recluse would be, but was also intrigued by this dirty replica of the godson she loved.

"How did you come to speak so well you ragamuffin?"

"By reading, listening and learning, my family were rich but fell on hard times through no fault of their own."

How did these lies continue to trip off his lips so easily? It wasn't supposed to be so.

He continued to stare at her, never flinching as if to convince the old hag. He couldn't fail, his whole future depended on this and nothing would prevent him. He didn't think for one moment that it would be so difficult.

"I have always admired you and wanted to work for you. I will do so for nothing except a room and any food which is spare, I will prove to you my worth. That I promise."

"Then bring me a cup of hot tea."

He ran down the stairs three at a time along the hall down the stone steps and breathlessly into the kitchen.

"Tea for her Ladyship," he panted.

He watched as a tray was set with silver pot, sugar and milk jug, and a cup of the finest china, he was anxious to be off. He wouldn't be able to run as fast without spilling the tea.

He grabbed a tea towel and wrapped it around the pot, removed the tray cloth and was off. Running, running back the way he came, before entering the room he quietly removed the items from the tray wiped the spills off and replaced the tray cloth, discarding the soiled tea towel he knocked at the door.

Her ladyship was very impressed but said.

"You will have to be quicker than that or my tea will be cold."

"Would you like me to pour, your ladyship?"

"No I don't want a dirty urchin pouring my tea. Tell cook to find you a room with a bell."

He made a small nod of his head trying to hide his joy, picked up the tea towel outside her room and ran back. He was determined that however she treated him, however rude or cruel, he would carry on working for her; it was the only chance he had.

This was the beginning of an adventure, nothing or no-one would stop him now, whatever he had to do he would do it. None of the staff stayed long and the Hall continued to decay. Sometime previously there had been a head housekeeper who was in charge of a great number of staff, but because of Lady Goslings cruel tongue they had decreased never to be replaced. Harry knew that they had little work to do and spent the majority of their time feet up snoozing. He ignored all the insults which Lady Gosling hurled at him and continued to be at her beck and call. He knew that in the end all of this unkindness and misery would pay off. He spent the time when Lady Gosling was having her afternoon sleep, in the library, learning everything he could, or walking around the huge hall and the grounds taking everything in and storing it in his mind for future reference. Lady Gosling got more and more feeble and forgetful. So far Harry hadn't had a day off nor had he been paid a penny.

One day she summoned him, it was late summer and a few days previously she had received a letter from her godson so she was in good spirits.

"I have been thinking, you need to have some more suitable clothes if you are to continue as my man servant. Take the Argyle and go to 'Browns' I will telephone them and they will provide you with suitable attire."

She waved her hand with its blue knotted veins in a manner of dismissal.

"Your ladyship if I could be so bold, I know that you miss knowing what is happening in the rest of the world including India where your dear god son lives,(he knew nothing of the sort) so I wondered if you would consider having a daily newspaper and if you were too tired I could read it to you (he was well aware that she could not read anything close up to her but wouldn't admit it). He nodded and left the room wondering what on earth an Argyle was. He thought all the way down the stairs, whatever it is, it can't be in the house he thought to himself.

Then it dawned on him it was the car which he had seen in one of the barns. He ran to find it.

He had very rarely seen this car or any other come to that, but he recalled that when he was small all the children would line up to watch it being driven down the lane by a man in a peaked cap.

The old barn doors with peeling paint scratched along the ground as he opened the garage. Sunbeams danced in the sun, and there she stood. He jumped up on the seat in front of the steering wheel which seemed to be so high up. What was he to do now?

Moments later a man approached.

"My name is Mason Season, I work in the grounds. Are you having trouble?"

Harry admitted that he was. Mason jumped aboard and soon sorted it out and Harry with great trepidation drove off. He didn't see any cars on his journey. He arrived at Browns the shop which only the toffs used so they were less than pleased to see him until they realised that it was Lady Gosling who had sent him, when their attitude changed. After measuring him, he was given more clothes than he had ever seen in his life time and told to collect the ones which were not in stock a week later.

Arriving back, not without a mistake or two in the Argyle, he ran up to his room to try on his new clothes, he had never felt so excited and prayed that Lady Gosling was still having her afternoon sleep. He just wished that he had access to a mirror.

He had just fastened the last jacket button when the bell rang.

He as usual ran like the wind to her room all this exercise and food had made him stronger and fitter.

She looked at him in a very strange way.

"My darling godson she said opening her arms, I didn't know that you had come all that way to see me."

Harry had experienced this misunderstanding several times and knew that however he played it the result would be the same. If he went along with the silly old bat she would no doubt realise and be very angry. If he told her, the same anger would ensue. At least that way was the quickest.

"It is not your godson, my Lady, it is Harry." His mouth attempted to reach nervously for a smile.

For a moment she stared in silence, then, she let out a loud noise like a screeching owl attacking its prey.

"Get out get out of my sight you er, er nobody and don't come back."

He just managed to get out before a brass candle stick hit the closed door.

When he arrived back in his room he wasn't surprised to hear her lady ships bell ring again, no doubt she would have forgotten what had happened only minutes before.

It was raining and as usual water ran down the inside of the broken glass and lay in puddles on the already water marked floor. The flag stones dipped unevenly. For once it didn't bother Harry, he was tired. Through the windows could be seen heavy swathes of long forgotten trees drooping onto the earth. "You rang, my Lady," he said in a voice which belied his tiredness." I have been thinking, Harry, I would like to have a daily newspaper. I'm surprised that you didn't think of it but what can one expect. See to it," she waved her hand in dismissal.

He returned to his cold dreary damp room.

CHAPTER 19

In August1915 England had been at war for a year, apart from the occasional Sopwith Camel flying over Rudlingden Hall where Harry had worked for four years, he was not affected. Lady Gosling having forgotten about allowing Harry to have a daily newspaper remained oblivious of the grim news concerning the effects of industrialized war. Harry was an avid follower of news. He was well aware of the dreadful conditions the men had to suffer such as trench foot, rats everywhere in the trenches. A fear that as their comrades were slaughtered they may be the next or worse still, severely injured when they knew that the prospect of a slow painful death in such a place as inevitable. No help would be forthcoming.

Three years later as Rudlingden Hall fell further into disrepair, there was very little work to do, The only staff who worked within the Hall were the kitchen staff and a handy man who didn't do anything handy or otherwise, Lady G had long since run out of personal staff, butlers, maids and so forth, every one of them had left long before Harry had arrived mostly because of the fear of mental and physical abuse, Harry tolerated it, he had plans. He didn't inform Lady Gosling, but forged each one of the remaining staff an excellent reference and a week's money in advance. They were all happy with the situation and he did what little extra work involved himself. He had learnt by watching the cook how to prepare the simple meals Lady Gosling asked for. His stack of hidden money was looking healthy.

Visitors seldom came. Once or twice a girl who appeared to be a bit older than himself would arrive, but as Lady Gosling had already seen her from her lofty tower she would ring Harry and tell him she did not want to see this person. The only other visitor whom she sometimes saw was her solicitor.

Harry now had more responsibilities. He spent his spare time studying, and had now progressed to reading about paintings and fine art. He would find a figurine or picture in the house and take it with him to the library and read about its heritage and value, before going he would leave it in the library, the sunniest room in the building.

Mason Season still worked in the grounds and refused to leave. Harry didn't see him and continued the habit of leaving his wages near the great door. Mason had a son who was usually with his father as his mother had died in child birth and there was no-one else to care for him. On the very odd occasion when Harry saw them he was unnerved by the boy who stared at him without saying a word. Harry didn't like children. He remembered his siblings too well, snotty nosed whining creatures.

One day when he had helped Lady Gosling into bed for her afternoon sleep he saw on the dressing table a piece of paper. Once he heard her snoring he opened it. It was her will. The solicitor had visited the previous day, so she must have for some reason put it on her dressing table.

She had left everything to her godson Hector Gibson Ffiske not one penny for him after all the work he had done, all the abuse which he had endured and all the unpaid hours. It also read that her daughter Cecelia and her offspring Arabella were to receive nothing. He replaced it and went downstairs. He felt cheated; what on earth would he do after she died? He would certainly be without a job, he had saved some money from the wages and had intended to sell some of the favourite books, paintings, and figurines which he had systematically stolen and hidden. And how long would that last plus, if he found employment it wouldn't be as lucrative or as easy as the job he had. All he could wish for would be that she would live a long life for him to find a way to make more money. That night was once again sleepless. The next few days were a nightmare each plan he thought up was in some way flawed.

By an awful coincidence the following week a telegram arrived. It was from HMS *Medina*, and stated that Lady Gosling's godson was on board. Evidently his parents, his Ayah and Barriers had been savagely murdered during a native uprising. He was carrying all the necessary papers to prove who he was and would dock at Southampton in two weeks time.

Harry, re read the telegram trying to think what to do. That night proved to be another sleepless one, he lay awake deliberating, his anger increasing. He couldn't let all his plans go to waste. This boy who had never worked a day in his life, would just march in destroy everything and dismiss him. He had imagined that when Lady Gosling realised how much work and abuse he had been subject to on a daily basis that she would leave him a considerable amount of money. He would by then have substantially increased the amount of things which he had pilfered; the paintings and objet d'art which he considered was what he deserved. Now this had all been ruined.

The night was long, culminating in a huge headache, but he had devised a scheme that was fool proof and would give him everything he had ever wanted, and more. Lady Gosling rang just as he had made her pot of tea and toast. He took it to her.

He intended to spend the day refining his plans, as well as tending to Lady Gosling's few needs which had diminished over the years he had been in her employ. He had decided not to let her know of her godson's impending arrival. She wanted to take her afternoon sleep so he helped her to lie on the top of the bed and poured her a cup of tea.

He needed to take a walk to clear his head and to put everything into perspective. He also had to think of all eventualities. It was one of those hot summer days when the trees seemed to be overloaded with fresh green leaves, the sky an amazing blue with white fluffy clouds lazily moving across it. He walked around the lake. The water sometimes had a calming effect on him. The swans, ducks and water hens swam around the small central island without a care in the world. The water was still; Harry looked across and saw what he thought was Mason Season fishing. He wasn't quite sure as he had seen so little of the man so he moved nearer to be certain that it was Mason fishing for carp. They exchanged waves; sitting about two yards from his father was William, the young lad stared at him. Harry always found his gaze to be disconcerting and unsettling and quickly returned to the Hall.

The day before he was due to meet the great ship *Medina* he drove to Witches Wood, a large and unused forest. The local people avoided going into the wood as there was a curse on it placed by local witches, or so they believed. His plan was a very daring one but he had no option but to carry it out.

He had a spade with him and began to dig a large hole. The earth was bone dry so it took him longer than he had expected and even though the woods were cool he was hot, sweaty and out of breath. He stood back to envisage the size and depth of his work, feeling satisfied he hurried back. Her ladyship would be furious if she knew that he had left the Hall without her permission. If she caught him he may begin to believe in witches curses.

He could hear her bell the moment he opened the door, and ran as quickly as he could to her room, he could feel the sweat running down his back.

"I will have two lightly boiled eggs for my tea with my usual thinly sliced, crust-less bread, a little heavier on the butter, it was too sparse the other day, kindly inform cook."

Harry couldn't help but remember the last time eggs were requested, she had hurled them through the air at him. He only just managed to duck as they crashed to the floor because apparently there was a shortage of butter. As the cook was long gone the lack of butter was solely his fault.

"Yes, your ladyship," he said.

He went straight to the kitchen and selected the sharpest knife from the drawer and gave it an extra rub on the stone which was for that purpose, he wrapped it carefully in a cloth and added a box of vestas. Then he made her ladyship's tea, making sure that the butter was spread evenly and thickly on the bread and placed everything on the prepared tea tray. He felt edgy and agitated, not because there was a fear that she would hurl it at him, he was used to that, but he was forcing himself to go over and over in his mind what he must do the following day.

He decided that for the very first time he would have a glass of whisky, it always calmed her ladyship down so maybe it would work for him. He couldn't bring himself to eat anything but definitely felt more at ease after drinking the alcohol.

The bird song woke him, immediately he felt wide awake and knew that all his plans had been made it was too late to change anything. The day had finally arrived.

Quietly he opened her ladyship's door, he could hear her snoring. He tiptoed to her bed his heart pounding. His hands shook as he reached for the spare pillow and gently placed it over her face. She didn't make as much as a sigh it seemed so quiet and peacefully still. He left it there for some time, terrified that when he removed it she would jump up and scream at him, she didn't, she looked just the same; he even bent down low to listen for her breath there was none. She was dead.

After removing the silver framed replica of her godson and making sure that she looked as if she still slept, he left and went down to the kitchen, collected the knife and Vestas he took the Argyle and drove to Southampton. Fear had left him, he was now elated.

He watched in amazement as the black and tan *Medina* serenely docked. He had been reading about it, but never ever imagined it to be so vast. He had learnt that it had carried King George V and Queen Mary on the very first trip which an English Monarch ever made to India. He thought of the grand opulence which Lady Gosling's godson had enjoyed. He watched with great interest as the passengers began to disembark and wondered how these very wealthy people had gained all their riches, the beautiful clothes, the ladies with their floppy huge hats and dresses trailing along the floor, the very way they carried themselves, the servants who meekly followed burdened down with hand luggage, he wanted a life of the rich not the one which he had been born into. Harry felt inferior.

After what seemed to him to be a long wait, a youth followed by several Indian stewards, one wheeling a barrow of trunks approached him.

The youth extended a hand in greeting.

"I am Hector Gibson Ffiske, you must be one of my new servants."

"Indeed I am," Harry said through gritted teeth.

"Are all of my other servants and my godmother aware of my arrival? As I had to depart so quickly I was forced to leave most of my belongings behind so my godmother will have to arrange to purchase some replacements."

Harry was busy helping the stewards to load the Argyle while Hector stood waiting, he just ignored him.

"I shall need a bath when we arrive, one can never feel totally refreshed aboard a ship. Will you arrange it?"

"I certainly will, sir."

"I hear that Lady Gosling is totally ga ga, so maybe it will not be too long before I receive my inheritance, plus one won't have to write those infernal letters any longer I will also inherit my share of the business. My parents and servants were killed by those dreadful Indians. My Ayahs saved me by shutting me in a cupboard so then when everyone had been killed and the despicable Indians had dispersed one found one's self alone. Looking at all those dead bodies was quite disagreeable. I hear there is a war on in this country, but it won't affect me of course."

Before long they reached Witches Wood and Harry turned into it.

"Where on earth are we going I am not used to travelling in this uncomfortable way?" he asked.

"We just have to take a short walk before we continue our journey." Harry told him.

"Don't be long about it, young man, the whole thing is adding to my discomfort, and I will have a word with Lady Gosling when we arrive don't you think that I have suffered enough?"

Harry finally stopped and walked silently onward followed by Hector. Then quickly he turned and without hesitation plunged the knife deep into his chest so hard that the tip actually protruded out of his back. Hector had a look of horror on his face as Harry pulled the knife out. He made a small groan and fell. Harry pushed him quickly into the hole before much blood could stain the floor of the forest. He then began to shovel the mound of dry soil on top of him; he flattened it down and spread the red brittle leaves over his grave. It looked the same as it had done prior to its disturbance. He was sure that his clothes and skin would very soon decay or be eaten until only his bones remained. He was pleased with himself, pushing the knife in hadn't been as difficult as he had imagined. He smiled when he recalled the look of horror and disbelief on his pompous face as the knife was plunged into him. .

He went back to the Argyle and searched for Hector's papers and a set of his clothes.

He discovered that Hector had been two years his senior. He stripped off his own clothes and replaced them with those of the late Hector. As he had not had his hair cut in all the years which he had toiled for her Ladyship he used the sharp knife to hack off his own long tresses. It had been a long hot summer so Harry once he had formulated his plan had purposely spent many uncomfortable hours laying in the sun He then burnt his own clothes and hair scattering the ashes over the grave.

He felt tired as he left and drove back to Ruddlingden Hall. He had begun his plan and so far it had gone without a hitch. There was much more to do, but before that he had to, for the first time, have a bath in Lady Gosling's private suite and wash his hair. Now that he was Hector Gibson Ffiske. He had to learn to, act like him, talk like him and forget that Harry Gibbs ever existed.

Lady Gosling or, his godmother, looked paler as he walked past her.

"I have arrived back from India, dearest Godmother," he chuckled to himself.

After wallowing in the water he began to feel a little more like his altered ego. He found some grease in one of her cupboards and liberally spread it on his hair, used her comb to part his now greasy hair and flatten it out in the fashion of the day. He put a little rouge on his cheeks which seemed to add to the resemblance and dressed in his clothes, He now even looked like the seventeen year old Hector Gibson Ffiske.

"I have just arrived at my godmother's, Lady Gertrude Elizabeth Gosling at Ruddlingden Hall and to my horror she appears to be dead in her bed, I am so shocked I need some assistance," he told the police officer on the telephone.

"My name?"

He paused.

"Oh yes, it is Hector Gibson Ffiske. I have just arrived back from Bombay India."

The police arrived with a doctor and went as directed to Lady Gosling's room where the body was examined.

"She looks like an old lady and I would think she died simply of old age, her old ticker just gave up. No need to intervene further. I would say just notify the funeral parlour," the doctor said.

Harry, now Hector, sighed with relief.

The Doctor scribbled on a death certificate and handed it to the policeman.

"May I just ask you a few questions, Mr Gibson Ffiske?" The sergeant said.

"But of course sergeant."

"I don't imagine that I will be of much help but I will do my best," he put on a false smile.

Hectors stomach was in knots, he tried to give the impression of grief and sincerity.

"I feel very distraught."

The policeman sat down opposite him and removed a pencil and writing pad from his pocket.

"So how did you come to arrive from India?

He had prepared what he was going to say and practiced it many times.

"I escaped from being assassinated. My parents and my servants were all killed in an Indian uprising. I travelled back here on the *Medina*. To my dear godmother."

He hung his head and sniffed a lot, for impression.

"She had sent her manservant to collect me from Southampton. He thought the world of her and she of him. When we arrived here we rushed up to her bedroom as Harry, her servant, was concerned that she had needed him while he was away and I because I hadn't seen her for so long was anxious to see her lovely old face."

He paused for a little while.

"Harry was so very upset that he had to go for a walk, that was hours ago and I haven't seen him since, I have looked all over the house and grounds and not only can I not find him, all the servants have disappeared, the hall is a shadow of its former self, it has fallen into disrepair, everything is just … so upsetting. I don't feel that I can take much more, officer, I really can't."

He hung his head in mock distress.

"Ah here is the undertaker, he will take your godmother away now, and then the funeral director will come and see you."

"I really don't think that I can spend the night here," Hector said. "Is there a hotel in which I can book into and be alone."

"We will sort that out for you, sir."

"Will you please continue to look for Harry Gibbs, I am so worried about his whereabouts?"

Harry Gibbs was obviously not found, even though he was under their noses. The newspapers were full of interviews with many different people including Harry Gibbs's family.

Hector didn't move back into the Hall, he had spent many years in this crumbling wreck and now he didn't have to stay any longer. He was at no-one's beck and call, every one respected him and he enjoyed that. The funeral was arranged. It featured in all the newspapers, even the nationals. Anyone who considered themselves to be important dusted down their black attire and put on a sad face. The church was full to capacity, people she had vaguely known and some who just pretended to know her arrived. The service went as well as funerals do. The Hymns had been suggested by the undertaker, The rector spoke of a fine lady, even though he had never met her and smiled his vicar type smile saved for such occasions while wondering what the after funeral food at the hotel would be like. His wife had gone to see her mother and he didn't fancy pre-heated shepherd's pie yet again.

Hector, also wearing a false look of devastation accompanied by the obligatory half smile, had a word with some of the mourners, just wanted the whole thing to be over so that after the will had been read he could get on with the organising of the estate and look forward to a life of luxury, something he could never have dreamed of. It was coupled with, at the back of his mind, a feeling of apprehension and fear.

He had shaken so many people's hands thanked them, and wished that they would all go away. No one liked the nasty old bag anyway.

Just as he thought that every hand had been shaken a small attractive young lady approached, she had sparkling green eyes and obviously came from a wealthy family by the way she dressed and spoke. She extended a kid gloved hand.

"I am so sorry to meet you in such circumstances."

She said her head on one side in an attractive manner.

"My name is Arabella Gosling. I am the late Lady Gosling's granddaughter. I know that you have been in India, and my meetings with my grandmama have been infrequent of late. She was not an easy person to get on with, I found, but I read about her death and thought that it would be the right thing to do to pay my respects, so here I am," she let out an attractive giggle."

"That is so awfully kind of you," Hector said in his new and well-practiced way.

"Are you staying somewhere around here? Or do you live close by?"

"I am staying at the Axe and Cleaver."

"What a coincidence so am I."

CHAPTER 20

The next morning, while having breakfast Arabella said to Hector.

"I did meet you once many years ago I assume you do not recall it, you must have been about eight at the time, a bossy child as I remember, you expected everyone to be at your beck and call. The servants who came with you did as you ordered. I think I felt a little sorry for them. My grandmama doted on you but hated me, so I hadn't visited a great deal. I thought your father was a pompous man. I'm sorry to tell you, maybe I should keep my opinions to myself, I apologise."

Hector began to panic, but outwardly kept his cool.

"No, I certainly don't remember, but I do have a frightfully bad memory. You have every right to your opinions."

Hector's throat felt tight, were these feelings going to continue to crop up frequently?

"I presume Mason Season still works here? I caught sight of him at the funeral, nasty vindictive fellow."

He must be very careful what he said, and remember that he was now Hector Gibson Ffiske who had not been in the country for more than a week or so.

"Oh yes, I haven't had chance to talk to him as yet and know very little about the chap. What do you intend to do with your time here, I expect you are anxious to return home?"

He told her in an attempt to change the subject.

"Oh no, no I am in no hurry, It is rather nice to spend some time here, it is a shame that grandmama let the Hall descend from its former glory into the state it is in now. I'm sure your Papa would tell you how magnificent it used to be, when he visited before he went to India of course. So many servants dashing around, then she ran the place with a strict hand and the decor was beautiful, so very beautiful, so I was told."

Arabella stared into nowhere in particular as if recapturing past memories.

Hector changed his mind and thought it to be a good opportunity to learn about something which he may be able to use for his own benefit in the future, while indulging Arabella in her reminiscing.

"I had no knowledge of what occurred after my last visit as I obviously returned to India. The only contact I have had has been through my dear godmother's letters, and nothing about trouble was ever mentioned."

"Ah India, so romantic you must tell me all about it."

"To tell you the truth Miss Gosling I haven't got over the dreadful shock yet. I would find it comforting to hear you talk about Lady Gosling and the Hall, I really know very little about it all."

It was clear that Arabella loved to talk about anything connected with herself and her life. She settled herself down and began.

"My grandmama was the only child of the Dean of Corrigan, and she married Lord Henry Maxwell Gosling. They had one daughter, my mother, who was spoilt and precocious. At that time my grandparents were very friendly with your mama and papa. They started the business together, long before you and I were born. It continues today."

Hector was finding the information fascinating and told her so. Arabella was in her element, she too was enjoying herself.

She began.

"The twenty or so female servants slept in the attic under the eaves at the rear of the hall, they consisted of an assortment of women, from the Lady's maid, who dressed and generally tended to grandmama's every need and who was considered to be the most important, down to the scullery maids. I assume grandpapa had a similar arrangement with the male members of staff. The House keeper saw my grandmamaevery morning and was told what food would be required for that day she would return to the kitchen and order whatever was required from the tradesmen who made their daily visits. The order would be delivered later in the morning. None of the other servants were ever addressed. They were invisible as far as grandmamawas concerned. All the male servants slept in the bedrooms on the floor below the females. Having any contact with the females after the evening meal had been eaten resulted in instant dismissal. Of course that was all before I was born."

Hector wanted to hear more and more, it did occur to him however that what Miss Gosling said came out a little too easy, as if it was, contrived, staged somehow, but he was probably wrong.

"So what was the cause of the trouble to make Lady Gosling change so dramatically?"

"We can talk about that at another time, Hector, it is very complicated."

She stood up,

Hector's head was thumping, he felt confused and wanted to learn more, but realised that he would have to wait for the time being. He had plenty of other things filling his brain. He had no idea about how he was to sell the hall and all its grounds, he didn't have any idea what it was worth and if he asked anyone surely he would be duped. Then there were all the works of art which he so much admired, he had done some reading about the subject, but certainly not enough. What was Arabella talking about, trouble, when was he supposed to have visited. What about his life in India? There seemed to be far too much for him to learn, he felt dizzy with it all, he was playing a part in a play, a part which he had not rehearsed sufficiently. He decided to take a walk, to be alone and to clear his head.

As he strolled along he gazed at the high trees with the sun shining through causing a dappled shade on the ground and along to the clearing and the lake it felt somehow unreal to him, maybe all this was one long illusion and soon he would awake and find himself back in the dirty wooden house, the screaming children, hunger and fear surrounding him.

"No, no!" The words flew out of his mouth before he knew it.

Mason Season was in the process of packing up his fishing gear, he looked as if he had had a good catch.

"Were you talking to me?" he shouted.

Hector knew it was too late to just leave, it would seem too strange.

"Me?" "No indeed I wasn't," he approached him.

"I thought I saw some ruffians in the far wood, I'm sorry if I startled you."

Mason carried on packing up his things.

"I see Arabella Gosling is here, no doubt seeing if her ladyship had left her anything. That is hardly likely after all the trouble she caused."

Hector was trying not to get too close to Mason, he saw that his face was like beaten leather his dark greasy hair receding from his high forehead, his mouth looked cruel even though a smile lingered on his lips. Hector kept his head down as Mason purposely and slowly got up from the tree stump which he had been sitting on and approached. Hector wanted to turn round and run his legs were shaking, fear had now descended into anger, he wasn't going to let this common man ruin all the hard work he had put into this, he deserved to be the victor it was crucial that Mason didn't recognise him, his heart felt as though it would burst, his breathing was laboured his head which was full to bursting was thumping and whirling around at an alarming speed, Mason's words echoed in a sort of void.

"I reckon that there is something odd going on. I've seen you once or twice and in comparison to the child Hector you bear no resemblance. I can't put my finger on it, but my guess is that you are no more Hector Gibson Ffiske than I am."

With one hard impulsive push, Hector, saw to it that he discharged Mason Season into the dark water and with the rod ensured that he didn't surface, the weeds helped as they tenaciously grasped his legs and dragged him down. When the bubbles had finally ceased Hector felt satisfied that this man would now never be able to reveal what he knew. He sat down heavily on a tree stump to regain his breath and composure, when he heard a child scream. He turned round swiftly and threw the rod on to the ground, in the distance he saw not only Mason's son William but Arabella watching him.

CHAPTER 21

That day felt like the worst day of his life, even thinking back to it brought him out in a cold sweat. He had killed Mason Season because he knew too much, and now Arabella and the child William Season knew of the murder. He had trouble sleeping and had re-occurring nightmares. The one he suffered from the most was suffocating Lady Gosling. In it he took the pillow off her face and the real Hector rose up laughing hysterically and then slowly changed into a skeleton covered with soil. He would wake up in terror and dare not go back to sleep for fear of its return.

He had lied to Arabella, by agreeing to her suggestion that Mason had been saying terrible things about her, he couldn't imagine what these things could be, but that was the least of his problems, so he just went on with it.

She seemed to remain calm, almost pleased, and told him that she would sort it out. A few days later, she arranged for the young William to be sent to a faraway very expensive boarding school which would be at Hector's expense. She had explained to the matron that the boy was very difficult was a habitual liar and in her opinion mentally unbalanced. The matron was used to this sort of child she told Arabella. Lots of cold baths and a strict regime would soon sort him out.

For her part Arabella saw it as a way to gain from the experience. Whatever Mason had allegedly told Hector about her was probably true, fortunately he didn't believe him, so to protect her honour he had killed him which suited her very well. He really must hold her in high regard. She must never reveal the truth of her past. That was extremely unlikely as she was such a very clever, devious woman. Hector was now paying for both of their rooms in the Axe and Cleaver

While eating their nondescript meal, Arabella casually asked.

"When do you intend to begin selling the Hall and grounds Hector?"

She asked him as they were entering the room which the landlord referred to as the dining room but bore little resemblance to one.

"I don't know Arabella it will have to be soon I suppose, as I am running out of money and cannot live on credit for much longer. There are also the beautiful pictures and lots of other valuable artefacts; I just do not know how to actually go about any of this, thus the delay."

He very reluctantly told her then added for effect.

"You see I didn't ever have to think for myself in India so I know nothing about these things."

Fortunately I have had a great deal of experience in this field, if you need any advice."

She coyly looked down at her knees.

How on earth do you know about such things at your age?"

My family's profession was a Valuer and Auctioneer, your parents own a great many shares, too. Were you not aware of that?"

He shook his head.

"I learnt a great deal from my papa and now I can put my knowledge to help you, as you so kindly defended my honour.

Obviously we two must stick together as we share a secret never to be told. "

"I am really quite thirsty should we go and have a glass of some sort in the bar?"

His mouth was dry as sand, his head was throbbing some sort of ominous feeling was creeping like a worm into his very soul. He agreed.

"I will do all the negotiating for you and sort everything out, on one condition,"

The worm continued to gain momentum on its destructive journey, the horror continued.

I realise now that you are very fond of me or you wouldn't have performed the way you did with Mason Season, and I am fond of you, too, so it seems to me to be natural and as it is leap year too, that we marry."

Hector was aware that there was going to be a price to pay for her silence and also her help. He didn't think that this would be the cost. He didn't have a choice except to face the gallows, at this moment in time he didn't know which was worse.

They were married on Saturday July 1st 1916, she was twenty. His birth certificate stated that he was eighteen, in fact he was sixteen.

She moved into his small cramped room in the Axe and Cleaver as they both considered the Hall to be not a fit place to stay and Arabella didn't cook.

Hector knew very little about sex and had spent his teen years in a broken down stately home, the only female with whom he had any contact was a batty old woman. He had heard the grunts and groans of his parents on a regular basis and the steady process of babies arriving accompanied by the screams of his mother, and then later the drunken appearance of his father. He also recalled the amount of times one or the other of them walked around with a black eye or several bruises. If that was what marriage consisted of he wanted none of it and he didn't intend to, he would keep his distance whenever possible. He discovered that he didn't like sex at all and did his best to avoid it. It seemed to him to be a messy sort of affair. He learnt that if he didn't engage himself in any sort of physical contact, or a dreaded kiss, she would be quite amiable and the subject was never discussed.

Hector was beginning to think that being married to Arabella was proving to be not a bad thing after all. He looked at her in a different light. She laughed giving him a glimpse of how lovely her face was, her green eyes being the focal point, her lips topped with a perfect bow. She was small and petite, the pearls she wore around her neck twinkled as she lovingly touched them. He was very tempted to give her a squeeze but decided not to risk it as they must get on sorting out the things in the Hall, some they would keep and some they would sell by auction. They found many unexpected items.

"Are you concentrating on the matter in hand, Hector? We have spent far too much time discussing my background and there is a great deal to do."

"Yes, dear."

It would by no means be the last time that he uttered those two small words. They continued the search of the Hall, and discovered a great deal of Victorian Staffordshire pottery which neither of them liked so all of this was placed into the 'For sale pile.' A Foley dinner and tea set complete and unused went into the same pile, as did a great deal of Majolica and Minton. They decided to save a couple of Llewellyn Jewitt busts just because Arabella seemed fond of them. Hector didn't argue, he was learning. All the undamaged paintings by assorted artists were placed in the 'For further investigation pile'

The Obadiah Sharratt Flat backed mantle plaque, Hector liked, it seemed to be pertinent somehow, as it said. 'PREPARE TO MEET THY GOD.' on the front. They argued a little as Arabella didn't like it even though she thought that it would be quite valuable, but in the end Hector won. There were dozens of pieces of Mason's iron stone ware in various forms. They decided to keep one or two pieces and also included the Galle cameo vases which Arabella liked. The rest would be sold. They were both tired. Tackling the library and the paintings would have to wait for another day. They returned to the Axe and Cleaver for a meal.

The following day Arabella said that she would have to go into town to sort out some business.

Hector had, a few weeks prior to this when he found out about the arrival of the dreaded godson, learnt about the location and the route the *Medina* would take. He had then found a large book on, *Life in Colonial India*. He decided that he would save that to read at another time, that time had come. The documents and book he needed were in the bottom of his trunk. He lay on the feather bed and began reading the documents first.

He really knew nothing about any of this and his inadequacy made him panic. His hands were shaking,

The first document was headed:-

LAND REGESTRY

GOSLING GIBSON FFISKE. LAND REGISTRARS VALUERS AND AUCTIONEERS

Ruddlingden Hall

Ruddlingden.

(a) To include.

All land and building in approximate 50 acres, lake, woodland and gardens to be included.

The second document was headed.

Land Registry.

GOSLING GIBSON FFISKE LAND REGISTRARS VALUERS AND AUCTIONEERS

Retail establishment High Street,

East-Thorpe-on-Sea

(a) To include.

Double fronted retail outlet used as land agents' offices premises

.

Two more floors used currently used as storage areas.

(b) To include.

Land situated on the promenade on which are built six superior, large 4/5 storey terraced houses in the Victorian style, Two of the buildings and an impressive theatre are owned by the Gosling Gibson Ffiske Estate.

All land from Sea Road to End Road amounting to 30 acres. Containing slums for the lower classes.

There seemed to be lots of other jargon which he couldn't be bothered to read, it was much the same except the location differed. Brigtown and Harrindan. He heard the sound of Arabella talking to the landlord of the Axe and Cleaver and he quickly put the paper work back into the bottom of his trunk. She came into the room.

"I have told Mr Toll that we will have chops for our meal, as that seems to be the only thing that he is able to serve. I am totally sick of this place, Hector, I am not accustomed to living in such cramped conditions."

"Well, my dear, we must make a concerted effort to sort everything out and move to somewhere more suited to our needs. How did you get along with things?"

She hesitated for a moment and turned away before saying.

"Oh well enough, Are we to dine early as I haven't eaten since this morning and I'm terribly hungry?"

"So all your business was completed to your satisfaction, my love?"

She seemed a little ruffled.

"Well enough, Hector, she repeated, now can we concentrate on our meal?"

The one thing that Hector noticed but decided not to mention was that Arabella's pearl neck lace was missing.

CHAPTER 22

Arabella had gone away for the day again so Hector spent his time reading the book he had found called *Life in Colonial India*. He was planning what to tell Arabella, or anyone else for that matter, about his mythical life in a place which he had never visited, Poona.

Of one thing he was sure, unless he was pressed he wouldn't talk about it, but it was best to be prepared. He did recall seeing the name on some correspondence from Hector to Lady Gertrude. That would be the place which he had lived. And the area he had grown up in. He spent the whole morning studying and trying to remember everything.

He decided, as it may not be too long before she returned, so he would go to the Hall and sort out some more things. The whole task seemed to him to be such a muddle that he didn't know where to begin. It seemed that they had done so much when in fact they had only scratched the surface. He wandered around aimlessly while trying to digest all that he had learnt about India and hoping that the subject would stay as a resident in his transient brain.

"Are you there, Hector?"

It was Arabella's dulcet tones. Hector turned, rounded the corner and came face to face with her.

"I haven't made much progress," he told her as he brushed a hand over his face to emphasize the point and added that he was sorry, which was of course untrue.

I really do not know where to begin, what to do, or have anything constructive to say; I need your help and advice."

He added for effect.

"Don't worry about anything, my love, I have sorted everything out. Nothing has been omitted."

She had a sanctimonious look on her face, a gesture which gave him the impression that he should be in awe of her ability. She stood, legs slightly apart hands on hips. It was then that Hector realised that he could never love her, but she was useful and he wouldn't be able to live without her. This was the price he had to pay, although not what he would have wished. He noticed that the pearl necklace had returned to her neck and the large diamond rings glistened as usual.

"We are to sell the Hall and the contents which we do not want, by, auction."

We can now sort out where we wish to live. I have made my choice which I am sure you will agree with. The auction will be the spring of next year. I will ask them to look out for anything from the arts and crafts era, you know, William Morris."

"Fine, splendid well done Arabella"

Hector thought even though he didn't understand a word, he realized that all these problems had never occurred to him when he carefully made his evil plans.

"Come," she said grasping his hand. "Let's go and look at a picture of my choice of house."

They found two dusty seats and a table and she spread the document out.

"Well," she said. "What do you think to this fine specimen?"

Hector looked down at the vast sheet of paper including a picture and plans of the house. The Promenade, East -Thorpe on Sea. A fine Victorian four storey terraced town house with large attic room situated in a prime position opposite the Humber estuary. This impressive large building is one of a terrace. There is a large cellar which at the moment is not used. The ground floor consists of four large rooms. There are beautiful polished wood stair cases to each floor together with spacious bathroom with running water. The lease for the present occupants is due to run out shortly.

All the land, buildings and a theatre are owned by Gosling, Gibson Ffiske Land Agents Valuers and Auctioneers. Only one house of the terrace does not belong to the above, namely the Corner House

"As we are both shareholders, the usual rules apply."

"Do you like it?"

"Yes I like it very much, my love, so can you explain to me how we go about getting hold of it, you are aware of my limited knowledge of such matters."

"It is very simple, dearest. I went to a board meeting this morning I didn't inform you as I knew that you would not want to be involved"

He nodded thankfully.

"We own 90% of the shares of the property between us. So we will receive that when the Hall is sold and of course the actual money from the estate. The amount realised from the fine arts and antiques which we intend to sell will be considerable. There are Lady Gosling's personal possessions and monies which she left to you. Don't bother yourself, my dear, it is all going terribly well, just leave it to me."

"Oh I see I didn't realise."

He couldn't help but think that it couldn't be that simple.

Arabella inwardly chuckled.

"Let's carry on sorting out the things for an hour then it will give you time to inwardly digest what I have told you."

Hector recalled East-Thorpe on sea on the documents which he had found and secreted in his chest. He was alone in the library, his most favourite place. He pulled out some books, behind 'the book of common prayer,' and 'Burkes Peerage' he discovered some fairly new newspaper cuttings, he suddenly recalled putting them there when Lady Gosling and the real Hector had died, it all seemed so long ago. Then he found the solid silver picture frame containing Hector Gibson Ffiskes brown creased picture which he thought he had discarded. He quickly put them underneath his jacket. Arabella made him jump.

"Have you sorted out which books you want to keep, I will do mine then we can put them all together, as I recall my name was written in some of them."

It was at that point that a thought jumped into Hector's brain, why hadn't he thought of it before. He sat on the library steps.

"Arabella how is it that your name was Gosling, the same as your grandmama's when surely you would have taken your father's name?"

She stood silently with her back to him as if he hadn't spoken but the feeling in the air told him that something unpleasant was about to be forthcoming, the silence continued. Should he repeat what he had said or just keep quiet.

"I told you before several times, Hector, that things were awfully complicated and I just hoped that you would forget about it. I don't honestly think that it would do you any good to know about it. Now this is all that I will say and I refuse to talk about it ever again. The only shameful thing that I will tell you is that my mother was not married when she had me. She didn't reveal the name of my father, but I am sure that my grandmama knew who it was and that is what most distressed her for all those years. When my mother told her parents, Lord and Lady Gosling, that she was pregnant my grandpapa dropped dead and my grandmama lost all interest in the Hall, all its contents and me. She wouldn't speak to me even if we passed in the Hall then she paid for me to go to boarding school. I was very angry so I stole a lot of her jewellery. She paid my nurse to take me away as she never wanted to see me again. She wouldn't see anyone if it was at all possible. She longed to see you though, didn't she? So now you know, Hector. We all, I am sure have secrets which we keep, including you. But some of them we should be allowed to keep. All the tales I know about the Hall are things people have told me. I have never seen my mother. End of story, Hector."

Hector thought of the evil things which he had done and wondered if in the end, they would be the death of him.

CHAPTER 23

Part 3

Octavia woke up, it was light so she grabbed Blue Ted by his paw and padded downstairs and into the kitchen. Rube wasn't there, maybe it was too early. She looked at the clock. She had been told that Rube came when the big hand was on twelve and the little hand was on seven. The big hand had joined the little hand on number seven, so that wasn't right. She went into the pantry, her feet were frozen on the stone floor, having located the milk on the gantry she carried the bottle into the kitchen and found her mug, She poured herself some, and returned to her bedroom, not without difficulty as she had Blue Ted in one hand and her drink in the other, no hands left for the stair rail, only a tiny bit was spilt.

"Right," Octavia crossing her legs asked her companion "Shall we read about A B and C." Blue Ted said nothing.

Picking up her well-worn book she said out loud.

"A is for apple," she took a mouth full of milk. "B is for ball, C is for cat D is for ...."

Her door opened. "Rube," she said, rather too loudly.

"I'll give you, Rube you little minx, did you by any chance go downstairs and get yer sen some milk?"

Octavia nodded, leaving Ruby in no doubt that she was indeed guilty of the offence.

"How many times have you been told?" she responded in her usual manner hand over her mouth, "Oops."

Ruby tutted and sitting beside this three year old whom she adored, asked her if she would like some toast.

Yes please, with Jam, you can come and share some with us too, can't she?"

She asked Blue Ted who declined to comment.

Ruby made the toast and did indeed join them, with jam covering Octavia's face and a tiny blob on Blue Ted's nose, she reminded Ruby that today was going to be a special day and she had to be a good girl.

I know, Tavia you've told me."

Suzannah, walked bleary-eyed into her daughter's bedroom, and sat heavily on her bed.

"Good morning, Suz, do you want some toast or are you going to have your bath first?" Ruby asked.

"Bath first I think thank you, Ruby, Tavia you are really such a very lucky little girl to have Ruby bringing you your breakfast I hope you said thank you to her."

Octavia nodded.

Octavia was dressed with a great deal of care in her new clothes, despite her complaints her hair was plaited neatly with beautiful red bows tied at the bottom. Suzannah drove Octavia to St Vincent's private school, where she had an appointment with the headmistress, Miss Lucinda Levington-Banner.

When she was shown into the inner sanctum which was Miss Levington-Banner's Office, she could smell the old boarding school aroma, it seemed to permeate every boarding school she had ever been in. It was a large room with more space than furniture. The centre was occupied by a huge oak table and the usual sort of accoutrements decorated the well-polished surface none of which seemed to have ever been used, they were just there for decoration and to prove what an important headmistress she was. The headmistress extended a veined hand and greeted her ignoring Octavia. When she was standing she was a very small person but for some reason when sitting she seemed to be much taller she had some sort of presence somehow.

She had two strong white teeth decorating her bottom lip resembling washing hanging out to dry, her spectacles occupied the tip of her nose, her grey hair was thin and greasy, she wore it pulled back to the base of her neck in some sort of complicated knot. She told Suzannah to sit down in a school maam sort of manner. Octavia stood beside her mother, she had taken a dislike to this woman who on close inspection smelt of the mop which Rube did the floor with, She, because of the lack of a chair had decided to sit on the thick pile carpet under the table. This person was sitting with her legs exposed for Octavia to see, they were slightly apart her long silky drawers, in a pale pink, had elastic bottoms which nipped her legs just above her knees, the remainder were clad in very thick brown stockings, her shoes were shiny black lace ups. Octavia thought the whole thing to be so funny and somehow naughty.

"Where on earth is the child?"

Presuming this referred to her Octavia stood up.

"Hello," Octavia said with a smile on her face.

This woman didn't answer, which Octavia thought to be rude so she decided to stare at her small black beady eyes. Suz said it was rude to stare but Octavia thought this woman deserved it.

"We will just take some further details Mrs Season."

Octavia continued to stare.

"What profession is your husband in?"

"I'm divorced."

There was a silence in which Octavia noticed an enlargement of the woman's eyes, but wasn't listening to a word she said.

"I'm very sorry but I am afraid that we couldn't even consider lowering the standards of our school by having the child of divorced parents."

Her face seemed to draw back like a tortoise into its shell. Suzannah was angry it had never occurred to her that she would be rejected. For a moment she was going to tell this ugly Mrs No Body what she thought, but then decided it would be a waste of her time and she would rather leave with her dignity intact.

She stood up, grasped Octavia who hadn't listened to a word, by the hand and silently left the room.

Suzannah was still angry when they arrived home. She was sitting in the kitchen with Ruby, both drinking tea. Octavia had run upstairs changed her new dress for a more comfortable one grabbed Blue Ted and raced downstairs, she had an important thing to tell Ruby.

"Rube, I've got something very, very funny to tell you."

She covered her face with her hands and began laughing as Ruby hoisted her onto her lap."

"I saw this very horrid woman's knickers, I did honestly," her eyes were wide like saucers.

Suzannah and Ruby stared at each other whilst trying very hard not to laugh. It didn't last for long as they both howled with laughter.

Octavia loved attention and this was one of her greatest hours, she jumped off Ruby's knee.

I'm going to tell Perce about this really funny thing."

Suzannah had spent some time thinking of how she could solve the problem of her daughter's education. In the end she decided to ask Josiah. He had contacts with lots of people through Kingston Constructions Ltd. Of which Suzannah had some shares. Marcus was only a few months older than Octavia and Josiah had secured a place for him at a local boy's boarding school as a day boy and he would be starting in September.

A lady answered the phone with a high trill, "Kingston Construction." When she managed to speak to Josiah she asked.

"Josiah, it's me can you find a private tutor for Tavia as you won't believe it but, she has been turned down for St Vincent's because I'm divorced."

"Do you want me to have a word with her for you I have crossed swords with the old bat several times?"

"No thanks I don't think that would result in a fair education for her now that I've met that odious woman. I've decided to have a tutor for a while then maybe send her to a state school or apply to a private school further away when she is a bit older. The only worry is that she would then have to be a boarder and I really don't want that for her. She is so anxious to learn and it would be a pity to knock that out of her"

"I will sort it out don't fret, I know plenty of people who owe me a favour."

As promised he drove home and contacted the person who he considered to be best suited.

"Do you want to come with your Pa to see Tavia, Marcus?" he asked his son.

Marcus jumped up and down and ran to the door.

"What about a kiss for your ma, sweet one." April said.

He ran, gave his mother a peck on the cheek, and ran off and into his pa's Rover.

The back door opened and an excited Marcus ran in.

"Tavia," he yelled.

"Marcus, let's go on the beach, yes? We can jump off the sea wall."

"Pa," Marcus said. "Can I have some money for me and Tavia to have an ice cream please?"

"Here you are two bob each. How many three penny ice creams can you buy for that? "

"I will have to work it out, Pa."

They ran over the road to the railings, looking over at the sand a long, long way below, they held hands.

"One, Two, Three Jump." they said together and with a bump they landed on the soft powdery sand, laughing as they did so.

The tide was coming in and as they ran along the beach to the American Ice cream stall. They could hear the whoosh, whoosh of the water as it hit the beach a few yards away.

"Now then Tavia Season, I can see you have your partner in crime with you, two cornets I guess?"

"Yes Pleeeeze," they said in unison and sat on the sandy beach cross legged lick, lick licking.

Meanwhile Josiah and Suzannah were sitting at the kitchen table eating Victoria sandwich and drinking coffee.

"I have found you the perfect tutor for Tavia. She is called Matilda Sanegar, posh name eh?"

He continued to enjoy his cake.

"I must say she sounds terribly grand. Thank you, Josiah, I knew I could count on you," he glanced at his watch.

"She will be here for your inspection in about half an hour. The nippers should be back by then."

"I shouldn't be too certain about that, Jo, you never know what the pair of them are getting up to when they go to the beach, Tavia goes for ages when she's alone. Ruby tells me off, but she slips away when I'm not looking. She will soon be four and everyone knows her, so she is safe enough. It's amazing she always finds her way home at meal time.

"I'm pleased to tell you that my latest plans for the old Theatre have at long last been accepted."

"That's really good news, Jo, I am awfully pleased for you, you deserve it. As the posh Miss Sanegar is coming we had better go into the drawing room. I'll ask Ruby if she can rustle up a tea tray."

"You must show me the plans for the new theatre when you get them,."

She said as they walked through.

Ruby was just coming downstairs from cleaning and Suzannah asked her for tea when the tutor came.

"Will do, Suz. Do you know them two bairns haven't come back yet?"

Octavia and Marcus were having a great time. They ran into the incoming tide and splashed each other then jumped the break waters, the sand stuck to their clothes.

"Let's go to your Pa's Bazaar and see what we can buy for our one and six."

Octavia took the remaining money out of the tied up hankie in the leg of her knickers, and the pair of them raced across the road.

Outside the Bazaar hung buckets, spades and 'kiss me quick hats'. Inside was a cornucopia of goodies.

Miss Sanegar had arrived. She was immaculately dressed in a pin striped navy blue suit with padded shoulders and a long straight skirt. She wore bright red lipstick which complimented her olive skin. Her dark eyes were just visible beneath her heavy black straight fringe. She had just taken a seat and was delicately drinking her tea, when the door swung open and two laughing children ran in. They both wore sun hats, had dirty faces and their clothes were wet and covered with sand.

"The hats were two bob, Pa, but we got them for one and six each."

"This is Miss Sanegar," Suzannah said in embarrassment.

Both of the children greeted her and Marcus offered her a dirty sandy hand, which Miss Sanegar politely refused.

"We better get you home young man Lord knows what your ma will say."

"Octavia go upstairs make yourself clean and respectable, change your clothes and get rid of that ridiculous hat, please."

Octavia ran off upstairs wondering what that strange lady had come for.

"I am so dreadfully sorry about the state of my daughter Miss Sanegar. She does not always look so dirty and unkempt, I promise."

Octavia returned with Blue Ted, a clean face and a change of clothes.

"Better?" she asked cheekily.

"Sit down over there please," her mother pointed to a seat opposite. Tavia wondered what had caused Suz to be acting in this strange way but she did as she was told.

"This is Miss Sanegar and she will be coming to teach you some things."

"What sort of things, Suz, I know most everything?"

"I can see that I will have a hard task on my hands, but one that

I hope we will both enjoy, when would you like me to begin?"

The first lesson didn't go too well. Miss Sanegar spread alphabet cards in order on the office table.

"Right, Octavia, how many of these cards can you name? Don't worry if you can't name some of them just yet."

Octavia wasn't a child who worried about anything she spent a few moments looking along the line of cards then said.

"All of them."

To emphasize the matter she proceeded to repeat them all A to Z.

Miss Sanegar was a little surprised and was preparing to dislike this precocious child.

"Do you think that you can spell a word out for me please?"

"What word do you want?" Octavia was getting bored.

Miss Sanegar was getting agitated.

"Any word, you choose."

Octavia spelt out Blue Ted.

"I know that's two words, so please may I go and fetch him from my bedroom?"

Miss Sanegar was quite taken aback she would have to make the lessons a bit harder. She nodded to Octavia who ran out of the door and up the stairs.

She picked up Blue Ted from her bed, left her room and glanced out of the rear window. Percy was feeding the chickens so she raced down Ted under her arms and went into the garden.

"Percy," she shouted. "Can I pick up my favourite chicken Mabel please?"

"It'll depend on what sort of mood she is in, Tav, you know Mabe." Octavia ran around the garden yelling to the chicken, who definitely didn't want to be picked up.

Suddenly there was a loud shout from the door.

"Octavia, what do you think you are up to we are in the middle of a lesson come back to the office immediately."

Octavia hand over mouth looked at Percy who was grinning.

"Oops."

"Now, you sit yourself down there at once and do not dare to leave this room again unless I give you permission. Do you understand?"

Octavia was so shocked, she had never been told what she could and couldn't do in such a nasty way before, she felt like crying. She nodded as she cuddled Blue Ted.

"Right, now we will continue, mathematics!"

She gave Octavia a sheet of sums additions and subtractions, simple ones which five year olds would have to learn. She was going to explain to Octavia what the + and − meant, when Octavia grabbed the piece of paper and with her lower lip stuck out completed the sums without saying a word and pushed the paper along the desk to her tutor who she had decided she didn't much care for and would rather be on the beach.

"I will just go and have a quick chat with your mother. Mrs Season. Could I have a word with you in private please?"

Octavia was nowhere to be seen she had disappeared the moment that Miss Sanegar had presumably ended the lesson.

"We will go into the drawing room Ruby will bring us some tea. How did Tavia manage?"

"Well it is very hard to say really."

Ruby came in with the tray of tea and was thanked.

"Please feel free to speak your mind about my daughter I won't be offended."

Suzannah told her whilst pouring the tea.

"To be truthful I find her to be a mixture of a very clever and unruly child."

"I don't really understand what you mean. To me she is just Tavia, the only child I have ever been in close contact with."

"Hmm maybe that is the reason, do you spend a great deal of time teaching her."

"Definitely not, she spends a lot of time reading and writing. She chose to keep my old boarding school books, To me they must be terribly boring but she loves them and writes lots of things in her 'Secret Book'. She also likes to be on her own or with Marcus Kingston. His father is on the schools committee and brings her school books. She likes just running around doing childish things, so I more or less let her get on with, it that way we are all happy. She does ask an awful lot of questions, to any one and every one, to be honest she chooses what she wants to do, and does it. She makes friends with grown-ups, particularly Ruby who she much prefers to me. To tell you the truth I don't think she realises that she is a child."

"Does she belong to the library?"

"I believe that she is too young don't children need to be five"?

"If that is alright with you I will take her tomorrow and we will sort it out then?"

"Just check with her, will you?"

Miss Sanegar wasn't too pleased having to ask a child if something was alright, she believed that children should do as they were told, but went back into the office to see Octavia who was nowhere to be seen, she left the room, and Ruby told her.

"If yer looking for Tavia, she's chasing Mable."

CHAPTER 24

When the doorbell rang, Suzannah was already waiting for the visitor with a feeling of apprehension. The policeman looked very young. He introduced himself as PC Burton and went, as directed, into the drawing room, removed his helmet and sat down.

"I am here because we have reason to believe that your husband may have committed a murder."

"I am divorced and have no contact with my ex-husband nor do I want any."

"We are well aware of that, Mrs Season, but this murder took place when you were married."

"I still cannot imagine what I have to do with the matter."

Suzannah's fear had now merged into anger.

"We have reason to believe that Mr William Season caused the death of your parents in 1943."

"I wouldn't be at all surprised."

"This has only just come to light when we had arrested a Mr Matt, former garage owner on another matter. He then admitted to the offence of aiding and abetting Mr Season by tampering with a motor car, allegedly owned by your parents Mr and Mrs Gibson Ffiske."

"What has all this to do with me? I have never been involved in anything William did, and I had no knowledge of this offence."

The constable scribbled all this down onto his pad.

Suzannah stood up, feeling that this would instigate the end of the conversation.

"We will leave the matter there for the time being."

"Never mind the time being. If you or anyone else from the police force question me on a subject of which I know nothing, I'm afraid I will take the matter further and view it as harassment."

The policeman left.

The next agenda for the board meeting, at Gibson Ffiske and Marsden's office arrived by first post. She went into the kitchen knowing that Ruby would soon be making tea for Percy and Fred. She would cast a cursory glance over the dreaded agenda while she enjoyed a cup of tea with Ruby She didn't enjoy these monthly meetings, at least the Kingston construction meeting was less formal.

"Ready for a cuppa, Suz, You look a bit angry?"

Suzannah told Ruby of her visit from the police and enjoyed her most welcome cup of tea Ruby somehow managed to make Suzannah feel better over any situation she found herself in. She briefly scanned the agenda. Ruby said.

"I'd stake my life on William doing the dirty deed, I would. Now that orrid man may get caught. There are a lot more secrets to be found out about the goings on with im and your family than we know of, none of it ever made sense. For instance why were there two sets of identical pearls, rings and watches, except one set was fake, the one your Ma was wearing when she was murdered and the real ones was in the bank vaults, and that is only one mystery ain't it. Did you ever find out what that little key fitted?"

"No, I didn't Ruby, I think that there is a tiny key on both sets of pearls, the genuine ones are in the bank vaults I think the reasoning must be if any one robbed her of the jewellery they would only get fakes. If I let myself dwell on all the mysteries I swear I would go mad. I gave the paste ones to Tavia for her to use when she does her dressing up, she pretends she is a princess and all sorts of things. I presume one of the keys is still on that set. I gave up trying to answer all the contradictions and I really don't care either way, as long as we are left alone or I regain my interest."

"I know all about the dressing up box, Suz, I av given her stuff for it and also tidied it up enough times." Ruby told her.

"Don't do the clearing up for the little monkey, Ruby, tell her to do her own and just leave it, she won't ever learn if you do it for her."

Autumn seemed to be arriving sooner than usual. The mellow sunshine held an unexpected early calmness. Suzannah, clad in a warm coat left the house. As she walked down the stone steps from her front door, her mind was far away, concentrating on the evening's meeting. She had at first made up her mind to walk the short distance to the office that was before she saw three women who she had, trouble with before. She felt in her pocket for the keys to her car, thinking that at least they wouldn't be able to follow her if she changed her mind and drove instead.

"Not content to get divorced and have a married man for your fancy piece, you now ave a bleeding Dago to teach your kid. You stuck up cow."

Ruby who had been looking out of the front window with Octavia, dashed out.

"Not you three no goods again, ain't you got ote else ter do but cause Mrs Season trouble?"

"Yer used ter be one of us, now look at you, Ruby Jacks. Mrs good for note grovel arse."

Suzannah, avoiding any eye contact with the three women silently got into her car and drove off. Ruby returned to her baby sitting.

The meeting was as usual similar to every other, except Mr Marsden, a small dignified man, asked her if he could have a word in private at the end of the meeting.

"I wanted to see you, Mrs Season because after we had a talk concerning your interest in your ancestors, I warned against you pursuing your quest in learning more about them, for reasons which I considered unwise for you to know. I now realise that I was out of order. If that is what you have decided to do, although I know that it will only bring you sadness. It is for you to decide, not me. I know the family from long ago, particularly your mama and papa. Only you should make the choice my dear. I am giving you this copy of the Rudlingden News, I'm sure that you will find it of interest if you want to contact me for any reason, please do not hesitate to do so. Whatever you decide to do, I hope that you will find contentment I have written my number on the top of page one of the newspaper."

With that he wished every one good night and was gone. For some reason Suzannah experienced a sinking feeling in the pit of her stomach as she accepted the paper left and drove home, thinking that she would read it when she went to bed, until then she would try and put that matter and the one of the nasty women to the back of her mind. It hadn't altogether been a very good day.

"I just wanted to tell you that me and Rube have read the book which Miss got for me from the library I can have as many books as I want you know.

"I'm sure that I can find my own way there, but Miss said no. I'm going to bed, night, night, and no, Suz, I won't forget to clean my teeth." She gave her mother a gentle look of disgust.

She reads a damn sight better than I can. She is so clever there ain't many words she can't read and they are usually ones that I can't either but, she tries and tries and gets there in the end."

Suzannah rose and put the kettle on.

239

"Thank you for baby sitting and sorting those awful women out for me, Ruby, I just don't say a word to them now no matter how rude they are, I keep hoping they will stop bullying me."

"I won't bother avin a cuppa thanks, Suz, I'm off ome ter me bed."

Suzannah took her cup of tea and the newspaper to bed with her. The front page headlines of the Rudlingden Reporter read.

GRUESOME FIND IN WITCHES WOOD

Men working on the new road through Witches Wood came across the skeleton of a man said to have been possibly 18 years of age at the time of his death. The remains were taken to the town's mortuary for examination. Police told our reporter the young man had been murdered, possibly by a stab wound to the chest as one of the ribs appeared to be fractured, prior to being buried. They think that the murder must have taken place possibly over 30 years ago. So there is little for them to work on.

At that time Harry Gibbs, who worked for Lady Gosling disappeared after collecting Hector Gibson Ffiske from Southampton, where he had sailed back from Bombay in India, and fled to stay with his godmother Lady Gertrude Gosling at Rudlingden Hall, after his parents had been killed by natives. According to sources at that time, Gibson Ffiske and Harry Gibbs are believed to have returned to find, Lady Gosling dead in her bed, Harry Gibbs, apparently distraught, left saying he needed to take a walk, and has not been seen since despite exhaustive searching by the police. This new find comes 3 years after the remains of a body were found when workmen were filling the vast lake which was situated on Lady Goslings land prior to building work. This body was believed to be that of local gardener Mason Season. It was believed that Mr

Season, a widower, had a son William who the police were unable to locate. Investigations continue.

Suzannah wondered why Mr Marsden had thought that she would be interested in the article. It must have been because her father's name was mentioned and also she had been married to William Season. Somehow it didn't seem to ring true. Her concern increased the more she thought about it. It couldn't possibly have been a coincidence that three people were dead, or murdered in what, would seem to be the same location at more or less the same time. She was sure to be awake all night trying to make some sense of it all. Tavia must be asleep in bed. So she went downstairs and made herself a cup of cocoa and retired.

The following day Ruby thought that Suz was quiet but decided that if she wanted to talk about what was troubling her, she would.

"Have a good meeting last night, Suz?"

"Not really Ruby. I always think that they are a waste of time."

On reflection the only thing that she was thinking about, apart from Mr Marsden's advice, was the fact that all of the years shares would be going into the bank that month. Consequently there would be a call from the bank. She would have to go and see them, which she found to be tedious.

"Those orrid common women didn't upset yer did they, Suz?"

"Golly no, I've got used to their vulgarity after all this time."

The doorbell rang, Octavia got to it first.

"Hello, Miss."

Miss Sanegar followed her into the office.

"Are you enjoying the book, Octavia?"

She settled herself down with her pupil opposite in the office.

"Yes thank you, I read it to Rube last night when Suz was at a meeting."

She handed it over to Miss.

"I can't keep up with you." Miss Sanegar told her laughing.

"Well it was only thin, if I have read all the books you gave to me why can't I go to the library on my own or I will be missing some books which other children might get?"

"Octavia I've told you already you are too young, you can only get books on my ticket at the moment. We could always go together sometime."

"Spiffing."

"Today I think it would be a good idea for me to get to know you better."

Octavia still had her bottom lip stuck out to make sure that Miss noticed it. She didn't.

"Please may I ask you a question first? What are oozes and lbs?"

"You have very good manners Octavia, and that is very interesting question. Have you been reading your mother's cookery books?"

She nodded.

"They are weights and measures, so that you get the correct ingredients in your cooking. Ask Ruby to show you."

"My question is; do you have a lot of friends?"

"Yes, I suppose you want me to tell you all their names which I must say, is a very boring thing to do."

Octavia counted on her fingers with a fed up expression on her face and said.

"Blue Ted, Rube, Marcus, Percy, Fred, Jo, Suz

Oh yes the cockle man, Sid from the Candy Floss stall and er Mr Ice cream man.

I nearly forgot Mable."

"I see. Why do you call your mother Suz?"

Octavia tutted in an exasperated manner, and rolled her eyes.

"Because that is her name, well it is Suzannah really but that is a bit long, like everyone calls me Tavia except you. If we didn't all have names then everyone would be mixed up and so that is why names were invented.

"Why do you say please and thank you?"

"Because you don't get what you want if you don't and it's called good manners"

"That's very commendable.

"What does that mean?"

"Well I suppose in its simplest form it means well done."

Ruby came in with the teas.

Miss Sanegar thanked her and Octavia said.

"Thank you, that's very commendable Rube."

They drank their tea.

"Please can we go to the library, Miss?"

Miss nodded.

Later after piling all the special books on her bed she ran down to see the chickens.

"Percy where is Mabel? And I can't see Chubby either."

Percy felt really uncomfortable as they had both been sold because they weren't laying and by now were probably residing in someone's oven.

"Well er some very kind people were quite lonely, and really, really fell in love with Mabel and Chubby so I knew you wouldn't mind as we ave lots of chickens, and we will soon be getting some tiny yellow ones for you to find names for. As it won't be many months before Christmas yer see, a lot of people like to buy chickens for presents. It's a nice thing to give lonely people ain't it, Tav."

Percy wiped his brow and congratulated himself.

"I think that would be a very kind thing to do Percy. We can tie a nice bow of ribbon around their necks with their names written on them. Don't you think?"

Octavia was beaming and jumping up and down. Percy thought that a bow of ribbon wouldn't be what they would be having around their necks.

CHAPTER 25

The doorbell rang it was Miss. Octavia came dashing through with the book in her hand and escorted her to the office, they sat down.

"I've been reading the book," she told Miss.

"Jolly good, there are some hard words in it and I thought that you may find it a bit too grown up how far did you get?"

Octavia looked at her with a blank expression on her face.

"You told me to read it so I did."

"Octavia, I'm asking you how much of it you managed to read."

Octavia stood up and put her face close to Miss's.

"All of it, that's what you wanted me to do isn't it?"

Miss wasn't pleased at Octavia's attitude, but realised that she was wrong, too, so said nothing she couldn't believe that her pupil could have read it all so decided to asked her what it was about.

Octavia crossed her legs in a grown up manner and told her all about the book.

Miss Sanegar told Octavia.

"I will give you another book before I leave, and I will return tomorrow."

As she was leaving after the lesson was over, she felt as confused as ever. In all her career she had never met a child as clever but with such a strange attitude, she caught sight of Ruby.

"Can I have a word with you, Mrs Jacks?"

Ruby nodded apprehensively.

"I am a little concerned about the rules imposed on Octavia's behaviour. She seems to be very well mannered but...."

"Well yer see Suz woz brung up in a boarding school which woz strict and when er mother made her cum back Suz din't know ow to make decisions and so she won't goin to let Tavia suffer like that so she lets Tavia decide wot to do, so she will learn by er mistakes. Tavia chose to ave good manners as if she dint no one took notice of er, see. She is a lovely little soul but I can understand what you mean, she never stops askin questions, things that you wunt think any child would want to know sometimes I don't know the answer to em, and she never forgets ote"

"Well, that's one way of looking at it, thank you very much I understand her much better now, unfortunately I don't think the teachers or pupils at her new school will have the same view. I will come back again tomorrow if that is alright with Mrs Season as there are a few things which I need to go over with Octavia."

Octavia was sitting on her bed reading her new book .Her new book wasn't very long but it was funny it was called *Ted's Adventures* so she was reading it out loud to Blue Ted. He didn't appear to be interested but she continued, after a while she decided to take him on the beach. She walked down the bouncy wooden steps to the sand below it felt a bit cold and it was very windy. She cuddled Ted close to her. The deckchair man was picking up the few now abandoned chairs. He waved to Tavia and she waved back as did Blue Ted then they continued on their way. There was hardly anyone on the beach, the Punch and Judy man had gone. Tavia didn't like him or Mr

Punch anyway. She could taste the salt in the wind. The sea was ebbing away, the foam was as white as white could be she thought the reason that the tide came in was something to do with the moon, but the moon would still be in bed for a while yet. She had asked Perce, but he didn't know any more than that, and he was busy scratching Jelly her favourite pig's back, so she decided to help scratching too.

It was much better on the beach when there were people to talk to or children to play with. Her blonde hair knotted in long strands behind her and her green eyes were beginning to sting, time to go home, her bare arms were covered with goose bumps. They called them that because they looked like a goose when it had lost all its feathers, Percy had told her that. Yes, she thought she would go back and talk to Percy. He was very clever and knew lots of things.

"Why do pigs have snouts and chickens have beaks Perce?"

Percy pushed his spade with great force into the ground and thought for a moment. He really wished he and Ruby had had children but maybe one day so Tavia was a substitute. He removed his well-worn cap scratched his head and said.

"Well you see the good Lord thought of everything, pigs as to furrow push in the ground for food like apples as ave fallen, and chickens likes seed so they ave pointy beaks to peck. In the far of jungle giraffes ave long necks so as they can reach high trees for the leaves they like to eat."

"What about lions, Perce?"

"Well they ave right big gobs so that they can eat other animals."

"I don't think that I am too fond of lions, Perce."

When she got inside she asked Ruby.

"What are gobs?"

Suzannah read and re read the newspaper article concerning the three unaccounted for deaths. Surely her father couldn't have been involved, much as she disliked her parents this was too much to contemplate. She had for some months now refused to get involved with any more searching in the house. She was sure that there would be much more to find and like a small creature, it gnarled at her brain no matter how. She tried to stop thinking about it she kept herself constantly busy in an effort to get rid of the small creature.

She went to the bank to sort out something she had wanted to do for some time, send a donation on a regular basis to widowed wives. She donated to several such good causes, it made her feel useful. As usual another matter she knew nothing about, cropped up, which meant she needed to visit her solicitors again she felt inadequate and depressed about the whole damn thing. She needn't have worried.

Mr Bush explained to her that there was a request from a local person concerning the sale of all the bombed land next to the three houses she owned. He showed her a copy of the extensive plans which included a theatre, thus replacing the previous one, many houses, a public house and several Bazaars. The land belonged to Gibson Ffiske and Marsden, who would retain it, making the buildings leasehold unless otherwise decided by a vote at the meeting.

The matter would be placed on the agenda for the next meeting.

Even Suzannah didn't have to think about who this "local person" may be. She wouldn't say a word, well maybe she might hint at least it made her chuckle to herself. A few days later the agenda for the next meeting popped through her letter box. Josiah was conspicuous by his absence. Ruby commented on the fact, adding how many scones they would save!

On her next visit Miss Sanegar decided to teach Octavia some history and geography, a subject she was sure that

Octavia knew nothing about. Her fifth birthday would be in October so she would qualify for the September intake at the local state school. The Park Road School Miss Sanegar continued to be concerned for the child, she had to admit that she had grown fond of her but she feared for her future for several reasons. She was exceptionally bright and could go far but not at the local school. She was in for a very hard time and both her and her mother were totally unaware of what the outcome would be.

"Today Octavia we are going to concentrate on History and Geography. Do you know what that means"?

Her pupil looked pensive.

"Is history about bad things that happened long ago before even you were born and geography, mmm well is that about other countries far away that nobody has been to"?

"Well done, Octavia, you are very nearly right."

Tavia was pleased to be right and even more pleased that Miss was pleased.

"So tell me what you know about say, history?"

Tavia wiggled about in her chair and looked at Blue Ted as if for inspiration.

"Well … I think that King Henry actually had a lot of wives, too many if you ask me and so he chopped all of their heads off. Well geography I don't really know very much except that Australia is a long way away and England is little."

"Er right we will begin from there then." Miss, wondered where her pupil had found out this amount of information.

When asked she flicked back her long blond hair and said.

"I think I must have read about it or asked Perce, he knows most things."

She rolled her green eyes and crossed her legs importantly.

"Were you interested in these things?"

"I quite liked bad King Henry, but it must have been a bit too many wives to kill especially if he had any children. I don't much care for fathers and I am pleased that I don't have one, if I did it might be bad like him and chop Suz's head off, and she wouldn't much care for that."

Miss decided that she had better not pursue that line of history. It would take a little time to for her original ideas to rearrange themselves.

"I think it would be good for you to write a story about what ever subject you like and I will read it tomorrow now we will learn about Geography?"

"Super."

Suzannah drove her black Austin along the promenade to the meeting. The mellow sunshine of late autumn held with it a sharp stab of the icy winter which was just waiting to put in an appearance. The wind hissed through the bleak branches of the leaf bare trees, the water was steel grey as it rushed up to the sandy beach. She shivered from both the cold and the thought of the meeting to come.

Mr Marsden was already in the back room of the offices rubbing his hands together in front of the small electric fire, He greeted her fondly.

Miss Watson his secretary busied herself putting the minutes of the previous meeting on the large table, the three other partners would attend, and she would copy down the relevant details of the meeting. The plans of the proposed building work submitted by Mr Josiah Kingston lay in the centre of the table. His application was the first item on the agenda.

After much discussion the meeting agreed to forward the proposal to the East Thorpe - on - Sea, planning committee with the recommendation for approval.

Josiah would be pleased. As expected he arrived the very next morning, Suzannah was determined not to comment on the subject, two could play that game.

Ruby, who was ignorant of anything about the situation, moved the kettle further onto the heat of the Aga in preparation of the usual refreshments. Percy followed him.

"Bit parky out yonder, even the pigs ave stayed in their ouse as Tavia calls it. Where is she anyway"?

"You never know with her." Ruby told him as she poured the boiling water out of the big brown kettle on to the tea leaves.

"Aven't seen you in a while what's been up with yer?"

"Nothing in particular, Rube, you know this and that," he cast an eye at Suzannah who was pouring milk into the cups and said "There are some bits and bobs in the parcel, Suz." for which she thanked him.

Tavia ran in, she as usual was full of chatter everyone was pleased to see her as usually she was too busy to put in an appearance. She had a piglet under her arm which everyone found funny except for her mother.

"Octavia take that piglet back this instant and put it back in the sty."

"Please may I give it something to eat first as it is small and the others don't let him have any food."

"Tavia it's a 'Her', and ask Percy what it would like after we have had a cup of tea. It is very rude to come in and not say hello to, Jo."

"Oops I'm very sorry, Jo, hello I'm pleased to see you," she looked at her mother for approval and sat down at the large kitchen table still nursing the pig.

"I'll tek it bak to its mother, Tavia, she will be frettin."

"I have decided she is called Bella." Tavia crossed her arms.

Wasn't there a meeting at Gibson Ffiske and Marsden last night, Suz?" Jo casually enquired.

"Yes there was, Jo, do you want another scone"?

Josiah handed her his plate, which obviously was meant to answer in the positive.

Suzannah busied herself buttering more scones and passing them round, Josiah had bought some butter in a parcel he had put on the table.

"I'll be damned pleased when this blinkin rationing finishes. It plays hell with people's lives. Good meeting was it, Suz"?

Suzannah nodded.

"Many there?" he shifted, uncomfortable in his chair.

She nodded once more, enjoying it.

"The usual people."

"Please may I get down?" Tavia asked her mother. "I need to go and see if Bella has settled down."

"You may," her mother said

"For goodness sake, Suz, did my planning permission come up?"

CHAPTER 26

September 1948

It came as a bit of a shock to Suzannah, when, in the middle of the night she decided to have her three houses converted into one hotel. Why hadn't she thought of it before? Josiah had asked her to be the sole partner in his company 'Kingston Building Constructions'. She had foolishly agreed even though she knew nothing about the subject. It was only after everything had been signed and sorted that he admitted to her that his knowledge was only slightly better than her own. He told her that he had an adviser so everything would be fine. The plans had been passed, it only left them to find the builders, carpenters, labourers and anyone else who would be needed in this massive construction. He made it sound simple, it was not, and they both had an awful lot to learn in a very short time. There were many sleepless nights and much more money than they had anticipated before the land could even be cleared. They were advised to make Kingston Building Construction, a Limited company to safeguard their properties. Suzannah had been too busy to think about her three houses let alone take notice of Miss Sanegars concerns for Octavia when she began school. More plans had to be passed for the large hotel. For once in her life she was excited. Ruby was worried.

Suzannah was rushing along the road with Octavia in tow, wishing she had chosen to come by car to take her daughter to her first day at school. She would be the youngest in the class as her fifth birthday wasn't for three weeks. The letter from the school had stated that school uniform was not compulsory but preferable, so Octavia was dressed from head to foot in grey and navy with a red tie. She carried a leather satchel of which she was very proud, it contained all her new writing materials in a wooden pencil box. Ruby cried as she plaited her hair and added two red bows, she looked so grown up.

"Don't cry, Rube, I'll be home at tea time, then I can tell you all about my day."

All the mothers were allowed to go into the child's class room on the first day. When they entered everyone looked around. The women who had caused Suzannah so much trouble whispered between themselves and ignored her. Suzannah was used to this and Tavia didn't notice. Only one other child wore the uniform. The teacher approached and introduced herself as Miss Ingham. All the teachers had been told about Octavia by the head mistress. She was shown her peg in the cloak room then returned to her class room. Octavia saw a wooden play house which she immediately ran to. Suzannah realised that her daughter didn't need her to stay as she looked out of the little window and yelled.

"Bye, Suz."

Suzannah was pleased to go home, she had had enough of screaming children, who clung on tenaciously to their mothers. She had more important things to consider. Ruby was very quiet. When asked if she had something worrying her she burst into tears.

"What on earth is wrong, Ruby?" Suzannah asked, Ruby was usually such a lovely jolly person and Suzannah cared very much for her and her welfare.

"What do you think is wrong that poor little mite at school with all those rough children to bully, her she's not used to it and I miss her."

Suzannah put her arms around her and wiped her tears away,

"How thoughtless of me, Ruby, I'm so very sorry I have been so wrapped up with other things to take any notice, I have been selfish, please forgive me."

Ruby was so full of something she could not explain. It was all consuming.

Building of the hotel had begun everything was in total chaos. She had a great deal of paper work, organizing and telephoning to do. Josiah was usually there at some point during the day to check on his work force and when required, do a tour of the building work with Suzannah. He also had other building projects in progress, his theatre, and making preparations for his house building project on the land where he had grown up. Ruby just did what work she could. Suzannah didn't have time to think about her past worries and although very tired, she was happy.

Octavia's day was not quite as she had imagined, Miss made all the children do what she wanted. Octavia, when she was bored, always went down to the beach. Today the playground would have to do, at least it was somewhere new to explore, so she left the class room oblivious to any sort of rule. Miss Ingham went out and gave her a good telling off.

"Octavia, this is your first day at school, and I will try to overlook your behaviour. You go outside at play times and lunch time and in between that you do as I say."

"Why?"

Miss Ingham ignored her, dragged her in and made her sit down on one of the tiny chairs. Octavia stuck out her bottom lip. She didn't know what she had done wrong but decided that Miss Ingham would go on her 'do not like' list. At play time she saw a large lardy boy called George shouting at a tiny red haired girl. His cheeks were so fat that his small mean mouth almost disappeared amongst the fatty jowls, his piggy blue eyes stared at her as he shouted 'Ginge' and 'Carrot' punctuating every word with a push to her shoulders, she began to cry'.

Enter Octavia Season, hands on hips approaching him, wearing her don't mess with me face.

"Leave her alone you big fat bully or I'll kick your shins."

She turned on her heels and putting her arm around the little girl took her to sit on a seat.

"Just because he's a boy don't let him be horrid to you." Octavia told her. The girl had red, corkscrew curly hair, pale skin with a smattering of red freckles adorning her sad face.

"He lives down our street and he won't leave me alone," she began to cry again." "

"Don't you fret I'll sort him out" Octavia reassured her, my name is Tavia by the way, Teacher calls me Octavia which is my real name but she doesn't know any better."

"My name is Ruth, Ruth Jolly, why do you talk so different and know what to do?"

"I didn't know I did. My other Miss told Suz that my diction needed a bit of tightening up so that might be why. Suz talks exactly the same as me but Rube doesn't."

Ruth hadn't understood a word, but said.

"Will you be my friend?"

School dinner didn't go down too well either and Octavia told them that she didn't like lumpy dirty coloured potato or fatty meat.

The teachers said to each other.

"See what comes of a child from divorced parents, she is going to be trouble mark my words." Everyone agreed.

At home time, all the children paraded out Octavia and Ruth were hand in hand,

"This is my friend, Ruth." Octavia told her mother excitedly.

They became firm friends, Octavia tall slim and confident and Ruth tiny and timid.

Ruth loved going to her friend's chaotic house where you could do as you wanted and never get told off, the exact opposite to her mother who ruled their council house with a rod of iron, while brandishing her duster.

After the Christmas break Suzannah and Josiah could begin to see the end in sight. Ruby had now been delegated to take Tavia to and from school, a task which she enjoyed. It was a cold, cold, dark winter's morning when she donned her brown zip up boots and faced the halo's of street lamps reflecting on the pure white of what appeared to be virgin snow, to collect Tavia. The large white flakes continued to fall. The white sky was a sign of more to come. Suzannah had received a letter of complaint about her daughter's behaviour. She was far too busy to acknowledge it. If she had read it she would have learnt that the teacher's opinion of her daughter was not a good one. She was disruptive when the teacher was reading the class a story, saying she had already read the book. She finished her maths, spelling and story writing before any of the other pupils, and became restless. She was noisy at lunch time, complaining about the quality of the food. She did not seem to take chastisement seriously. But then her mother didn't take the letter seriously either, and filed it in

B.I.N.

Ruth and Octavia continued to be the best of friends In the middle of January a new boy started in the class. His name was Ali Terimo. He had to sit alone and Tavia could sympathise with that as she was also segregated from the other children sometimes. He wore a very sad expression and his big brown eyes darted back and forth, as if he was frightened of something, he was, as expected bullied. The teachers had an

257

explanation and ignored this treatment. That was until Tavia, stepped in. It resulted in her getting the cane once more and it hurt. She had told Suz about it and she told her to behave then she wouldn't be punished. She explained it to Blue Ted, but teddy bears weren't much help. She put a cold flannel on her blistered hand, she dare not tell Ruby about the teachers treatment as she imagined that Ruby would hit them all and then she would be blamed and get the cane again, Octavia wasn't happy.

The winter seemed to be never ending and caused disruption everywhere, pupils were allowed to wear their coats in class. If they owned a coat. The large amount of snow seemed to create an eerie silence outside, and inside the children's breath could be seen like smoke out of a chimney. It was a white world but the children enjoyed the icy slides at play time and the snowmen and snow balls which they painstakingly constructed. Everyone, that is except Ali Terimo. Octavia encouraged him to join in their fun at play time as he seemed to just stand in a corner, shivering. If he did join in, George would approach until Tavia intervened.

"Don't you dare to be rude to Ali, you horrid fat boy."

"My ma says that e should go back to where e came from e don't belong ere."

"You and your ma should learn some manners."

Ruth continued to spend a great deal of time at Octavia's house. Although Mrs Jolly, Ruth's mother, was very nasty about Suzannah, which was no surprise to Ruby, who knew the horrid woman. Mrs Jolly liked the fact that she didn't have to buy food for her daughter and the house was always spotlessly clean, as she was determined to keep it at all costs. Her husband, when not at work, could normally be found, in his shed with his paper to read, his primus stove kettle and tea. He couldn't remember the last time his brown stained cup had been washed, and he loved it. On the other hand Suzannah didn't notice another child in the house.

"Ali's mother won't let him come here to play."

Tavia said to Ruby on the way home from school one day, "Ruth comes so why can't he, Rube?"

"Probably, cos'e's black and his parents don't want im mixin."

Tavia gave this a great deal of thought then said. "I think you are mixed up, Rube, I've never seen him black."

"I'll ave a word with is ma Tavia, OK?"

School was an absolute nightmare for Tavia, everything Miss Ingham taught she had already learnt or read so she grew even more bored and confused she hated school and was sure that everyone disliked her but she didn't care about it she was naughty because she needed attention and stimulation.

The children went into dinner one day in spring. On the menu was tough ox liver with white tubes running through it, white watery cabbage and lumpy grey potatoes.

"This is absolute rubbish, and I'm not eating it."

Tavia was as usual stating the obvious, which wasn't appreciated. She pushed her plate away. Opposite sat George whose parents had eight children to feed.

"Give us it then, yer don't know wot yer missin my ma says that you are a stuck up snob and no wonder your dad left yer once e ad a look at yer."

There was a silence the teachers looked at each other with dismay, wondering what to do. Before they had decided, Octavia climbed over the dinner table spilling food everywhere and got hold of George's hair and screamed.

"You big fat liar, I don't even have a father I never ever did.

So put that in your pipe and smoke it fatso." Emphasizing her point, she smacked his face while still holding on to his hair. "I hate you and would like to kill you."

"That will do, Octavia, you naughty, naughty girl."

Octavia was unceremoniously escorted to the headmistress's room.

"What have you been doing this time?"

Octavia felt hot and her head was hurting.

"Why do you all pick on me when piggy George is so awfully cruel to Ruth, Ali, and anyone else he doesn't like? You don't take any notice of what I have to say. I have already learnt everything from my other Miss so I am bored when I have nothing to do, but you all don't care. All your friends say nasty things to Suz so none of you are kind, you are all horrid George never does his work, he can't do sums or spelling and can't read. I can and I keep getting the cane because I'm clever my other Miss said that."

"I will ring your mother and tell her to pick you up and take you home until you have calmed down, Octavia."

Octavia stuck out her bottom lip.

When she arrived home, her mother told Ruby that she didn't know what Tavia had done.

"The head teacher talked a whole lot of absolute garbage which I don't have the time or inclination to listen to."

Tavia ran to Ruby sobbing.

"I hate school, I hate George and I hate all of the teachers too."

"Bless your little eart you sit on Rubes knee and ave a cuddle."

Octavia snuggled into Ruby's bosom.

"What would you like me to make for your tea?"

Ruby wiped her tears away and noticed that she seemed to be very hot.

Octavia was fast asleep, Ruby kissed her tear stained face.

Suzannah popped her head round the kitchen door and told Ruby that she and Josiah were going to inspect what the workmen had done since the last time they had looked.

"Suz, I don't think Tavia is very well she seems to be very hot and she has fallen asleep."

"I'll get Josiah to carry her upstairs to her bed."

"I reckon I'll stay for a bit like just to keep an eye on er."

"You know what Tavia is like, she hates being chastised and she has probably worn herself out."

"I'm still stayin, Suz, it's not like er ter be so upset."

But Suzannah had gone to see Josiah.

Ruby stayed for a couple of hours. She undressed Tavia, put her night gown on, wiped her face with a cold flannel and got her to drink some water. She seemed to be more settled and Ruby thinking that Suzannah might have been right she kissed her and went downstairs.

"Golly are you still here, Ruby, you must be hungry, I'll make you some food."

"No thanks, Suz, I'm goin ome now, please keep an eye on Tavia."

Octavia woke. It was dark and she felt very cold. She pulled her blankets and slippy blue eiderdown up over her and went back to sleep. She woke up some time later and pushed all the bed linen down she felt hot and her head hurt. She tried to remember what had happened. Oh yes some people had been very nasty to her at school and she came home and sat on Rube's knee. She drifted back to sleep. She woke and wanted Blue Ted, he usually sat on her bed, she found him. Now her throat was sore. She fell asleep once more, she really wanted a drink but didn't want to go and fetch one, so she returned to slumber land.

She felt a cold hand on her forehead, it felt very comforting. It was just starting to get light.

"Rube, is it you? I don't feel very well. Please may I have a drink?"

"You can, my pet lamb, do you want some nice cold water or a cup of tea?"

"Water please, is it morning? I won't feel like this for ever and ever will I?"

Ruby reassured her and turned the light on.

Tavia immediately put her hand over her eyes.

"Glory be. You've got the measles so yer ave."

She quickly turned the light out and went to fetch a glass of water for her.

She soon returned with the water and a Beecham's powder.

"This should make you feel a bit better and I'll get Suz to ring Dr Summers when she wakes up."

"I don't much care for the taste, Rube."

"No well they aren't made for yer to enjoy, they are to make yer feel better, so get it down yer."

"I think I got the measles because of podgy George. He's so horrid I hope that he gets double measles. Look at my arms, they are covered in red spots and they itch, will they go away soon, Rube?"

"In a while my love, would you like some toast?"

Ruby asked.

"No thank you, I'm not hungry my throat hurts and toast will be scratchy, do I have to go to school today?"

Later Ruby woke Suzannah up with a cup of tea.

"Tavia has the measles, Suz, will you ring Dr Summers?"

"Golly that's all we need isn't it, Rube."

Ruby wasn't very pleased at Suzannah's attitude, she had been meaning to have a word about it for some time.

"I don't think that the child did it on purpose to interfere with your most important work."

Ruby walked out and went downstairs to make Percy and Fred a drink. She felt angry and had left Suzannah before she had lost her temper. Suzannah must have sensed this so after quickly drinking her tea, she went to see her daughter.

Octavia was curled up her arms round Blue Ted.

"How are you feeling, my pet, she asked?"

"I don't feel very well to tell you the truth, Suz, Rube says it's the measles."

"I think I got it because George said that I've got a father, but he looked at me and really hated me so he went away. I didn't know I had one, was I so horrid, Suz?"

Suzannah, had, without realising it, dreaded this moment all her life, she had locked it away in a cupboard in her brain with lots of other dreadful things.

"Well you see, Tavia, for reasons which you are too young to understand your father went away and I got a divorce. You try to sleep now. Dr Summers will see you later. "

Tavia thought about this, she had never seen this divorce it must be better than a father or Suz wouldn't have swapped him for one. When she was better she would look for it. This would be difficult as the house was in such a mess at the moment and she had no idea what a divorce looked like.

Dr Summer's cheery face appeared round Tavia's door.

"Now then, you poor spotty girlie, are you feeling unwell?"

Tavia nodded enjoying the attention.

"Well, we will have to get you well very soon."

He sat on her bed listened to her chest felt her pulse and her hot forehead.

"She will have to stay in bed for a week or so, her spots must be bathed daily in per manganate of potash then a liberal amount of calamine lotion applied. The curtains must remain closed. I will give her some medication too, and I will return in a few days, any problems give me a ring."

CHAPTER 27

All was quiet, the workmen had gone home as had Josiah and the Jacks family, it had taken a lot of persuading for Ruby to leave Tavia, but Suzannah had managed it in the end. After giving Tavia boiled egg and soldiers for her tea, covering her with calamine lotion and spooning medicine down her throat, she reluctantly went home. Suzannah, taking a sigh of relief sat at the kitchen table with a much wanted cup of tea, to rest her weary bones and read the evening news paper in peace.

The heading on the bottom of the first page caught her eye, it read ....

'Police are still searching for Mr William Season in connection with an alleged murder which took place in January 1943. His accomplice, a garage proprietor, admitted his small part in the crime and has named Mr Season as the perpetrator of the murder of Mr and Mrs Hector Gibson Ffiske, the parents of Mrs Suzannah Season whose ex-husband is the elusive suspect of the crime, was approached some time ago about her ex-husband's whereabouts but refused to comment. Mr Josiah Kingston a local business man was not available for comment. He and Mrs Season are partners. They jointly own Kingston Construction Ltd, and are presently working together on several building projects in the town, one of them is reported to be the largest hotel and restaurant in the area. If anyone has any information concerning the whereabouts of Mr Season would, they please get in touch with the local police.

The case continues.'

To say that Suzannah was angry was an understatement. Her hands were shaking and her head thumping, just as she had thought that things were progressing well. Bang, something else rears its ugly head.

The phone rang, she was tempted to ignore it, but thought better of it.

"Suzannah, this is April, have you read tonight's paper? It says that you and my husband are partners, and we all know what that means, how could you? This may ruin my life not to say that of my sons."

"Just a moment, April, can you imagine how awfully angry I feel? You know that these insinuations are not true. We are business partners nothing more."

"That is not the point Suzannah true or not, it makes out otherwise in the newspaper. I have my standing in society to consider."

"Oh yes, April and I suppose that I don't? I have had to tolerate years of abuse and just when I think that it has come to an end, this happens."

"Just you see to it that my son and I are not implicated in this."

The phone went dead.

Josiah was at the doors of his solicitors before it opened the next morning, walking up and down like a regimental sergeant major.

Suzannah rang the newspaper offices, and April ate a box of Dairy milk obtained from an illegal source.

"Don't you think that my spots are getting better Doctor, me and Blue Ted think that they are?"

"I am sure that you are both right, Octavia. Do you feel like eating something yet?"

"I think that we would like some buttery mashed potato please."

"I will see what can be done. I believe that your little friend Ruth is waiting to see you. I will send her up and sort out this gourmet meal with Ruby, see you in a few days."

"Oh, Ruth, I am so glad to see you I have been so very fed up, come and sit on the bed with me and Blue Ted."

Octavia was happier than she had been for days and days. Ruth's grin nearly stretched from ear to ear.

"I have missed you so much, and I have loads to tell you. I have had the measles anyway so I can't get it two times Dr Summers says."

"Ruth I must tell you this secret, the reason that I got the measles was because George told me about my pa. I've found out from Suz that I did have one but she swapped him for a thing called a divorce, have you ever heard of such a thing?"

Ruth was wide-eyed in amazement. And crossing her arms said.

"What do they look like? I am sure that if my ma knew, she would like one instead of my pa. She always says that if she could sell him for half a crown she would. I never see him he lives in the shed so I don't really care what she does with him." Tavia was very interested to learn that pa's weren't much good.

"I don't know what divorces look like or where Suz keeps hers. No one will talk about it, not even Rube. What if it gets thrown out with all this rubbish that the workmen make? I reckon if we ask Marcus he will know, or be able to find out boys know about that sort of thing."

"I must tell you this, Tavia; Porky George pushed Ali down the stone steps at school and he had to go to the hospital. He has got a broken arm and has got this white hard plaster thing on until it gets better, I told Miss that George did it on purpose but she said that George told her that he never did, and that I should keep quiet about it, but I saw him do it, no one listens to me. I think that Ali's ma is moving house so he will go to another school. My ma said that our school has got bad repu repulsion or something." Octavia listened with interest then said.

"The reason that George gets away with everything is because he has a huge big pa and when he is home from sea he gets full of booze and loses his temper I overheard Ruby talking about it to someone at the door, when I sneaked out of bed one day."

The door opened and in came Ruby carrying two plates of steaming snowy white mashed potato with a generous knob of butter melting down the sides like lava from a volcano.

"Get that down yer sens and enjoy it," she smiled.

Josiah came later in the day after Ruth had gone home to do her ma's errands which was her Saturday job. Marcus was with Josiah who had decided that if his son was to get measles it was better now than when he was a lot older.

Octavia was listening from the landing.

"I've sorted out the business in the newspaper, and not only will we get a retraction we should get some cash. Can't have these riff raff papers making up lies about us decent hard working people."

"I don't think that it will make a dash of a difference Jo, people in East Thorpe are always willing to believe all the horrid things about us. Is April alright about it now? "

"April is never alright about anything," he laughed his loud echoing laugh.

"Go upstairs son and have a word with your friend, see if she wants an ice cream and go to the corner shop and get them," he handed him a shilling.

"Marcus," Octavia said, "I need to talk to you about a very important matter."

"Shall I go and get us an ice cream first my pa's given me some money?"

"OK but don't be long, an ice cream will be nice on my throat."

When he returned the ice creams had begun to melt, "I had to lick them both."

He told Tavia.

"The thing is Marcus," she said in between licking.

"I need you to find out what a divorce is, what it looks like and where it could be hidden. Suz has one and I'd like to test it out to see if it's better than a father. Pleeeze Marcus it is very important."

Marcus had just got down to the end of his cornet the part where it is very soggy.

"Hang on Tavia, while I finish this."

Octavia continued to eat hers, trying to control her impatience.

"What is this thing a 'vorce' never heard of one."

He wiped his sticky hand down his grey short trousers.

"Divorce;" and it is something a lady gets instead of a man. Like Suz got one instead of my pa."

"What for, my pa is OK he gives me money and stuff, my ma only just wants to kiss and cuddle me YUK."

"Promise me, hand on heart that you will find out, I NEED to know and you are my friend so you do things for friends, like I hid your catapult from your Pa. do you remember?"

"Yes I'll do it or give it my best shot. Get it - best shot - catapult?"

They both giggled.

They could hear Josiah's heavy footsteps climbing the stairs Tavia quickly wrote on a piece of paper and handed it to him before the big man came into the room.

"Now then, poorly little one, are you feeling better?"

The bed squeaked as he sat down.

"Yes, thank you for the ice cream, Jo, it was very nice."

"I have got some news, better than an ice cream for you," he told her.

Tavia's eyes opened wide.

"You know that you hate your school and that brat George?"

He asked while wearing his very, very smiley face.

"You don't have to go there any more. That awful headmistress with the silky pink knickers ...."

Both the children laughed out loud.

"Well she has retired."

"Does that mean she's dead, Jo?"

"No, Tavia, it means she has left her job and another person is to take her place, someone you know. Miss Sanegar!! So now you can go to her school."

Octavia jumped up on Josiah and gave him a great big hug.

"Yuk." Marcus said screwing up his face.

When they arrived home Marcus went upstairs and unfolded the note which Tavia had handed to him it read ....

'DEVORS.'

CHAPTER 28

1952

Suzannah with Tavia and Ruth in her car visited Madam Daphne, Clothes for the Discerning.

Madam Daphne ingratiated herself "Oh Mrs Season what a pleasure it is to see you again, how Octavia has grown, and who is this little girlie?"

As usual Suzannah was in a hurry and had no time for false pleasantries.

"I need a full uniform for Tavia for St. Vincent's and this."

She handed her Tavia's previous school uniform.

"Please will you alter these items to fit this one, Ruth, they are all clean?"

"I will need to measure Ruth, well both of them really, but it shouldn't take a tick," Suzannah hoped not.

At first Ruth was mortified at the thought of Tavia going to a new school. Tavia explained that her school was only a short distance from Ruth's, and she could still visit her house whenever she wanted and come for weekends. The other bonus was having a proper school uniform, which would make her feel important and give her confidence. Tavia had also taught her how to deal with Porky George. So things didn't seem quite so bad. Next term George was to stay in the same class anyway, and not move up with the rest of them. So I won't see much of him and if he starts being horrid I will yell Dunce, dunce. She had told her friend proudly. Mrs Jolly was pleased to see her daughter s new attire after all it would save her having to hunt around jumble sales for clothes for Ruth. She was, however, a little concerned about what the other inhabitants of the area would call her so she decided not to thank Suzannah for the clothes

Octavia settled down very well Miss Sanegar had, knowing Octavia's abilities, put her in the year above her age group. She now enjoyed school and after each weekend, she couldn't wait to get back to school. She always did her homework on time and was anxious to learn.

Work on the hotel had proceeded apace throughout the year. Suzannah had spent many days and nights regretting her rash decision to begin such a huge conversion of three large Victorian terraced houses into one hotel while she and Tavia were still in situ. The upheaval had been tremendously stressful Ruby had been marvellous and supported Suzannah when she was down in the dumps or told Tavia off when she was naughty. Now it all seemed to be nearing completion and was habitable once more. Sometimes Suzannah forgot what it was actually like previously.

Mr Plant the surveyor/architect had proved to be a gentleman in every sense of the word. Winter and summer he wore a checked trilby hat the only time anyone saw what was beneath was when he charmingly doffed it to greet anyone accompanied by a slight bow thus revealing a parting of his mousy coloured hair approximately an inch above his left ear. The remainder of his locks were combed up and over his shiny pate. His moustache resembled a shaving brush which rested onto his lower lip. He wore beer bottle bottom wire spectacles, which seemed to increase the size of his watery blue eyes tenfold. He was devoid of the slightest sense of humour, He tolerated even Tavia's endless questions with patience and called her Miss Octavia to her delight. His skills were endless and faultless.

His plans for the conversion had prevented the total removal of any of the internal load bearing walls. This was good as there was still a vast open looking space. The entrance was now in the centre of the entire building. The doors to the Corner House and the former rented house were blocked up. The ground floor consisted of a large restaurant area and bar looking out on to the outdoor eating and recreation area. The vast kitchen spanned the original Corner House and the original dwelling. The impressive entrance and reception area included stairs offices and toilet. Upstairs there was eighteen bedrooms and three attic rooms one for Tavia one for Suzannah, the other being made ready for the head chef, who was yet to be appointed. Both Tavia and her mother had settled down in their respective rooms.

There was a small rear car park anticipating the new trend for motor cars which were now not only for the very rich. Percy had been given a stall to sell the remainder of the produce from the hotel. He had traded this for the loss of some of his previous allotment. This made him one happy fella.

Suzannah wanted the hotel to be completed before the summer holidays, which were only a few months away. The workmen had nearly finished and were anxious to return to the work on the houses and the theatre which had been planned for the bomb site. She and Josiah were going through all the applications for the various jobs which the hotel would require and deciding which of them to invite for an interview. The decorators and design specialists were coming the following day, so Suzannah felt a little stressed, Josiah didn't. He considered that sort of thing to be Suzannah's department. He had been promised by the newspaper they would print a retraction in that day's copy so he was more interested in that.

The afternoon went reasonably well they both agreed on most of the candidates, so Suzannah would have to type all the letters which at her speed, one fingered, would take a lot of time. She would soon have a secretary to do all that thank goodness. Ruby could help her with the recruitment of the domestic staff. She stood up and stretched her aching back.

"I think it is time we had a break. The newspaper will have come, so you can read it if you like and see if the editor has kept his promise."

She went into the kitchen. Ruby had been very quiet the last few days or maybe it was her imagination. She didn't have much time to enjoy a chat with her because of the organisation going on.

"I'm just making a pot of tea Ruby I presume that the men have had theirs, would you like one pouring?"

"No thank you, us workers ave ad ours."

Suzannah thought Ruby was joking so just laughed. She heard Josiah shouting.

"Damn and Blast cheeky buggers."

Carrying the tray of tea she went to see what the fuss was about.

"Just you look at this, Suz. I've never heard the likes."

He pointed to a small article at the bottom of the first page it said ....

APOLOGY

We apologise for the error in a recent copy of our newspaper

Mr Josiah Kingston and Mrs Suzannah Season are no longer partners.

Josiah's face was bright red and he was furious.

"I'll go, when I've had my cuppa and strangle the buggers."

"Jo, you will be wasting your time, it's easier to just forget it."

"Forget, be damned I'm not letting the sods get away with it this time, It won't do our reputations any good or that of the hotel and all my other projects. No, Suz, I've come this far and I'm not letting them win."

He drained his cup and left. Suzannah felt too tired to feel angry, she was used to being abused.

She took the dirty cups into the kitchen to wash them up, Ruby looked up and said. "I'll wash them there cups, that's what I'm paid for."

"You don't seem to be yourself lately, I'm sorry that we haven't had our usual chats, but I've been so busy, I have probably neglected you. I need to have a word with you anyway."

Ruby swiftly turned round.

"I thought that me an you woz more'n just er, er workers together, I thought we woz friends."

Suzannah looked at her aghast.

"You, Ruby are my best friend in the whole world. What on earth have I done to make you feel otherwise?"

"You can say that, but still get rid of me. I don't fit in anywhere in this new hotel thing, so I'm thrown out, after all we ave bin through together."

"What on earth are you talking about, I couldn't manage without you to organise all the cleaning staff, maids and such?"

"Yer mean yer ain't getting rid of me?"

"Come here and have a hug, you silly thing."

They had a cuddle and Suzannah realised that she had taken it for granted that Ruby would understand.

"I am really sorry, Ruby, I wouldn't hurt you for the world. It is totally my fault. Will you please take on the job? I couldn't think of anyone more suitable. You will naturally get a rise and instead of you doing all the work, you can tell the others to do it. When we interview the domestic staff, you must be on the interviewing panel, OK, that is what I needed to discus with you?"

Ruby beamed. "You mean I'm goin to be important, be in charge of other folk, I never dreamt of such a thing."

"You will always be important to me, Ruby, I can't imagine how you could think otherwise. We will continue to use Percy's produce in the hotel and the remainder he'll be able to sell on a stall which will be placed on the edge of his allotment. He should do a good trade once people get to know where it is and it will be all his and of course your money."

Octavia had moved into her newly decorated room and Suzannah into hers, the remaining attic room was finished and waiting for the new occupant. The editor of the evening newspaper had been dismissed.

Josiah was reading the newspaper when Marcus found him. He slid his hands in his short grey flannel trouser pockets, wondering what would be the best way to approach this tricky subject. He pulled up his grey woollen socks for the second time and asked.

"Pa, can I ask you a question, some chap at school wants to know?"

"And what would that be, son?"

Josiah was worried in case it may be about sex, and sighed with relief when his son said.

"What exactly does a divorce look like, is it awfully large or, well, how would one notice it, or find it, if it were hidden, that sort of thing?"

His father lowered his newspaper with force.

"Have you been talking to Octavia Season by any chance?"

Marcus looked at him wide-eyed.

"No, that is to say, yes I always talk to her when we go to visit, why would you think of Tavia?"

"Keep the big fellow out, son." Josiah tapped his nose.

"Just don't have anything to do with it, it will only cause upset."

He went back to his newspaper.

"Well this fellow at school asked me to find out for him as he is trying to search for his ma's so that he can sort of get to his pa and see which is best his pa or the divorce. Do you see?"

He pulled his socks up again.

Without moving his paper Josiah said.

"When we go to see Tavia son, just tell her you don't know anything."

When Marcus returned to school he questioned a chum with divorced parents, and got the low down on the situation. He breathed a sigh of relief, now he could face Tavia and be the bearer of his vast knowledge on the subject.

CHAPTER 29

The following weekend Marcus arrived with his pa to the nearly erected hotel, the girls knew that he must have some news of the most important question concerning the divorce. He had been conspicuous by his absence for a little while, not at all like him.

The three dashed up to Tavia's bedroom, Ruth and Tavia perched themselves on her bed.

"I really like your new bedroom, Tavia," Ruth said. "I have to share mine with my sisters and they are so so..."

She stopped abruptly as Tavia was giving her a look, which meant for her to be quiet.

"Right Marcus" Tavia said "You stand near the window and me and Ruth will sit on the bed so that you can tell us about the extreeeeeemly important subject of divorce."

"You can be so bossy sometimes you often forget that I am the boy of the group."

"Come on Marcus let's hear what you found out about you know what."

He coughed importantly as he rested his arm casually on the window sill to emphasize his importance.

The two girls sighed and looked at the ceiling.

"Well a chum of mine has parents that are divorced and he sees them both but lives with his mother except that he is a boarder."

The girls tutted; Marcus was in control of the situation so ignored their rudeness.

"It's pretty simple actually," he paused to cough for effect.

"It is just a piece of paper," he examined his finger nails.

"How can it be just a piece of paper, that's rid er ridic stupid?" Tavia asked

Marcus changed position and put his hands into his pockets.

"If you keep interrupting me how can I tell you?"

"Come on don't dilly dally or me and Ruth will lose our tempers."

"What you two seem to have forgotten is that I went to a lot of trouble to get this information, and all I seem to get is you two girls being bossy. Anyway. When a man and a lady get married and the man starts buggering about, the lady gets fed up of it and goes to see this bloke called a judge who sorts it out. The man, because he is the one who has done the beggaring about, has to go and live in another house. The judge gives the lady a piece of paper called a divorce so they are sort of un-married. The lady can get married again if she chooses another man who doesn't like buggering about and behaves himself. The man can, too, as long as he gets someone who doesn't mind his buggering about much. If your ma wanted she could get married to a nice man and you would have a new pa."

The girls stood up "I don't want a new pa thank you very much specially as the last one spent his time buggering about, it might be catching, like measles." Octavia said hands on hips.

"They aren't much good anyway." Ruth said as she wondered what buggering about was.

"My pa is ok" Marcus said grudgingly.

Tavia felt better even though she didn't have the vaguest idea what buggering about was, come to that neither did Marcus. He just hoped that the girls wouldn't ask.

Josiah got out of his car and rushed in to see Suzannah who was in the newly organized office.

"You will never believe what I am going to tell you, Suz. "He told her laughing until his face was red. "You know that the police were searching for William Season."

"You will never guess where he had been all the time. Only inside prison!"

Hearing her ex-husband's name caused a shiver to run down her spine.

Josiah leant forward across the desk.

"He has been in prison for fraud."

Josiah laughed so that his corpulent stomach wobbled like a jelly.

Suzannah tried to see the funny side but it was with great difficulty.

"Is he going to go for trial then, Jo?"

"He will, when I tell the police, stupid buggers. I can't believe that they didn't know when he was under their very noses."

Suzannah felt a surge of fear but told herself that she was being stupid.

"Have you noticed that I have got rid of the editor of the newspaper too? Power, I love it," he chuckled.

She nodded trying to put William's trial at the back of her mind. She knew she would be called to appear, the thought of this terrified her. Merely seeing him made her tremble. She told herself that at the moment she had too much to occupy her mind that the trial should be the last thing she needed to think about.

"Well," she told him. "As you know the interviews begin next week as does the decorating everything has been ordered." She handed him a piece of paper.

"These are the dates and times of the interviews. The ones marked with a red dot are the ones which Ruby needs to sit on too. We also have to arrange her uniform fitting and the others as and when."

"Well you don't need me for that. I'll just be at the interviews. OK?"

"The deciding who to employ, too, Josiah don't forget that, I know that you want to get on with your bazaars, theatre and houses but I can't do all the other things alone," she said sharply.

"Sorry, Suz, I will help whenever, you click your fingers," he laughed.

She realized that she was taking out her feelings of stress concerning the trial on him so she just smiled.

Octavia was diligent where her homework was concerned without ever being reminded, the moment she came home from school she would have a glass of milk and begin to do it. She was very proud that she always received a star and never a 'See Me' on her work. Today was Friday; school finished early that afternoon as they had extra homework to do, she always got it completed before Ruth came after her school ended for the weekend, so that they could play together. Miss Sanegar always told the school homework first, play second. What she said was law according to Tavia.

"Story first," she told Blue Ted who didn't seem to be too interested. She enjoyed writing stories best so she really ought to do her maths history and geography first. She changed her mind and tackled the other subjects. Then she got out her story book. Octavia's work was always neat and tidy Suzannah told her it was a shame she didn't feel the same about keeping her clothes tidy as the dirty ones were thrown in the corner on the floor. Suz made her pick them up but Ruby was kinder and picked them up for her.

"Hmm," she said as she read what her story had to be about this week.

"Write a story from your imagination about something unusual," she read out loud.

She opened her writing book and thought about this subject. To her horror there was only one clean page left in her book, why hadn't she noticed before.

"Suz - Suz," she yelled as she ran down the stairs.

She told her mother of her plight. "Will you take me to the shop in the car, as I've run out of paper and need some now to finish my homework before Ruth comes please - please, will you."?

"I'm afraid I can't I have two interviews and then a meeting tonight, you should have thought about that before, you will have to walk down the promenade yourself or wait until tomorrow."

"I haven't time, Suz. It's very important."

"Have a look in my room and see if there is any paper. Now I must go. My first person to be interviewed is waiting. Hope you have picked up your dirty school uniform and not left it for Ruby to do."

Tavia stamped her feet, but her mother had already gone. She ran back up the stairs and along to her mother's room. She searched everywhere then recalled seeing a very big thick old book with metal corners and a tiny lock. Perhaps there would be empty pages in that. Locating it was easy but when she tried to undo it she failed. It was locked. Then it suddenly came to her that in her dressing up box there was a little key on a string of white beads. Like the wind she dashed to her bedroom and searched in her box, at last she found it. Returning to her mother's room she discovered it fitted. She didn't even have to remove it from the pretty necklace.

Back in her own room once more she looked inside The pages smelt strange. At the beginning of the first page it read.

This book belongs to
Arabella Gertrude Gosling.
Ruddlinden Hall.
Private do not look inside.

It seemed to be written in a childlike hand which appeared to alter as the book progressed amongst the first few pages was written.

I really hate my mother for leaving me with this horrid nurse. I hate my grandmama as well, she won't speak to me or allow me into her room and now I am told that I am soon to start as a boarder in some school which I am sure that I will hate. Why can't my nurse be nice to me instead of beating me and taking away my dinner. I HATE HER MOST OF ALL.

Several pages later in the same writing but different coloured ink, was written.

I decided that If I killed my nurse I may not have to go to school, that would teach her a lesson.

I waited until she was yelling to me from the top of the stairs, but she didn't know that I was already hiding behind the landing curtains. I crept up and gave her the biggest push ever. She did make some noise, but not much. I watched as she tumbled down, what a hoot, I laughed as quietly as I could. She didn't make a sound at the bottom. I ran like fury down the north stairs out through one of the rear doors and on into the copse. I was getting pretty fed up after waiting ages for something to happen. I wasn't sure what but it didn't. I lie down on the crispy leaves, I was hungry but I knew that my supper would be out of the question if she was dead, so I went to sleep.

It was getting dark when I heard people shouting my name. I stood up and shouted back.

No one bothered to ask me if I had pushed her, they just said that she must have slipped. The only bad thing was that she wasn't dead yet. But she would never walk or anything even if she did live. So that was better than nothing. I also got a grand supper that night so it turned out to be better after all.

Octavia was fascinated. At first she thought that it must have been some story that a little girl who she didn't know had written a long time ago.

Funny sort of story, and what was it doing in Suz drawers. Maybe her teacher would like the story, or would it be cheating when it wasn't really her own made up story.

She turned over a few pages and saw some very grim drawings of people with huge big daggers sticking out of them and red blood running out. Underneath it said.

This is what I will do to the people I hate. It said in red letters. Especially those, who sent me to this terribly, awful school.

A few pages later Octavia read.

Today the headmistress sent for me. She said that I was extremely talented and at the top of my year, she wondered why I didn't have any friends.

I told her that I didn't like anyone. Then she changed the subject and said that she was in receipt of a letter from my grandmama, telling her that she had received a visit from my mama who at last had revealed the name of my papa. The situation would continue whereby I would not have any visitors, the present monitory situation would continue.

The headmistress said that as I was clever but extremely unsociable it may be better if I change to a school which would be more academically suited to my needs. One had been found and my grandmamainformed me.

I would be moving the following week at the end of term.

On the last day I found a huge brick, as the car was waiting to escort me I hid round a corner and threw it at the headmistress's head, she fell to the ground covered in blood I ran round and got into the car, and was gone. No one had seen me and I later found out that she was dead.

Octavia thought that she had never read a book like this before, it was compulsive reading as well as frightening. Ruth and her homework were temporally forgotten.

She flicked through the book there was so much to read. She stopped at one point for no particular reason. It read.

I succeeded in conning that stupid man and he believe me I just need to keep my nerve and be terribly clever. I can very easily do it after all my experience. I'm an absolute wiz at this sort of jape.

There was a large heart drawn in red, inside it were the letters Ha Ha.

The only teeny weeny problem will be getting rid of that cad Marsden, without spoiling my contacts at GF and co. I'll sweet talk him make a few promises and give him a gift.

The following page made even less sense to Octavia who was starting to lose interest until something caught her eye. It read.

I am furious, I went to all the trouble to have a paste copy of my pearls and give them to him saying it was a love token worth thousands of pounds, he threw them back in my face, what an ungrateful bounder. It's over, and much easier than I had imagined.

Octavia looked anxiously at her clock. Golly she must get back to her room Ruth will be coming soon and she needed to write her story first. She would take the book with her. She closed the book and locked it, before returning to her room.

She slipped the book under her bed. The door opened and Ruth marched in

"Mr Kingston let me in," she told her friend." I was first out of the school gate and ran all the way here," she said.

"What have you been doing at school today?" Tavia asked while trying to decide if she would show Ruth the book now or wait until she had read it all.

"Same as usual really, teacher gave us a spelling test, with hard words in it, I got seven out of ten but the very best result from a yuckie boy was only eight so I didn't feel so bad. I bet that you would have got ten, Mrs clever clogs."

They both laughed, "I've got something very strange to show you, Ruth."

Ruth interrupted. She had made up her mind.

"Strange was one of the words in our spelling test today, and I got it wrong."

"Golly that doesn't matter much, Ruth, it's spelt S T R A N G E.

"I know that now don't I"?

"Anyway I must show you my strange thing."

Octavia reached under the bed and pulled out the book.

"It's got murders and nasty horrid things in it, really, really awful, honestly but really spiffing at the same time."

"Where did you get it from Tavia, not the Library?"

Octavia began to tell her all about how she had found it, and then showed it to her. Ruth was shocked.

"Who wrote all that nasty stuff and what did they do it for? Do you think that it is really, really true or just pretend?"

"I think we should ask Marcus don't you Ruth?" she nodded.

"We must keep it a secret though, only us three must know about it."

Tavia couldn't sleep that night for thinking about the book.

CHAPTER 30

As soon as breakfast was over the next morning, they rang Marcus to ask if he could come to play. He told them that he would be there later with his pa.

When you come they hinted, we will have a big surprise to tell you, but it's going to be our secret they teased him. Despite his pleading they refused to let him know anything else and rang off.

"Don't forget that I have to do my mother's errands today," Ruth reminded Octavia.

"Why is it always you that has to do them on Saturdays, Just tell your mother that it's not er conv, convene, that it should be your brother's or sisters' turn? Anyway why can't she do her own shopping, you have to go to school all week. I've got a good idea, me and Marcus will come and help, then you can come back to my house when the jobs are done, and you can stay until tomorrow."

"You have never been to my house before, it's not posh like yours and things don't happen the same way."

"I don't live in a proper house any more I live in a hotel, well nearly, and I much preferred it when it was a normal house."

"You'll soon change your mind when you see mine Tavia. It is not a normal house either."

288

Marcus wasn't very pleased when he was told he had to go with the girls to do errands before he would be shown the secret.

"I've never done errands, and I don't think that I much care to begin now."

Tavia soon piped up.

"I will give you a clue to the secret then, it's a very mysterious book, a horror book, nasty things happen."

"It's not about buggering about again is it? I'm not asking my pa any more questions."

"I promise that the parts that we have read hasn't got any buggering about in it, has it, Ruth?"

Octavia crossed her fingers as she still hadn't any idea what it meant. The subject of the once vitally important divorce had taken a back seat since she had discovered the book.

Ruth shook her head.

They arrived at Mrs Jolly's house, an ordinary pre-war terrace.

"We have to go to the back door in case we dirty the porch." The three of them walked around the rear of the house, down a narrow passage way, in through a green painted gate, past a shed, down the back garden and to the door which Ruth opened.

Mrs Jolly was in the kitchen dusting.

"I've bought my friends with me, mum, they are going to help me do my Saturday errands then I can go back to Tavia's until tomorrow."

They still stood at the door and did not dare to enter. One look at Mrs Jolly's scowl was enough to put anyone off. She certainly didn't live up to her name. She wore a flowery apron, her hair was encased with a turban like scarf and she held a duster which seemed to be attached to her, as she continued, even while talking, to wipe everything in sight. She had a long thin mean face and a snipe nose. Her mouth had long forgotten how to smile, maybe had never learnt how to, her white skin hadn't seen any sun for many a year. Tavia took an instant dislike to people who didn't have smiley face and this woman was at the top of her list.

"This is Marcus and Tavia my friends, I stay with Tavia most weekends but you have never met her."

Through the door they could see the cardinal red tiled kitchen floor was covered with newspaper and a coconut mat. Newspaper covered the oven top. Tavia stared as she wondered what reason she had, maybe Mrs Jolly liked to read while she polished so why didn't she put them on the table tops like normal people, she was very strange, she could possibly be a killer like in the book.

Ruth had obviously thought about what Marcus said.

"Why can't Margaret, Peter, John or Joan have a turn at doing the errands for a change, mum?" Mrs Jolly was clearly not pleased.

"Margaret is at work at the jam factory and the boys seem to be training to follow in their father's footsteps and idle their time in a shed. Joan isn't capable of doing what she is told. At least with them out of my way, it helps to keep the house clean. So Ruth that leaves it to you."

She was dusting the top of the small table.

"Are you sure that Mr Jolly is actually in the shed?"

Tavia asked, thinking that he may be lying on the shed floor with one of Mrs Jolly's best kitchen knives sticking out of his back. She may have killed him there would be blood all over the place. Mrs Jolly ignored the question, which made Tavia even more suspicious.

"I'm sure that your posh friends don't have to demean themselves, but our life is a bit different I'm afraid. They are the idle rich and can afford to divorce their husbands when they don't come up to standard."

She handed Ruth the list. Tavia was furious at the word 'divorce' being mentioned and had to keep her hands tightly closed for fear of hitting her. Marcus too had evil thoughts directed to the woman.

"One pound note to pay off the slate at the grocers, a list of things to be delivered by the boy. A piece of Brisket from the butchers, pay no more than five shillings mind, it has to do for us all on wash day as well as Sunday dinner. Take your father's boots to the cobblers and I'll pay when e as done em, E'd better be quick like, or there will be no work for your dad until e as is pair of boots back. That will no doubt suit him, but not me."

"When we have done all this, can I stay at Tavia's for tonight and come back tomorrow afternoon, mum?"

"Makes no odds to me, Ruth, I'll have less mouths to feed and clear up after. Mrs Season as more money than sense so that is up to er, she can tek the lot of the family if she wants em." They headed for the door.

"By the way, lad, will you tell your dad that e more or less promised us one of these new council ouses ese building on the old gunnel site, and I presume when he's finished the toffs houses near er hotel," she pointed to Tavia, who wanted to tell her that it was very rude to point.

Marcus was furious and Tavia wasn't far behind. He said.

"If you want my father's office number I will give it to you and then you can tell him yourself, I'm sure he will consider it, especially as you have made us so welcome." Octavia and Ruth's eyes were like round balloons.

"I did warn you." Ruth said as they walked back down the path. Octavia couldn't help peeping into Mr Jolly's shed window.

"I don't blame your pa spending his time in the shed with your horrid mother in the house, he ought to get a divorce."

"Or stab her with a big sharp knife then you can come and live at my house er hotel." Tavia said with venom.

Ruth didn't look too sure about that.

When they finished all the errands, the three walked down the promenade to the little shop which sold nearly everything. Octavia bought a writing pad and all of them a bar of chocolate. Marcus had continued to ask when they could see the surprise, so he deserved chocolate and Ruth certainly did for having a spiteful ugly mother.

Octavia thought that Ruby looked very smart in her new uniform as she stood near the door to show it off. Not that her mother would notice.

"Oh there you lot are, I'll bring some milk and biscuits, Suz and Josiah are having a meeting, I thought that I would just try on my new uniform, do you like it?"

They all nodded.

Marcus couldn't wait to find out the surprise, and afterwards when he saw his pa, make sure that the Jolly's were put on the bottom of the housing list.

They sat on Tavia's bed. She produced the book and unlocked it. She quickly closed it as Ruby brought three glasses of milk and a large plate of homemade biscuits for them. They thanked her and dived onto the biscuits and thirstily drank the milk before returning to the book.

"I've never seen anything like it." Marcus said in disbelief as he flicked through the book, stopping to read and re read some parts before moving on.

"Have you read this bit?"

I was the only one left at school for the summer hols, that was not unusual, but after two weeks I was just so fed up I'd read all the books tore a few up in temper, and decided to abscond for a while I knew that they would find me anyway and drag me back and maybe give me a beating but it would perhaps be worth it. I collected all the money that I had and looked around to find some that I could steal, luckily some stupid teacher probably Miss Bedrose, had left the door to her flat open, she was on duty to take care of me, as all the other pupils had gone to stay with their parents or someone else. I went into the room, it was so easy, and stole loads of things including money. Lots of it. I just walked out of school no-one even noticed me. And caught a train to Ruddlingden, I did think someone would question me, but no-one did. When I got into the Hall I went up to grandmama's bedroom, she was so surprised. I had to laugh out loud. She wouldn't talk to me she just continued to yell. Stupid woman, so I hit her good and hard and then stole her casket of jewels and as much money as I could find. I wondered if she were dead as she just lay where she had fallen when I hit her, but she hadn't as I could hear her moaning. I left as quickly as I could. And got the train back to school, I had been gone all day and no-one had even missed me. That's how important I am to any one I had lots of money and a casket containing pearls and all sorts of great things. What a hoot, I had a huge laugh.

"We read that piece because we went on to read about this … Er wait a sec till I find it, ah yes this bit about when she was much older there are lots of just letters instead of names, she showed him the piece she had read earlier. Marcus there's so much to read. And we passed that bit and moved on, I can't understand, who wrote it, is it true, or just a story and why did Suz have it locked up in her room? It's a waste of time asking her as she never has time to talk to me. Maybe whoever wrote the book was the same as me, I'm not important to anyone."

"You are very important to us isn't she, Marcus?" he nodded.

"Maybe I should murder someone." Octavia remarked as she stared into space as if she was contemplating it which made Ruth shiver.

She then joked as she grabbed hold of Ruth's neck.

"Who should I choose?"

"It's time to go home, boy."

Josiah's booming voice sounded just before he opened the door,

"Oh pa we were just involved in something interesting."

"Well that interesting thing will just have to wait son."

Marcus got up and reluctantly followed his pa and remarked.

"Remember you two, we are the three musketeers and don't forget what they used to say."

Ruth said when he had left

"Who are they?"

"They are three men who go around on horses with swords killing folk, I've read the book. It's jolly good, all about killing bad people."

"I thought that you must have read the book, Tavia. Is there any book in the whole wide world which you haven't read?"

"Yes, this one," she said.

Neither of them slept too well that night, as their minds where occupied with the book.

The next morning after breakfast, the pair of them had a great time acting out murder scenes, but always at the back of Tavia's mind was her incomplete homework.

Ruth left for home late afternoon after she had enjoyed a big Sunday dinner.

"Everything always tastes so much better here, than it does at my house. We never have biscuits or cakes or - anything nice really, at tea time we just have bread and maybe jam if it is early in the week and my dad has been to work.

"That's because your mother is mean and horrid, tell her, Ruth. Say you won't do the errands if she doesn't do yummy food. I will ask Ruby to put lots of food in a box and give it to you to take home every week. You can hide it and eat it in secret."

"My mother would clip me round the ear hole and pinch the food if my brothers and sisters didn't find it first.

Octavia opened her new writing book. She had decided that instead of copying some of the book, she would make up a similar story, which she really enjoyed doing. She was undecided as to who she would kill in her story. Then she laughed to herself, it would be Mrs Jolly. She was never parted from her duster. That seemed to be a great idea to use for the killing. So in her story she strangled Mrs Jolly with her duster.

She was so pleased with her story, there were lots of gruesome bits, the best story she had written. She was beginning to feel tired so she quickly collected her clean uniform for the following day, went downstairs to the kitchen for some milk and biscuits. She saw a large knife left near to a huge piece of beef and found some bread which she buttered, Suzannah caught sight of her

"Tavia, don't you go using that knife you could easily kill someone, I'll do it for you."

"Thank you, could that knife really kill someone?" her mother finished the sandwich and put it and a glass of milk on a tray. Her mother added some fruit jelly and a piece of cake.

"It certainly would young lady, why are you thinking of murdering some one?" she laughed.

"I might one day. It sounds good fun."

Miss Sanegar had been handed Tavia's story on Tuesday as her class teacher was a little concerned about the contents.

Thinking that as she knew Tavia quite well and also how bizarre she could be it

lay on her desk until Thursday unread.

When Miss Sanegar did eventually read it she immediately sent for Octavia.

"I have read your story, Octavia, and I think that it is very disturbing."

"Did you like it, Miss?" Tavia asked.

"I don't really know what to say, where did you get the idea for this gruesome murder from?"

"Well it is supposed to be a secret, but maybe that doesn't count with you. It was from a book which Suz told me that I could have from her bedroom drawer."

"What was the book about Octavia?"

"Murder of course that is what gave me the idea to write it."

"Did you enjoy writing it?"

"Yes it was fun, I had to decide which person I would like to murder then the rest was easy, can I go now miss as I am missing my lessons?"

Miss Sanegar tried to get hold of Suzannah by phone but she was always too busy to talk. So she decided to delay sending her a letter and try to sort the matter out herself for a while. Knowing Mrs Season she would not act upon the knowledge anyway, or in fact feel it was necessary to do so.

CHAPTER 31

Now that Josiah didn't have to spend so much time at the hotel as Suzannah had it all in hand. He was concentrating on his theatre, amusement arcade, and house building, one of which Ruby and Percy had bought. A dream neither of them could have ever imagined would happen.

Suzannah was very pleased and proud with the success. She was motivated, for the first time and had an ambition which she could aim for. There were alterations to be made in the way things were organised and more ideas to be added. She was looking forward to it. Surely, she was over the really awful things that had happened to her in the past. Nothing could go wrong for her now. As soon as this wretched trial was over she could relax entirely and face the future with a smile.

Octavia was feeling really happy. It was half term. She had finished her homework and Ruby was taking her to a party later on. She had continued to read the murder book, as she had called it. She had no idea who this Arabella Gosling could have been and was more amazed as she read it. She knew that Suzannah was going to some court or other with Josiah, that afternoon

"Are you going to put your pretty party dress on, Tavia, or do you want me to come and help? Don't forget your new shoes and your present." Ruby shouted up to her.

All Tavia's party clothes were neatly laid for her to put on in, her excitement she placed the book open on her bed and instead of hiding it as usual she forgot about it as she ran down the stairs. "Ruby will you do my hair now please?"

Ruby got hold of the hair brush and Tavia's new ribbons.

"There is a letter for you on the table, Suz, looks like it's from the school."

"I'll read it when I get back, Ruby."

Suzannah had received a summons to appear before the court at Langden Dyke regarding William Seasons alleged murder of Mr and Mrs Gibson Ffiske, her parents. She felt that the matter was of no concern to her and regarded it as a complete farce and waste of everyone's time. There was little evidence to begin with and so after all these years it seemed that nothing more would be forthcoming.

"I bet you had forgotten that I was going to Claudia's birthday party didn't you, Suz?"

Josiah came in.

"Now don't you look like a princess?" he told Tavia, who did a twirl.

"Can we go now, Rube, we don't want to be late, do we?"

William, as expected, walked from the court, a free man with a smirk on his face.

Josiah had hoped that William would have been hung. Everyone knew that he had committed the crime. When he passed Josiah he handed him a letter.

"Will you see that Suzannah gets this please, don't do it for me, Josiah, do it for her, there are things in it that are vital she should know. She has been treated very badly by me and her parents I am truly sorry and need to make it up to her before I disappear out of her life forever. I have been transferred to the British embassy in Paris." Josiah snatched it from him with a look of hate on his face.

"I won't bother any of you again, if you promise to give it to her. She has to read it for her to understand things which she should have been aware of years ago. It will clarify a great deal and make her much happier."

"I promise." Josiah said between gritted teeth, he knew that in the past he hadn't always been an honest man, he had to fight all the way to the top but he would honour his promise to a man he hated. Suzannah approached and William quickly went.

"Will you promise me something? It is very important, I would never break a promise and I made this one because I believed it to be in your best interest. I know it will be hard for you as it is a very difficult thing to do. But as you know we all have to do things we don't like in life for the good of other people. Will you read this please?"

"Josiah, you are frightening me."

"Oh no, Suz, it is nothing to be frightened of it should make you happy read it when you get home."

He said echoing what William had told him. He drove her home she thanked him and went inside. Josiah was feeling happy thinking that everything would be much better for Suzannah who he loved more than anyone in the world although no one must ever know. He fell in love with her the very moment he saw her in Miss Elder's house.

The first thing Suzannah did once she had arrived home was to open the letter with some trepidation she didn't trust anything which was remotely connected to William Season.

It read:

Suzannah,

I can understand how much you hate me and I know that you are justified, I am also aware that you didn't read any of my letters or I would have heard from your solicitor. It is vital however that you read this and that you know the truth about your family then other things will become clearer to you and you at last will know the truth of who you are.

You may think that you know everything but I can assure you that you most certainly do not, and it is important that you do, so I am just letting you know the bare facts.

Hector Gibson Ffiske, who you thought to be your father, was in fact Harry Gibbs a common ambitious ruffian. He killed Hector, and stole his identity. He also smothered Lady Gosling your maternal great grandmother to prevent her finding out the truth. The only person who realised the deception was my father who Hector (formally Harry Gibbs) drowned in front of me and your mother. I was three years old and spent my life just waiting for a time when I could obtain my revenge, just waiting. Your parents must have thought that they could forget about their evil past, but I hadn't, and needed to get my revenge for the misery imposed upon me by your parents all the time I spent at that school, the harsh regime I never forgot the day your father pushed my father under the deep waters until he stopped breathing. I was getting older and older and had to act before long or I would have lost my chance of marrying you, a young naïve girl.

Your maternal grandmother was raped by Maxwell Gibson Ffiske on one of his visits making you legally a Gibson Ffiske. Although your father had assumed the name, he was not a Gibson Ffiske.

Your mother killed several people for the pleasure of it. I black mailed your parents with this information, making you marry me, then, yes I killed them. My intention was to obtain all their money which you would have inherited then obviously to murder you too. I would then have received all their wealth. At last I have unloaded the truth which you will have to live with all your life and although I don't have your money which I think I deserved. I have the satisfaction of hopefully ruining your life

William.

300

At first Suzannah just stared at the letter. It seemed as though something was preventing its contents entering even the periphery of her mind, illusion and fact were blending together she lacked the capability of separating them, or the will to do so.

How long she stood there she had no comprehension. Slowly her memory began to clear, returned from a place which was as yet unknown to her, then like a jigsaw it seemed to fit together and the past evils of which she had no previous knowledge prior to the letter, joined with the memories of her parents, and their then unexplained treatment of her, the puzzle was complete. She could never live with it.

Suddenly she let out a scream like a wounded animal and ran out of the hotel, across the promenade and onto the beach, her beach, the place where she belonged. Her shoes were cast off onto the yellow sand as she ran on and on. She glanced back once to see the hotels large sign 'SEASONS,' shining in the dim light.

The brown sandy water was cold but she felt nothing as she slowly walked into it, farther and farther, deeper and deeper. There were no echoes of times past as she embraced the water and peace.

THE END